THE
SPOOK
ROAD

ALSO BY SHANI STRUTHERS

REACH FOR THE DEAD
BOOK FOUR

THE
SPOOK
ROAD

SHANI STRUTHERS

Authors Reach
www.authorsreach.co.uk

ISBN: 978-1-9160626-2-7

ACKNOWLEDGEMENTS

In 2022, my family and I had the good fortune to travel from Chicago across the great American West, through South Dakota, Wyoming, Montana, and North Dakota. It was an incredible trip, with amazing sights to see, not least the Badlands. We kept to the main highways, but we took some backroads too, and how the world changes when you do! That trip was the inspiration for this book, so a huge thank you to my husband, Rob, for suggesting it. Also, thanks, Rob, for your help in the initial stages of this book, and to Lesley Hughes too for your feedback. Rumer Haven, thank you so much for your editorial skills, second to none as usual, and I'm so glad you're working on another set of books yourself—exciting times ahead! And thank you also to Gina Dickerson for another great cover design, plus formatting, and for just being great to work with. Writing a book is a labour of love; certainly, I loved writing this one, reliving my time in such a magical part of the world. I hope you enjoy it!

p.s. As the book is set in America, it is written in American English.

p.p.s. The Spook Road is real, it exists, but I've moved its location slightly for artistic reasons!

*Two roads diverged in a wood, and I—I took
the one less traveled by.*

Robert Frost

PROLOGUE

Two Years Earlier

Bullshit. All of it. I don't want to have to think about it anymore, to *worry*.

This *world* is bullshit.

And this road, it's fucking endless. Like so many roads around here. Dirt tracks, most of them, the wheels of this rusted hulk of a car I'm driving kicking up gravel till I'm lost in a cloud of dust. But there's comfort in that, in being lost. It's what I want right now.

To disappear.

If I did, if I vanished…well, they had it coming, my folks. There's nothing I can do to please them, *nothing*. What's that saying? Can't win for losing.

"You're drifting, Ethan," they say to me, they *yell*, Mom especially. "Running around all day, and for what? For who? Can't have it. *Won't* have it. Get a job!"

Damn!

The sound of my palm hitting the steering wheel is nothing compared to the roar that leaves my mouth. I've tried to find work! *Meaningful* work. And you know what? There's nothing. That's all this place is full of: a big fat nothing. I long for when I was a kid, for how simple life was. I could go to school, come home, watch TV, play on my

PC, rinse and repeat. They left me alone. They did that because they thought I was doing something *other* than chasing pixilated cars around a pixilated track, that I was studying.

It soon became clear I wasn't, though, when I flunked my classes.

I'm a disappointment. It's there in their eyes that they feel that way. The eldest of three, I'm supposed to lead by example. Thing is, I could never understand all that stuff my teachers shoved in front of me. And when you didn't, you had to raise your hand, of course, and ask. Yeah, right! In front of Johnny Latham? He'd crucify you! Him and those he ran with: Caleb, Ben, Leo, Julian, and Wax. They'd interrupt class constantly, the teachers getting so riled they'd lose track of what they were trying to tell you anyway.

If you *ever* asked for help, you'd be in for the worst time. *Creep. Fucktard.* That's what they'd call you. They'd follow you home along the dirt tracks, kicking up more dust, so much it'd damn near choke you, and then...*he'd* choke you, that asshole Johnny, for real. Have you up against the wall of Barnsley's Home Store, looking into your eyes as deep as a lover would as his hands encircled your throat, his goons shielding him, laughing like the crazies they were, and he'd say, oh-so sweetly, "Now why'd you want to go and do that for? Pretend to be smart when you ain't? Bother the teacher so?"

Not lover's eyes, *dead* eyes. Just nothing in them. Nor in those shitheads that worshipped him. Yet more and more, I found I wanted to be a part of it, to *belong.*

Because...what else was there?

Wyatt, South Dakota. Population 6,895. Six thousand eight hundred and ninety-five! So small. So...insignificant.

Seems to me if you're born here, you get stuck here. My grandparents were from here, my *great*-grandparents; my parents were childhood sweethearts at that frickin' school I went to as well, Randall High. I've got a sweetheart, and she *is* sweet, although…I'm no virgin, okay? That's something else you can't be in Johnny's gang, clever or a virgin. You lose it any which way. You try to get a taste for it… Shit! Shit! Shit! This steering wheel's taking a pounding. Why'd I ever get involved with them? Why am I such a loser? Was I born this way? Stupid after all?

I *hate* Johnny Latham, and everyone who hangs on his every word. And right now, more than anything, I hate myself. I *am* a disappointment. But worse still, I'm a coward.

They do stuff, that gang. Bully—there's that, of course—and no one, *no one*, goes against them. They won't 'cause they're also gods, to the bored shitless of Wyatt, anyway, therefore the young, those who don't pretend this is a pleasant neighborhood, some fucking utopia, they see it for the dead end it really is. And the stuff…it keeps getting worse.

Johnny tells us he has connections, that he can get good shit, and when he does, we have to deal it out, act like it's good shit too when it's not; it's the worst. Stuff that'll kill someone one day, not 'cause of the way you act when you're on it but 'cause of what it's cut with. "Deal it anyway," he says. "And don't ask questions." Again, those eyes of his penetrate, *daring* you to ask. And it's me who's the first to hang my head.

Best if I go. Just go. Into the wilderness, the Badlands, not for sightseeing, not this time. It's strange out there, unique, like how I imagine the surface of the moon to be, with jagged peaks for mountains and deep, waterless craters.

Off the beaten path, away from the crowds, a place of silence. Hot in summer, ice-cold in winter. Both beautiful *and* hostile.

That's where this road takes you. But this road…it's supposed to be bad too.

The Spook Road, it's known as—around here, anyway. You cross five bridges along it, and I've done three already, with another coming up. I can see it in the distance. Shades of the dead are supposed to hang from these bridges on wild, stormy nights, kicking and screaming, shadows of the dead in the trees too, a whole gathering of them, watching you.

Crazy. Just some lame urban legend that won't go away. The desert's full of tales like that. There's supposed to be skinwalkers too. Shamans turned bad who can now change form, their sole purpose to scare you all the way to death, but then what? They steal your soul? Even though it's as black as theirs? Would they really want it? The Badlands Banshee also gets talked about, especially at night under the covers, a flashlight casting its long beam. I used to do that with my sisters, Beth and Kim, tell them ghost stories, rile them real good! It was as though I were a skinwalker myself, as powerful. The banshee wanders the Badlands, her head thrown back and her long black hair ragged against the torn white shift she wears. She bares her fangs and howls at the moon—she *shrieks*. Beth in particular was frightened of her. She'd have nightmares, which I got the blame for. "You enjoy tormenting her, Ethan? Is that it? What's *wrong* with you?"

Clearly, what's wrong is that I was ever born at all.

My tires drum on the rutted surface of the fourth bridge, and the car shudders. Another eight or nine miles to the final bridge, then the road will change, like someone's snapped

4

their fingers. No more trees huddled by the side of the road, whispering like a bunch of old ladies; it opens into scrubland, becomes barren, harsher. But…it's *all* harsh out here.

On and on the road goes, no other driver behind me or coming at me, and the sun still high in the sky on this sweltering August day. There's never many people on it, not that I've seen, anyway. If you go to the Badlands, you take the highway. Everyone knows to keep away from roads like this. *Lonely* roads. But I don't mind them; I have the world to myself. A world where skinwalkers and banshees roam. Maybe creatures even worse.

Angry. That's what I was, and what I am now, all the damned time. One big useless bundle of writhing anger. But something else is creeping in as I continue traveling, something that would make me angrier still if it didn't have the power to swamp it.

Which it does, so fucking easily.

Fear.

It's in my veins, creeping up them from my feet, threatening to turn blood into crystals, to stop the ebb and flow of it, my heart thumping against the walls of my chest. Will I reach the fifth bridge, or will it have disappeared? I'll get trapped between them, and, as the sun wanes and the darkness comes, I'll see all the hanging bodies. It isn't nonsense after all.

Get a grip, Ethan! It's a crock of shit! A stupid, stupid myth. I've been up this road a couple of times before, and nothing happened. It was fine. Five bridges heading one way and the same five bridges heading back. Bridges *don't* just disappear. And lo and behold! Hallelujah! There it is, the fifth and final, after which I can breathe easier.

The tires rumble again, and the car shudders all the way over to the road on the other side. Johnny likes it on the Spook Road, said he's raced up and down it loads, day and night. "Ain't nothing there that'll scare me," he said. "But you princesses, you'd pee your pants."

Funnily enough, he's probably right. Thing with Johnny is, he *wants* to see the shadows.

I *don't* like it out here, even in daylight. There I go, fooling myself about that too. I just didn't want to be seen on the highway, I suppose, easily done when you know half the fucking people that use it. I *really* don't like it. The atmosphere…it's wrong. Too heavy. The trees will start thinning soon, but parts of this road are so hemmed in by them it's claustrophobic. They'd suffocate you if they could, their boughs reaching out, gnarled fingers getting closer and closer, tapping at the car windows like the shadows would if you stayed long enough to see them, to do what Johnny allegedly does and *test* the theory…

I'm done. I'm out. The land finally opens up.

The sun is fierce, heat rising in a hazy shimmer from the road to meet the air, creating something of a mirage. But it's there, all right, beyond it, the land. It always has been and always will be, long after we're gone, all the folks of Wyatt and the neighboring town of Murdoc too, which you pass through to get here. If you take the backroads, that is.

A landscape on fire. No flames, but if you set foot out there this time of day, the heat'll devour you all the same. Part of a national park, folks from all over coming to see it, but they keep to "designated areas." No one ever approaches it from this direction, goes this deep. It's no place for anyone. Not unless you were born to it, unless a land like this is in your blood.

I was born to it, but I still fucking hate it.

I fucking fear it.

A coward. The worst kind. The kind that was going to disappear. It'd be easier for my family if I did, but I can't even do that right.

Nineteen. How can you fail so hard at life at nineteen?

My foot slams on the brake, and the car comes to a violent halt.

The jagged peaks of the mountain range up ahead look like they could spear you.

If I *could* do it, carry on, drive through the day and into the night out here on the quietest roads of all, what would I see on the way? Would I emerge sane?

My mom's face appears in my mind, and it isn't red with rage or stricken with disappointment. Not this time. Her eyes are so watery, they glisten.

She seems to whisper something to me. What is it? Is it...what I hope for?

I just want someone to understand me!

I'm not like Johnny, Caleb, and the others. I haven't been as bad. I'm trying to break free. But how? In a small town like Wyatt, how can I ever hope to find myself?

My hand travels to the back of my neck as I continue staring at the peaks, the colors fierce too—red, yellow, purple, and blue, ever-changing—and I touch the pendant at my throat, the one Kim bought for my birthday, one half of a heart, and she has the other.   "You're my best brother," she said as she handed it over, and I laughed. "I'm your *only* brother," I replied, but she just shrugged. Her face appears alongside Mom's, and there's such innocence in it. She's nearly twelve. I have dark hair like my father, and she's blond like Mom. Her hair's always in pigtails, and freckles cover the bridge of her nose. She's cute and sentimental as hell. I don't wear this chain often. Truth is, I don't wear it at all. If Johnny and the others saw it…my girlfriend too…

It upsets Kim that I don't. She never takes hers off. I've put it on today, though, wouldn't leave the house without it, and I'm glad I did, never realizing before how much comfort it gives me, a sign of love, pure and genuine. So, fuck Johnny. And fuck the rest of them.

The sun is so hot, and the AC barely works. The heat is making me tired. Life is. If I pull over and close my eyes, just for a short while, I could find escape that way. Then, when I wake, my head'll be clearer. I'll feel…better. Lately, I've hardly slept at all.

I do it and let my eyelids flicker shut. I'll decide what to do after, whether to turn back or just keep going. Dreams. They're weird. They're forming in my head even before I'm fully under. I'm on a road, a long dark road, and I *should* keep going. Everything's so slow in the dream, languid, but there's also a sense of urgency at odds with it.

My body jolts. I'm breathing hard.

I've slept, but now I'm awake, although my mind…it's like that dust cloud from earlier has somehow managed to get inside it; everything's so hazy. I have to work hard to clear it. *Keep going. Keep going.* These words echo in my mind for the longest time.

From having slumped in my seat, I sit up, blinking hard.

The sun's fading; there's no shimmer anymore, all colors muted.

How long have I slept for?

I check my watch. *Hours.* How?

My breath hitches. Darkness—it'll come soon, take hold, and in the Badlands it's blacker than black. The stars and now, the coolness of an October morning greeting her.

She'd pick up her friend and colleague Ray on her way. He borrowed his mom's sedan when he could, but otherwise caught a ride with Shady, the pair of them always excited about what another day at the Mason Town Museum would bring, located thirty miles from their hometown of Idaho Falls, in Bingham County. Annie Hawkins, the owner, was also in today, curating, Shady and Ray usually taking turns helping her and greeting visitors.

There was Ray, standing outside his mother's house, a big grin on his face and his red hair sticking out at angles like it always did. Shady smiled to see him. Although they'd attended the same high school in Idaho Falls, Fairmont High, they hadn't been friends there, had only known *of* each other. She knew too how much he was teased because his hair, the names other kids would call him. They'd pick on you, a certain contingent, if there was anything about you that didn't make you a clone of them. She'd escaped pretty lightly, she supposed. Ellen and Bill were blond and blue-eyed, but she'd turned out a different color entirely— dark hair, dark eyes, and her skin not as fair, all courtesy of her Native American grandmother, Kanti—*she who sings*— whom she hadn't truly known about until recent years. Who died when Shady was a baby. *Hanged* herself…

Shady wound down the window.

"Hey, Ray! Ready for today?"

"Another day in paradise?" he replied, grinning. "Bring it."

Always grinning, that was Ray Bartlett. Probably even smiled through the teasing at Fairmont, but he'd had plenty of friends too; he was a popular guy.

They might've only gotten to know each other *after* high

12

---

the moon too far away to make a difference.

Mom. Dad. They don't understand me, but…I long for them. For Beth and Kim. For my family. There's a whisper in my ear, as though I'm dreaming still, but words different from before. My *own* words: *It'll be all right. It'll work out. Don't go.*

I want to believe it! If I can get them to understand me, my folks, not condemn me, I can be stronger. Stand up to Johnny, not get pulled deeper into his web, 'cause if I do, it'll destroy me like it'll destroy him, eventually, and everything else his life touches.

Badlands. Bad seed. That's what he is. And what I've been too.

But no longer. I want to change. That sleep *has* done me good.

Running ain't the solution. You can't be a coward forever. I'll leave Wyatt one day, but maybe now isn't the time.

I need to look out for Kim and Beth. Despite everything, I'm still their big brother. It's my duty to protect them. I've seen it, when we're out and Beth walks past, how the guys look at her. Not Johnny, though. *Thankfully.* He seems to look right through her. But she's at that age when guys take notice. Sixteen, blond like Mom and Kim, and pretty.

I turn the car around. The Spook Road's back in front of me, twisting and turning the way it does, always so secretive. The *longest* of roads.

Johnny's traveled it alone by night as well as day. And if he can, so can I.

He survived, didn't he? Said there's nothing to be afraid of.

Five bridges one way.

9

Five bridges back again.

Supposed to be.

But sometimes, just sometimes…one disappears.

BULLSHIT!

Nothing to be afraid of, not Johnny or his gang or some trashy made-up urban legend. I'm not a kid anymore, not a pushover. I want to belong, but not to them.

I can work my way out of this mess.

Somehow. Someway.

Make my folks proud of me, Beth too, and Kim, although…she's *already* proud.

My foot on the gas, I'm pressing down, *revving* that engine, more dust kicking up.

I'll get a job, something decent, maybe at that pharmaceutical company that's opened up in Murdoc. They're recruiting right now. I can start at the bottom, climb the ladder.

Imagine it: me, Ethan Wick, a kid from nowheresville, making something of himself.

I eye again what lies in front of me.

The Spook Road.

A backroad in the backcountry.

A dirt road.

Dirtier than ever…

In minutes, I'm back on it.

CHAPTER ONE

"Mom? You okay?"

"What? Oh, yeah, sure, honey. It's a just…I'm chasing invoices, you know? And da always the big guns that don't pay, that hold they can."

"Really? So, what're you gonna do about

Turning to face her daughter, Ellen Gro *those* smiles, adding such steel to otherwis "Sweetheart, I'm going to hunt them down pay."

Shady burst out laughing. "Savage! Tha Momma. One savage lady."

Ellen simply shrugged. "I'll take that as "Believe me, it was meant to be."

Their morning exchange over, Shad door, no time to grab coffee from the kitc work cut out running a stationery supp Shady's dad, Bill Groves, and Sha vocation—working in a museum.

"You'll be home for dinner?" Ellen c door shut.

"Only if it's meatloaf."

"It's meatloaf," Ellen assured her, S

school, but she was glad they had. Along with Josie Lea Wong, he was pretty much her best friend ever.

He opened the door to Shady's Dodge Stratus, a bit of a rust bucket, she had to admit, but reliable enough, and threw himself into the front passenger seat, the car rocking from his vivacity. They began the drive, thirty miles taking around forty-five minutes, give or take, on roads that grew increasingly quiet the farther they got from their hometown.

Mason in Bingham County was small compared to Idaho Falls, a welcome sign at the side of the road claiming the population was 690—a bit of give or take in there too, considering the sign was as old and rusted as the Stratus. Somewhat down on its luck, the town had a couple of diners and a handful of stores, all of which were functional, including a decent grocery store and a bakery that sold the best cinnamon rolls—as big as your head, almost—which she and Annie always shared whenever they had one. Not Ray, though. He'd have one all to himself, then complain when his belt needed loosening a notch again. All Mason was, was a thoroughfare. Plenty of people passed through it on their way to somewhere, but if they noticed the museum, if they needed a break, they'd stop. Some even *beat* a path to it after Ray had written an online article about one of their exhibits, a doll called Mandy that'd give Annabelle a run for her money. Luckily, she was contained in a hermetically sealed glass box and bombarded with all the good vibes that Shady, Ray, and Annie could direct her way, breaking down the darkness in her, bit by determined bit.

The museum was at the end of Main Street, several steps leading up to its heavy oak door. It wasn't just any old museum, though, and Mandy not the only object with negative energy attached, energy that could influence people unwittingly, *dangerously*. And so, it had become Annie's duty to locate and contain such objects, to negate them, something she'd always done and that her father had as well back home in Lavenham, England. She was like a secret caretaker, and now Shady and Ray had signed up to help shoulder the burden. Visitors were welcomed to the museum, which was open seven days a week except for Easter, Christmas Day, and New Year's Day, and there were some pretty fascinating things in there, a real eclectic mix. The public was welcomed not because Annie wanted to expose anyone to danger but because the *objects* needed exposing, to be dragged out of the darkness and into the light so they could be admired, just the beauty of them, what was good or interesting. A beautiful piece of jewelry, for example, or an ornament of some description. The people doing the admiring also helped to break down the attached energy, even if they never knew it.

The journey passed in companionable silence, Ray itching to put some music on, but it was her car, so her rules. Shady liked quiet in the morning, time in which to bolster herself, because when she'd asked Ray if he was ready for today, she wasn't simply being blithe. With a job like theirs, you never knew what was coming. Most days were pretty ordinary, but some weren't, and she just had a feeling about today…that it'd be different somehow. And so, even if he was always all guns blazing, she took advantage of the journey to prepare herself because she was the one who had the gift—who could hold objects and read them. Psychometry, it was called, inherited not from Ellen but Kanti, and because of constant practice and attention, gaining in strength. She was okay; she could handle it. Annie and Ray helped in that respect too, grounded her, as did her the moon too far away to make a difference.

Mom. Dad. They don't understand me, but…I long for them. For Beth and Kim. For my family. There's a whisper in my ear, as though I'm dreaming still, but words different from before. My *own* words: *It'll be all right. It'll work out.* Don't *go*.

I want to believe it! If I can get them to understand me, my folks, not condemn me, I can be stronger. Stand up to Johnny, not get pulled deeper into his web, 'cause if I do, it'll destroy me like it'll destroy him, eventually, and everything else his life touches.

Badlands. Bad seed. That's what he is. And what I've been too.

But no longer. I want to change. That sleep *has* done me good.

Running ain't the solution. You can't be a coward forever. I'll leave Wyatt one day, but maybe now isn't the time.

I need to look out for Kim and Beth. Despite everything, I'm still their big brother. It's my duty to protect them. I've seen it, when we're out and Beth walks past, how the guys look at her. Not Johnny, though. *Thankfully*. He seems to look right through her. But she's at that age when guys take notice. Sixteen, blond like Mom and Kim, and pretty.

I turn the car around. The Spook Road's back in front of me, twisting and turning the way it does, always so secretive. The *longest* of roads.

Johnny's traveled it alone by night as well as day. And if he can, so can I.

He survived, didn't he? Said there's nothing to be afraid of.

Five bridges one way.

Five bridges back again.

Supposed to be.

But sometimes, just sometimes…one disappears.

BULLSHIT!

Nothing to be afraid of, not Johnny or his gang or some trashy made-up urban legend. I'm not a kid anymore, not a pushover. I want to belong, but not to them.

I can work my way out of this mess.

Somehow. Someway.

Make my folks proud of me, Beth too, and Kim, although…she's *already* proud.

My foot on the gas, I'm pressing down, *revving* that engine, more dust kicking up.

I'll get a job, something decent, maybe at that pharmaceutical company that's opened up in Murdoc. They're recruiting right now. I can start at the bottom, climb the ladder.

Imagine it: me, Ethan Wick, a kid from nowheresville, making something of himself.

I eye again what lies in front of me.

The Spook Road.

A backroad in the backcountry.

A dirt road.

Dirtier than ever…

In minutes, I'm back on it.

CHAPTER ONE

"Mom? You okay?"

"What? Oh, yeah, sure, honey. It's all good. It's just…I'm chasing invoices, you know? And damn it, but it's always the big guns that don't pay, that hold out as long as they can."

"Really? So, what're you gonna do about it?"

Turning to face her daughter, Ellen Groves gave one of *those* smiles, adding such steel to otherwise soft features. "Sweetheart, I'm going to hunt them down and *make* them pay."

Shady burst out laughing. "Savage! That's what you are, Momma. One savage lady."

Ellen simply shrugged. "I'll take that as a compliment."

"Believe me, it was meant to be."

Their morning exchange over, Shady headed for the door, no time to grab coffee from the kitchen. Ellen had her work cut out running a stationery supplies company with Shady's dad, Bill Groves, and Shady had her own vocation—working in a museum.

"You'll be home for dinner?" Ellen called just before the door shut.

"Only if it's meatloaf."

"It's meatloaf," Ellen assured her, Shady out on the path

now, the coolness of an October morning greeting her.

She'd pick up her friend and colleague Ray on her way. He borrowed his mom's sedan when he could, but otherwise caught a ride with Shady, the pair of them always excited about what another day at the Mason Town Museum would bring, located thirty miles from their hometown of Idaho Falls, in Bingham County. Annie Hawkins, the owner, was also in today, curating, Shady and Ray usually taking turns helping her and greeting visitors.

There was Ray, standing outside his mother's house, a big grin on his face and his red hair sticking out at angles like it always did. Shady smiled to see him. Although they'd attended the same high school in Idaho Falls, Fairmont High, they hadn't been friends there, had only known *of* each other. She knew too how much he was teased because of his hair, the names other kids would call him. They'd pick on you, a certain contingent, if there was anything about you that didn't make you a clone of them. She'd escaped pretty lightly, she supposed. Ellen and Bill were blond and blue-eyed, but she'd turned out a different color entirely— dark hair, dark eyes, and her skin not as fair, all courtesy of a Native American grandmother, Kanti—*she who sings*— whom she hadn't truly known about until recent years. She'd died when Shady was a baby. *Hanged* herself…

Shady wound down the window.

"Hey, Ray! Ready for today?"

"Another day in paradise?" he replied, grinning. "Bring it on!"

Always grinning, that was Ray Bartlett. Probably even grinned through the teasing at Fairmont, but he'd had plenty of friends too; he was a popular guy.

They might've only gotten to know each other *after* high

school, but she was glad they had. Along with Josie Lea Wong, he was pretty much her best friend ever.

He opened the door to Shady's Dodge Stratus, a bit of a rust bucket, she had to admit, but reliable enough, and threw himself into the front passenger seat, the car rocking from his vivacity. They began the drive, thirty miles taking around forty-five minutes, give or take, on roads that grew increasingly quiet the farther they got from their hometown.

Mason in Bingham County was small compared to Idaho Falls, a welcome sign at the side of the road claiming the population was 690—a bit of give or take in there too, considering the sign was as old and rusted as the Stratus. Somewhat down on its luck, the town had a couple of diners and a handful of stores, all of which were functional, including a decent grocery store and a bakery that sold the best cinnamon rolls—as big as your head, almost—which she and Annie always shared whenever they had one. Not Ray, though. He'd have one all to himself, then complain when his belt needed loosening a notch again. All Mason was, was a thoroughfare. Plenty of people passed through it on their way to somewhere, but if they noticed the museum, if they needed a break, they'd stop. Some even *beat* a path to it after Ray had written an online article about one of their exhibits, a doll called Mandy that'd give Annabelle a run for her money. Luckily, she was contained in a hermetically sealed glass box and bombarded with all the good vibes that Shady, Ray, and Annie could direct her way, breaking down the darkness in her, bit by determined bit.

The museum was at the end of Main Street, several steps leading up to its heavy oak door. It wasn't just any old museum, though, and Mandy not the only object with negative energy attached, energy that could influence people unwittingly, *dangerously*. And so, it had become Annie's duty to locate and contain such objects, to negate them, something she'd always done and that her father had as well back home in Lavenham, England. She was like a secret caretaker, and now Shady and Ray had signed up to help shoulder the burden. Visitors were welcomed to the museum, which was open seven days a week except for Easter, Christmas Day, and New Year's Day, and there were some pretty fascinating things in there, a real eclectic mix. The public was welcomed not because Annie wanted to expose anyone to danger but because the *objects* needed exposing, to be dragged out of the darkness and into the light so they could be admired, just the beauty of them, what was good or interesting. A beautiful piece of jewelry, for example, or an ornament of some description. The people doing the admiring also helped to break down the attached energy, even if they never knew it.

The journey passed in companionable silence, Ray itching to put some music on, but it was her car, so her rules. Shady liked quiet in the morning, time in which to bolster herself, because when she'd asked Ray if he was ready for today, she wasn't simply being blithe. With a job like theirs, you never knew what was coming. Most days were pretty ordinary, but some weren't, and she just had a feeling about today…that it'd be different somehow. And so, even if he was always all guns blazing, she took advantage of the journey to prepare herself because she was the one who had the gift—who could hold objects and read them. Psychometry, it was called, inherited not from Ellen but Kanti, and because of constant practice and attention, gaining in strength. She was okay; she could handle it. Annie and Ray helped in that respect too, grounded her, as did her parents and all her friends: Josie, Brett, Carrie, Sam, and Teddy. They brought her back down to earth, *normalized* life. Nights together with the gang at their regular haunt, the Golden Crown, one of Idaho Falls' most esteemed establishments—in their view, anyway—were precious to her. In their early twenties, they still goofed around like kids.

As soon as they entered Mason, Ray burst into life again.

"Wanna grab a coffee before we head on in?" he said, sitting forward in his seat and pointing at the bakery.

Shady nodded. "Sure, I could use one. You want a cinnamon roll too?"

He contemplated. "Think I'll grab a donut instead."

"Nice idea. We'll get Annie one as well. Double caramel?"

"Okay," he said, brimming with even more excitement. "Let's do this!"

Another couple of minutes and they were inside the store. As usual, Mo was behind the counter, a middle-aged woman whom Annie, being a resident of Mason, was friendly with.

"Well, hello!" she said. "What can I do you for?"

"Good morning, Mo!" Ray replied as brightly. "I'll have a latte, I think, an Americano for Shady, and a tea, please, for Annie. Plus three of your finest double-caramel donuts."

"Coming right atcha." Mo—short for Maureen, Annie had told them—hopped to it.

Not even 9:00 a.m., it was quiet in the bakery for a Saturday. Probably it would stay that way until midmorning, when Mo'd get a lunchtime rush from all of around ten people. But like Annie with the museum, she showed up for work every day anyway, barring Sunday, and whatever the season, always making the most of holiday

15

traffic around Indigenous Peoples' Day, Veterans Day, and Thanksgiving, opening earlier then and shutting later, a true Mason legend.

There was another bout of silence in the store while Mo fulfilled their order, Ray ogling the cinnamon rolls despite having ordered a donut, and Shady standing idly, staring at nothing but a clock on the wall as it ticked away, three rows of shelves beside it filled with fresh pastries and cakes and bread rolls that would go to feed the good folks of Mason on this fine day. She might even pick up a sourdough baguette, pop out at lunchtime for it. Ellen made a mean tomato sauce to go with her meatloaf. It'd be perfect for mopping it up with.

If she'd had any unease earlier, any suspicion that today wouldn't be an everyday kind of day, it was gone. She was happy, relaxed, and looking forward to coffee and donuts and simply whiling away a morning at the museum. *That's* what she was musing about when the door opened and another customer walked in, or so Shady assumed.

A woman. No, not a woman, more of a kid, a teenager. Around eighteen? Her eyes were red rimmed and her nose a little pink, as if she either had a cold or had been crying. A pretty girl with blond hair and blue eyes, slight in build, dressed in jeans and a blue hoodie.

Ray smiled at her. "Hey. How you doing?"

Mo looked up too and welcomed her in the usual way.

Strange thing was, the girl was focused on Shady and *only* Shady.

"I've driven a long way," she said, ignoring the other two.

"You have?" A lame response, but it was the best a surprised Shady could offer.

Ray stepped closer. "Looking for the best donuts in

town?" He was seemingly oblivious to the fact she hadn't acknowledged him yet, or at the very least refused to take offense. He also appeared not to notice that she was clutching at something. "'Cause if you are, you've come to the right place. Well...the *only* place in Mason. But let me tell ya, they also do a pretty mean cinnamon roll. In fact, I might just order one right alongside my donut."

Despite his enthusiasm, he got no reaction, turning from the stranger to Mo, maybe for reassurance or something, then back again, still grinning but that grin slipping as, finally, it dawned: the girl who'd traveled a long way wasn't here for donuts, coffee, or friendly chat.

Instead, she held up what was in her hand, a gold necklace, and swallowed hard before once again addressing Shady.

"It's the Mason Town Museum I'm looking for. Shady Groves. That's you, isn't it?"

CHAPTER TWO

"Ah, there you are, you two," Annie said as they entered the Mason Town Museum. Then, giving only a slight frown, she amended the sentence. "There you are, you...*three.*"

Ray reached the counter first, handing over Annie's tea and donut before making the introductions. "This is Beth. Beth Wick. She's...um...come a long way to see us. From South Dakota, in fact. Almost six hundred miles."

"Six hundred and thirty-five," Beth amended, then more shyly, "It's *over* six hundred. I left right after school yesterday."

"My, oh my," Annie said. Despite having spent so many years on American soil, her English accent remained as strong as ever. "That's a long way indeed." She came out from behind the counter, took the time to thank Ray for bringing her breakfast, then ignored it while she got better acquainted with the girl. "How did you hear of us?"

Immediately Beth pointed at the doll in the glass case. "Because of her. Mandy."

Although the museum was privately owned by Annie, and something of a personal crusade, it had to make money if it was going to survive. Before Mandy, before Shady and Ray too, it had been running at a loss, Annie'd said, any private money reserves she'd plowed into it running perilously low. Post-Mandy, Ray'd had the idea to leak information about her onto social media. After all, he'd reasoned, who doesn't love a haunted doll? He was right; they did, and so the public had come, traveling like Beth had from far and wide, but not with objects of their own. Most of them didn't, anyway; they simply wanted to have a look at her, to *boast* that they had, having their photo taken right alongside her, then posting on Instagram with captions such as "Who's afraid of the big bad doll? Not me!" Harmless behavior. So far. And the museum was now breaking even, Ray also having raised the entry fee. Quite the businessman, was Ray, taking just another failing venture and turning it around. He also took care of museum accounts too, Shady having no head for figures. So, yeah, he was smart. He'd brought people to their door. And now he'd brought Beth.

Shady cleared her throat. "She's got a necklace she wants us to look at." Not true; she wanted *Shady* to look at it specifically. Not that Ray had ever put anything about Shady's gift online. She wasn't the one who needed exposure. There was, however, on their website a photo of the team with Mandy, and somehow, someway, Beth had zoned in on her, as if—Shady shook her head, no matter how imperceptibly—as if she'd *known* already.

Even now, as the four of them formed something of a circle, the girl kept glancing her way, her eyes pleading.

It was Annie's business, though. She was the boss, so she took the reins.

"Would you mind showing *me* the necklace?" she asked, holding her hand out, although in a friendly manner. Annie was in no way pushy. She was probably the kindest and wisest person Shady had ever known. Ray thought the same, had said so about a million times. Shady had her family comprised of Ellen and Bill, she an only child, but right here in front of her was her second family; that's how precious they'd become. A crazy red-haired guy the same age as her and a middle-aged English woman who dressed mainly in brown, and because of it known fondly (and secretively) by Shady as Rhapsody-in-Brown.

Beth hesitated. More than that, she clutched the necklace tighter and again turned her baby-blue peepers toward Shady, clearly wanting to hand it to her and her only. Shady could do it, she supposed, reach for it before Annie and see what she could sense. Annie wouldn't be best pleased, though. She was big on Shady using her gift in a controlled manner, Annie or Ray handling any objects first, sensing what they could, just how negative a vibe it had, before she got involved, and only then with them flanking her. Thing was, they were flanking her now, so would it really be a problem? And yet she couldn't do it, give in to the girl's wishes, the unease she'd felt this morning having returned with a vengeance.

Annie had not retracted her hand, and from being held captive by Beth's gaze, Shady looked away, indicating if Beth wanted help, she'd have to comply with what Annie had asked.

She handed the necklace over, Annie first enclosing both hands around it, holding it tight, then holding it up to what light there was in the museum, sometimes bright, but sometimes it would dim, particularly when a new object arrived, one that was potent.

The light *was* dimmer than usual, but the necklace glinted nonetheless. A golden chain, it had what looked like a heart on it, or rather *half* a heart.

still ringing in her ears, and in it was the weight of
1, grief and sorrow beyond imagining, fear and
. Annie had held the necklace, *easily* she'd held it,
1 Shady had, she'd had to fling it from herself,
carry that much weight, not yet strong enough.
landed at the foot of Mandy's glass case. And she'd
was absolutely certain, that the evil that possessed
as howling too, but with laughter.
when Annie had burst into action and scooped
ly and the necklace up, hurrying everyone along to
oom and closing the door behind them.
g downed half the water, Shady mentioned the
, Annie glancing briefly over her shoulder at Ray
before replying.
ps it's best we leave it for today. Let you recover
gth further."
would love nothing more than to leave it, not just
but perhaps forever. Even so, she heard herself
"Beth's come a long way."
..yes—"
six hundred miles."
now that—"
we go to the basement, take the necklace down
1 I'll handle it in a more—" she swallowed "—
manner."
nodded, her brown hair, peppered with grey,
lightly. "If you're sure?"
ere it was, in the brown of Annie's bespectacled
just an excitement but relief. The necklace was
arged, so of course she wanted to understand it.
her job, *all* their jobs, Shady's and Ray's too,
nly through understanding could they hope to

"This is yours?" Annie said, continuing to examine it, her tea growing cold behind her, Shady's coffee too. Only Ray was holding his drink and sipping intermittently.

Beth shook her head. "It belongs to my younger sister, Kim."

"I see," Annie replied, clearly a lie, because she was frowning again with something like confusion. "And why have you brought it to us at the Mason Town Museum?"

"It's one half of a heart, right?" Beth asked.

All three of the museum employees nodded.

"The other half belongs to my brother."

"Your brother?" Ray mused.

"Uh-huh. My older brother. I'm the middle child. Kim gave it to him for his birthday a couple of years back. She was, like, devoted to him, you know? That whole kid-sister, big-brother thing going down. She had his back when…when no one else did."

"They didn't?" Ray took a step forward to get a closer look.

"No. He was…I don't know…the black sheep of the family, you could say. Ran with the wrong crowd. Thing is, he was only nineteen; he could've straightened out."

"Could've?" Shady whispered. "What happened to him?"

Since they'd met in the coffee shop, Beth had had a defiant air about her. Now, her shoulders slumped as her eyes filled with tears. She looked defeated. Sad. Lost, even.

"Dear?" said Annie, also stepping closer, the necklace back in her fist now as, with her free hand, she reached out to gently touch the girl's arm in a gesture of consolation.

"I don't know what happened," Beth said after a while. "He left the house one day in August two years back, and we haven't heard from him since. He disappeared."

Annie made no secret of her confusion this time. "Disappeared? Gone missing, you mean? There's been an official investigation, I take it?"

"Uh-huh."

"A *thorough* investigation?"

"The sheriff said so, but as there's no body, it was never treated as a homicide." The girl reached out to Annie also, but only because she wanted to reclaim the necklace. "I brought it here because…because he's gone," she said, "and now Kim's gone too. She died last year in a car accident. Mom's a mess. She cries all the time, and Dad locks himself away in his home office, hardly speaks to anyone." Tears trailed down her cheeks, but there was also anger in her voice. "He did this! Ethan. When he went, when he took off, our family just…fell apart. And if he's out there, if he's keeping tabs on us, he should come back and help. Losing one family member is bad enough, but two…"

Beth couldn't continue, had lowered her head, trying to hide the emotions coursing through her. Even so, Shady felt every one of them, the girl's grief and bewilderment.

She also drew closer but didn't touch the girl, not yet. "We're sorry," she said.

In a museum full of things that harbored emotion, which people such as Beth had poured into them, empty vessels subsequently filled, the air seemed to crackle and hiss with the recognition of her suffering. Shady was sure no one else could hear it, but the atmosphere was so alive suddenly, with like calling to like across the aisles, the good, the bad, and the downright ugly. She didn't turn to look at Mandy sitting in the glass sealed box, but she could imagine well enough the doll's head lifting slightly as it took notice, as it *fed* off the grief Beth had brought into this large, lofty building

with her, Mandy's beady black ey[e]
for more of it, *encouraging* it.

They had to get Beth off th[e]
into the sanctuary of the base[ment]
examine the necklace properly.

Planning on doing that, S[hady]
entrance first and flip the sign to
to be any visitors this morning,
Mason who thought they migh[t]
the small-town museum had to [o]

Before she could put any di[stance]
the others, though, Beth's hand [s]

"Here," she said. "Take it."

No warning, no preamble[,]
reacted, did as she was asked.

Not just half a heart, a *cracke[d]*
And it *howled* at her.

* * *

"Better, Shady?"

Instead of the basement, the[y]
the back of the museum, Annie [p]
into Shady's hand and insisting

Behind Annie stood a conce[rned]
Beth, such a slight girl, the top
Ray's shoulder.

"Sorry," Beth muttered. "I'[m]
to—"

Annie hushed her, her ton[e]
"Allow us a moment, please."

Just the one? thought Shady

pacify it. As much as this was a crusade for Annie, as much as she could tell when an object "wasn't right," she didn't have Shady's ability, couldn't sense as deeply or see as far. And that ability had to be put to use somehow, do some good.

But to hear that howl again, something so…malignant.

Shady shook her head as she rose in an attempt to clear it.

She'd do as Annie'd taught her. Before it was back in her hand, she'd surround herself in white light, the light of protection, strong and pure, against which the darkness was powerless. She'd be prepared this time, not have it thrust upon her, and so it'd be different.

Surely?

Only one way to find out.

All four of them relocated to the basement, an iron staircase spiraling downward, Annie always holding on to the handrail for dear life and their shoes producing a clickety-clack that echoed through the entire building, enlivening it further.

Beth was given the option of joining them or sitting on a stool farther back. She could even wait outside the building if she chose, in her car, perhaps.

The girl didn't hesitate. "I'm staying right here with you." And again, it was Shady she was looking at, *fixating* on.

Beth clearly knew of Shady's ability despite it not being written anywhere, certainly not in any information to do with the museum. She knew because…she had an ability too? The necklace wasn't hers; it was her sister's, her *dead* sister's, and the other half of the pendant belonged to her brother, her *missing* brother. Perhaps that kind of thing, dealing with the dead or the presumed dead, people who were so close to you, your own flesh and blood, made you more sensitive. In that respect, Shady hoped she'd never find out.

In the basement, Annie flicked on the lights. She liked it bright down there, strip lights practically neon, but as with the light elsewhere in this building, they sometimes failed to reach their full potential. Perfectly aware of this, and to counteract it, she'd installed some standalone spotlights too, five of them, and so she went around switching them on as well, her lips tight together, indicating her own unease, perhaps.

Shady watched as Beth looked all around, her eyes wide and her breath ever so slightly ragged. More items were stored down here, most of them covered in white sheets and all awaiting attention. They'd have to wait a little longer. The necklace took priority.

Once Beth was seated, Shady joined her at the long and wide oak desk. Her own breath was unsteady too, causing her to remind herself she was safe. She'd not only employ the techniques Annie had taught her regarding the light, drawing it straight down from Source, but she also had her colleagues by her side, who'd snatch the necklace from her if she displayed any signs of distress, therefore breaking the connection. That was the plan, anyway. The theory. And no reason to distrust it. It had worked before.

Some objects, though… Shady couldn't help her mind wandering. A chair had been brought into the museum earlier in the year, heavy oak but stained such a dark color, practically black, and carved with a variety of symbols she'd never seen before. It had been practically dumped on their doorstep, the owner backing away before Annie'd had a

26

"This is yours?" Annie said, continuing to examine it, her tea growing cold behind her, Shady's coffee too. Only Ray was holding his drink and sipping intermittently.

Beth shook her head. "It belongs to my younger sister, Kim."

"I see," Annie replied, clearly a lie, because she was frowning again with something like confusion. "And why have you brought it to us at the Mason Town Museum?"

"It's one half of a heart, right?" Beth asked.

All three of the museum employees nodded.

"The other half belongs to my brother."

"Your brother?" Ray mused.

"Uh-huh. My older brother. I'm the middle child. Kim gave it to him for his birthday a couple of years back. She was, like, devoted to him, you know? That whole kid-sister, big-brother thing going down. She had his back when…when no one else did."

"They didn't?" Ray took a step forward to get a closer look.

"No. He was…I don't know…the black sheep of the family, you could say. Ran with the wrong crowd. Thing is, he was only nineteen; he could've straightened out."

"Could've?" Shady whispered. "What happened to him?"

Since they'd met in the coffee shop, Beth had had a defiant air about her. Now, her shoulders slumped as her eyes filled with tears. She looked defeated. Sad. Lost, even.

"Dear?" said Annie, also stepping closer, the necklace back in her fist now as, with her free hand, she reached out to gently touch the girl's arm in a gesture of consolation.

"I don't know what happened," Beth said after a while. "He left the house one day in August two years back, and we haven't heard from him since. He disappeared."

Annie made no secret of her confusion this time. "Disappeared? Gone missing, you mean? There's been an official investigation, I take it?"

"Uh-huh."

"A *thorough* investigation?"

"The sheriff said so, but as there's no body, it was never treated as a homicide." The girl reached out to Annie also, but only because she wanted to reclaim the necklace. "I brought it here because…because he's gone," she said, "and now Kim's gone too. She died last year in a car accident. Mom's a mess. She cries all the time, and Dad locks himself away in his home office, hardly speaks to anyone." Tears trailed down her cheeks, but there was also anger in her voice. "He did this! Ethan. When he went, when he took off, our family just…fell apart. And if he's out there, if he's keeping tabs on us, he should come back and help. Losing one family member is bad enough, but two…"

Beth couldn't continue, had lowered her head, trying to hide the emotions coursing through her. Even so, Shady felt every one of them, the girl's grief and bewilderment.

She also drew closer but didn't touch the girl, not yet. "We're sorry," she said.

In a museum full of things that harbored emotion, which people such as Beth had poured into them, empty vessels subsequently filled, the air seemed to crackle and hiss with the recognition of her suffering. Shady was sure no one else could hear it, but the atmosphere was so alive suddenly, with like calling to like across the aisles, the good, the bad, and the downright ugly. She didn't turn to look at Mandy sitting in the glass sealed box, but she could imagine well enough the doll's head lifting slightly as it took notice, as it *fed* off the grief Beth had brought into this large, lofty building with her, Mandy's beady black eyes, usually fixed, searching for more of it, *encouraging* it.

They had to get Beth off the main museum floor and into the sanctuary of the basement, where they could examine the necklace properly.

Planning on doing that, Shady would head to the entrance first and flip the sign to *Closed*. If there were going to be any visitors this morning, someone passing through Mason who thought they might stop and check out what the small-town museum had to offer, too bad.

Before she could put any distance between herself and the others, though, Beth's hand shot out and stopped her.

"Here," she said. "Take it."

No warning, no preamble, so Shady automatically reacted, did as she was asked.

Not just half a heart, a *cracked* heart.

And it *howled* at her.

* * *

"Better, Shady?"

Instead of the basement, they were in the staff room at the back of the museum, Annie pressing a glass of cold water into Shady's hand and insisting she drink it.

Behind Annie stood a concerned Ray and a bewildered Beth, such a slight girl, the top of her head barely meeting Ray's shoulder.

"Sorry," Beth muttered. "I'm really sorry. I didn't mean to—"

Annie hushed her, her tone gentle but authoritative. "Allow us a moment, please."

Just the one? thought Shady. She'd need several! That

23

howl was still ringing in her ears, and in it was the weight of the world, grief and sorrow beyond imagining, fear and anger too. Annie had held the necklace, *easily* she'd held it, but when Shady had, she'd had to fling it from herself, unable to carry that much weight, not yet strong enough.

It had landed at the foot of Mandy's glass case. And she'd swear, *she was absolutely certain*, that the evil that possessed Mandy was howling too, but with laughter.

That's when Annie had burst into action and scooped both Shady and the necklace up, hurrying everyone along to the staff room and closing the door behind them.

Having downed half the water, Shady mentioned the basement, Annie glancing briefly over her shoulder at Ray and Beth before replying.

"Perhaps it's best we leave it for today. Let you recover your strength further."

Shady would love nothing more than to leave it, not just for today but perhaps forever. Even so, she heard herself insisting, "Beth's come a long way."

"Well…yes—"

"Over six hundred miles."

"We know that—"

"Then we go to the basement, take the necklace down there, and I'll handle it in a more—" she swallowed "—controlled manner."

Annie nodded, her brown hair, peppered with grey, bobbing slightly. "If you're sure?"

And there it was, in the brown of Annie's bespectacled eyes, not just an excitement but relief. The necklace was highly charged, so of course she wanted to understand it. That was her job, *all* their jobs, Shady's and Ray's too, because only through understanding could they hope to

pacify it. As much as this was a crusade for Annie, as much as she could tell when an object "wasn't right," she didn't have Shady's ability, couldn't sense as deeply or see as far. And that ability had to be put to use somehow, do some good.

But to hear that howl again, something so…malignant.

Shady shook her head as she rose in an attempt to clear it.

She'd do as Annie'd taught her. Before it was back in her hand, she'd surround herself in white light, the light of protection, strong and pure, against which the darkness was powerless. She'd be prepared this time, not have it thrust upon her, and so it'd be different.

Surely?

Only one way to find out.

All four of them relocated to the basement, an iron staircase spiraling downward, Annie always holding on to the handrail for dear life and their shoes producing a clickety-clack that echoed through the entire building, enlivening it further.

Beth was given the option of joining them or sitting on a stool farther back. She could even wait outside the building if she chose, in her car, perhaps.

The girl didn't hesitate. "I'm staying right here with you." And again, it was Shady she was looking at, *fixating* on.

Beth clearly knew of Shady's ability despite it not being written anywhere, certainly not in any information to do with the museum. She knew because…she had an ability too? The necklace wasn't hers; it was her sister's, her *dead* sister's, and the other half of the pendant belonged to her brother, her *missing* brother. Perhaps that kind of thing, dealing with the dead or the presumed dead, people who were so close to you, your own flesh and blood, made you more sensitive. In that respect, Shady hoped she'd never find out.

In the basement, Annie flicked on the lights. She liked it bright down there, strip lights practically neon, but as with the light elsewhere in this building, they sometimes failed to reach their full potential. Perfectly aware of this, and to counteract it, she'd installed some standalone spotlights too, five of them, and so she went around switching them on as well, her lips tight together, indicating her own unease, perhaps.

Shady watched as Beth looked all around, her eyes wide and her breath ever so slightly ragged. More items were stored down here, most of them covered in white sheets and all awaiting attention. They'd have to wait a little longer. The necklace took priority.

Once Beth was seated, Shady joined her at the long and wide oak desk. Her own breath was unsteady too, causing her to remind herself she was safe. She'd not only employ the techniques Annie had taught her regarding the light, drawing it straight down from Source, but she also had her colleagues by her side, who'd snatch the necklace from her if she displayed any signs of distress, therefore breaking the connection. That was the plan, anyway. The theory. And no reason to distrust it. It had worked before.

Some objects, though... Shady couldn't help her mind wandering. A chair had been brought into the museum earlier in the year, heavy oak but stained such a dark color, practically black, and carved with a variety of symbols she'd never seen before. It had been practically dumped on their doorstep, the owner backing away before Annie'd had a

26

chance to question him thoroughly and ask *why* he'd wanted to get rid of it. Shady had known, though, the moment she'd set eyes on it. He'd done so because it was evil, and not just that, it had been *created* for evil, dark intent in every whittle of the knife. She didn't need to sit on it to know what a terrible object it was. Indeed, she'd refused to. Insisted instead that it be removed from the museum and put in storage somewhere, crystals and salt placed all around it until…Shady didn't know until when. Until she was strong enough to deal with it, she supposed. Which wasn't now. Which could be never. Her choice entirely—Annie was clear on that. It was *always* her choice how far she went and how deep she delved. People like them, *caretakers*, had locked away many objects like that chair, Annie had told her, until they could either be dealt with or left to rot. There were some in the world who would call such objects sacred. Annie called them profane.

Annie held on to the necklace while Shady prepared herself, Ray as wide-eyed as Beth, chewing slightly on his lower lip.

Just a necklace. Not even gold, but gold-plated. Something really cheap, bought in a store such as Walmart or Target, likely only a few dollars, mass-produced in China and sold all over this country, all over the world. Cashing in on sentimentality.

Annie asked Shady if she'd like to know more background from Beth before she began, but she shook her head.

It was a mass-produced item that had become unique.

It would tell her what she needed to know.

CHAPTER THREE

So far, so good. Shady had to remember that this was Kim's half of the necklace, who'd been a kid when she'd died, aged twelve.

Perhaps it was because she'd surrounded herself in light that she tuned in to joyful times at first, no matter how tenuous. Sitting at the desk, with the chain in her hand, it *pulsated* with memories, the kind you'd expect a kid to harbor. Ethan might have been regarded as the black sheep of the family, but this girl was a happy one, taking delight, as children should, in childish things. A new bike. She'd gotten that while wearing this chain and had loved riding the lilac Huffy through the streets of her hometown, taking great care to mind the traffic. She was a considerate kid too, more than willing to help with chores around the house. That's how she'd gotten the money to buy this chain, by sweeping the kitchen floor most days, tidying the living room, dusting around ornaments on shelves, and keeping her room neat. Another memory surfaced, a venture into someone else's room—Ethan's? All she could see was a shadow figure lying on the bed, and Kim trying to coax him or something in that way Shady could imagine a kid sister doing, being annoying, her voice becoming whiney, Ethan telling her to go away, turning on his side away from her, the kid wondering what she could do to cheer him up.

This chain offered the solution. *I love you, Ethan. Even if no one else does, I do.*

Shady sniffed. It was the sweetest of gestures. An only child herself, what she'd give to have a kid sister like that, someone in whose eyes you could do no wrong. You were a hero, simply by virtue of being older. Or maybe, just maybe, she was as perceptive in her own way as Beth was. When no one else could see the good in him, she did.

But the darkness attracted to the necklace pushed its way forward, as Shady knew it would. Kim had known innocence when wearing this necklace, and then she'd known grief, the brother she idolized disappearing and nobody knowing where.

It was drenched with bewilderment, heartbreak, and, above all, sheer disbelief. He wouldn't do that, take off without a word to anyone, to *her*. She trusted him on that, implicitly. Days passed, weeks, months, and still Ethan was missing, so she'd do as he once had and lie on her bed in a darkened room. In her hands would be the necklace, her lips moving all the while she clutched at it. *Where are you? Where've you gone? Come back!* Such fierce pleas, the child no longer lying down but on her knees, her hands clasped together as if in prayer, *shouting* those words, albeit silently, screaming them in her head. *You* have *to come back! Ethan, listen to me. We* all *miss you. We do!*

Did they, though? Because there was an anger that Shady didn't think belonged to the child. More shouting and screaming, this time loud enough for everyone to hear. *He* would *do that! Because he's immature, and he's selfish. Damn him for this. Damn him to hell!*

The Wicks were a family torn apart, as any family would

be having suffered such a thing, never imagining that they were to be torn apart even further.

A family trying to get back on its feet, to return to normal, some veneer of it. Kim back at school and a supportive network of friends around her. She was still wearing the chain, still clutching at it, almost a subconscious action now, although at other times it was intentional, always on the lookout for him wherever she went, scanning the crowds, the sidewalks, in between trees and bushes, places he could be hiding, spying on them, trying to reach out. *Because he wouldn't just leave us. I've told you! He wouldn't!*

Shady started. Those last words…it was as though they'd been thrown at *her*, not the parents, hurled in her face. *Listen to me!*

Immediately, she replied. *Kim? Kim, I am listening. Are you still attached?*

Hard to tell if this was an intelligent haunting and, therefore, something of her spirit clinging to it. Alternatively, it could just be an echo, a resonance. Since buying the necklace, Kim had worn it always. It was precious to her. So how come she wasn't buried with it? Had Beth retrieved it? When her sister had lain cold in the casket, the necklace glinting around her neck, had she reached in when no one was looking and taken it? If so, was it because she knew how significant it was, that it was the final link, not just to her sister but her brother too? And so, no way it'd go into the ground too.

It was Beth who'd later sit with the necklace and hold it, ask not where Ethan was but where they *both* were. When the car crash had happened, Kim had been wearing the necklace as she always had, one hand reaching up and

caressing it like a talisman. A woman had been driving her, with another child in the front seat—so a friend's mother, perhaps? Kim was in the back. Kim…who was craning her neck, searching, searching, searching. Thinking she'd seen Ethan again? Shouting. Unlocking her seatbelt. The woman turned around. *Put your seatbelt back on, honey. Honey? Listen to me. I said, put your seatbelt back on.* Kim was not obeying, continued to shout, although Shady couldn't hear what. Pointing? Was that what she was doing?

Shady echoed the driver. *Put your seatbelt on, Kim. Do as she says!*

A futile gesture. She knew the outcome, couldn't change it. The woman was reaching over now, only one hand on the wheel, her own kid beside her sitting there and frowning, not quite knowing what was going on. The woman mouthed something again. *I said—*

No more words, just a screech of metal as loud as the howl had been earlier, every bit as ear-piercing. There was the dull thud of the windshield glass too and tires skidding as Kim hurtled toward the dashboard, nothing more than a rag doll. There was gravel and the jewels of broken glass. A cloud of dust—so much dust that, briefly, it swallowed the car whole, along with whatever or whoever they'd crashed into.

There was silence within that cloud, which had now become something of a tunnel, and Shady, like a wraith, traveled down it. A long, long tunnel, with no end in sight.

What had Kim seen to make her act that way? What had she been pointing at? *Excitedly* pointing? Had she been right thinking Ethan might be close by and had caught sight of him?

She'd been the only fatality in the crash. The seatbelts

had saved the other two. What had possessed her to unlock herself? Everyone knew how important it was to remain buckled up, and she had been such a careful child. So why had she done it?

A thought made Shady flinch. *Had* she been possessed? By Ethan? Somehow?

Kim had so much faith in him. Was this how he'd rewarded her?

Regarded as the black sheep of the family, perhaps there was some truth in it. Maybe he was as selfish as his parents believed, this boy who lay in the dark in his room, who'd told his little sister, his adoring sister, to go away when she'd tried to support him. *Harshly* told her. *Leave me alone! I don't want to talk to you, to anyone, okay? I wish you'd all just fucking leave me alone.* What had his reaction been when she'd given him the necklace? Had he been grateful? Had he even worn it? Or had he felt embarrassed by it?

It *had* embarrassed him; Shady could sense it. Only Kim had worn hers.

There was something bad. In the dust. Following her.

She was continuing to drift through it, scanning like Kim would, not on the hunt for Ethan but for a way out. There was an obvious way out, of course: she could just let go of the chain, do as she'd done before, hurl it from herself. Something so…infected. But she didn't. She held on. Just for a short while more, to gather as much information as possible.

What was behind her? Or was it in front of her? Or to the side? *Both* sides.

What was it that…*surrounded* her?

The dust from the crash should be settling by now, beginning to clear. If it did, would she see poor Kim's twisted and broken body, a terrible sight that would have her howling too? Even so, she wished for it because *not* seeing was worse.

Whoever followed made no sound. They were drawing closer, though.

Creeping, silent creatures that would soon be able to touch her.

Shady frowned. It was she who touched things, not the other way around, who had the talent, the ability to read and to delve, deeper and deeper, to *know* things. Terrible things. Things that could haunt you, drive you mad. *Like they did with Kanti. Kanti could see this kind of stuff too, which is why she did it, hanged herself, because this...this is torture.*

She really should let the chain go, open her hand and drop it, break the spell. Try again another time. She was sure she was doing so and murmuring too for Ray and Annie, for them to help her. They were just feet away. They'd hear her. She now injected strength into her voice. "Help me, Ray! Help me, Annie! That's what you're supposed to do, isn't it? So where are you? Can you hear me? Can you?"

She was lost, and the dust wasn't clearing but forcing itself inside her mouth and nose, making her gag as she lifted her hands—free of the necklace, they had to be—and clawed at her throat. Scrabbled around there. Still no air. No way to breathe at all.

I'm hanging. Realization finally dawned. *I'm hanging, and so are others. That's what's all around me, hanging bodies.*

Bumping into her, swinging harder and harder. So many dangling corpses.

But not everyone was hanging. The one who wasn't was drenched in blood, limbs and face mangled. Kim. Walking toward her, if it could be called walking. Dragging a leg bent at an awkward angle from the knee downward, an arm angled unnaturally too. And like her sister's had been earlier, her eyes were trained on Shady—and *only* her.

When words left the child's mouth, blood splattered out too, gurgling up from deep inside like a fountain, globules of it. Shady wanted so hard to look away, but her neck in the noose was like being caught in a vice. She could only stare back as Kim spoke:

He wouldn't *have left us. You find him. Do it.*
Or stay there and hang.

bloodshot eyes, *tears* of blood staining the girl's cheeks, her hair matted with blood too. And the girl had stared back, unflinching and so, so demanding. *Find my brother*, the intimation. *Or else…*

Beth had taken the call, then held her cell up apologetically.

"Is it okay…?" she'd begun, and Annie had answered.

"The signal's erratic down here, in this entire building, in fact. Perhaps if you head outside, you'll be able to hear better."

The girl had nodded, then her eyes had roamed to the necklace.

"Don't worry," Annie'd assured her. "We'll keep it safe until you return."

A brief glimpse at Shady, and she was gone, heading back up the winding staircase, her absence giving them a chance to discuss what had happened. Shady saw no reason to hold back. She described it freely, Ray, already pale, losing any color in his cheeks.

He sighed when she was done. "What do we do now?"

A question Shady was busy asking herself.

"Kim," Annie said, "very sadly, is dead. She died not knowing where her brother had gone, after looking for him everywhere she went and, according to what you've just said, maybe even thinking she'd spotted him, hence why she unlocked her seatbelt and was pointing. She *wanted* him found. Obviously. And it's such a…desperate feeling. It must be. I can't imagine it. Don't want to. Always wondering. The sheer exhaustion of it! I'm sorry, I'm digressing. If she *had* thought she'd seen him, even if she'd imagined it, that's what you tuned in to, Shady, her desperation in the moments before death, nothing more

CHAPTER FOUR

"It was a threat? From a kid? A *dead* kid? Really?"

Shady eyed Ray. "Yep, a dead, previously cute kid. And by the way, Ray, Annie, thanks for not noticing I was in distress."

"You were?" Now Annie looked as concerned as Ray, as flummoxed. "I was carefully monitoring you. Your breathing was normal, your face muscles relaxed. Even the hand holding the necklace was relaxed. Shady, I'm so sorry. I'd have intervened straightaway if I had the merest inkling you were in trouble."

What *had* intervened was a phone call—not to any of the team, but to Beth. Her cell phone had rung, a tone Shady recognized: Ellie Goulding's "Love Me Like You Do," a somewhat sentimental choice. It had pulled her out of that fog she'd been in, a twilight place, bodies hanging on either side of her, she remembered with a shudder, and then Kim in front of her. A Kim so different from the one she'd first seen in visions, pre-accident, sweet, loving, and helpful, not yet a teenager, so she hadn't yet adopted typical teenage ways. A *great* kid, and then death had changed her—*immediately* changed her. The way she'd presented herself to Shady was nothing less than diabolic, something straight out of a cheesy B movie, Shady unable to look away, staring into substantial than that. She was pointing, I know, but was her other hand clutching the necklace?"

Shady shook her head. "I don't know. Maybe. Probably."

"I'll bet you a pound to a penny it was," Annie concluded. "And that she held on to it many, many times, during the day in school and at night in bed, until it not only resembled a broken heart, it became one, as potent as the one beating inside her."

"May I?" said Ray, holding out his hand for the necklace.

"Sure," Shady replied.

Ray wasn't psychic, but he tried his best to tune in, to practice, to help with those types of matters as well as accounts and the general running of the museum. With the necklace in his hand, he closed his eyes, Shady and Annie quiet, giving him the time he needed.

Only a couple of minutes later, he opened his eyes.

"Well?" Shady asked, ever hopeful.

"Nope, not getting anything. But if this was so precious to Kim, like she never took it off, if it began *channeling* her, why wasn't she buried with it?"

"Good question," Shady admitted. "In fact, I have a ton of questions. Why wasn't Kim buried with it, and why does Beth look at me the way she does, like she knows me, knows what I can do? It's more than a hunch. You wouldn't drive all these miles on a hunch. Does she want us to keep the necklace, try to dissolve the energy, or become more involved?"

"Become more involved. Definitely that."

Beth's answer as it traveled ahead of her on the staircase startled them. With the phone call having ended, she'd come back, *crept* along the length of the museum, it seemed, because they hadn't heard her, no footsteps from above echoing. But there she was on the stairs, *like a ghost*, thought Shady. Wouldn't that be surreal? And yet she wasn't. She was flesh and blood. There was something about her, though, something…secretive, and it unsettled Shady almost as much as her younger sister had.

Shady, Ray, and Annie remained quiet as Beth drew closer, waiting for her to expand on her wishes. First, she apologized for the phone call.

"It was my boyfriend," she said. "Checking up on me."

"Does he know why you're here?" Annie asked.

"Kinda."

If it was "kinda," then perhaps he should have come with her. That was a long way to travel alone, especially for such a young girl. And she looked tired, Beth, black rings under her eyes and the color of her skin ashen. Perhaps, though, if he knew more than "kinda," the boyfriend would have tried to stop her. It wasn't everyone in the world who agreed they were acting with good intentions. Some would class it as the devil's work.

"So yeah," she continued, coming to a standstill in front of them. Now that Shady had "met" Kim, she could see how similar they were, that if she'd lived, Kim would be a carbon copy of her big sister, perhaps even more beautiful. "I want you to get involved further. To help me." She hesitated only briefly before adding, "Help *all* of us."

"I have a question," Shady said, leading with the most pressing one.

Beth indicated for her to go ahead.

"The necklace was precious to your sister, right?"

"The most precious thing she owned."

"And your parents knew she considered it precious too?"

Again, a nod. "They did."

38

"So why wasn't she buried with it?"

God, the girl's eyes penetrated deep! They didn't miss a beat either when she replied, "She didn't want to be, that's why. She told me to take it instead."

* * *

Dreams. That's how Kim had told Beth about the necklace. So it transpired.

The girl didn't claim to be psychic. In fact, when Annie had asked her outright if she was, she'd looked horrified. "No," she'd answered. "I'm just me, normal."

Shady couldn't help but bristle. As she was psychic, what did that make her? Abnormal? And yet although her friends knew she had an uncanny ability to find lost objects—in fact, it amazed them how successful she was at that—none of them, with the exception of Josie, knew the full extent of it. The museum had some weird things for sure, Mandy, for example, but Shady wasn't sure the others believed the hype surrounding the doll; they were probably more amused by it than anything else, thinking it was just clever marketing. It was an easy ability to disguise, so that's what she did because...perhaps it *was* also a teeny bit embarrassing, altering the way people thought of you, and their expectations.

Beth was normal, or so she professed, but she seemed to think that Kim appearing to her in dreams and speaking to her was pretty normal too.

"Before Kim, you didn't have dreams about anyone else in particular?"

"Not like this, not so...recurrent." They were all back around the oak desk in the basement, the necklace for now lying there between them, glinting. "So yeah, she was just…there, in my dreams, really vivid, you know, like as real as you three are, as I am too. She kept touching her neck where the pendant was, kept saying something like 'take it.' And so, when I visited her in the funeral home, before…you know…before…"

"Before her burial," Annie said.

"Yeah, that. I asked for some time alone with her, and my dad agreed, gently helping my mom out of the room. God, she could hardly walk, she was so distraught! Alone with Kim, I reached into the casket, and…I took it, the necklace." Beth had to stop briefly and swallow hard. When she resumed, her voice was barely above a whisper. "Her skin felt so *cold*. It wasn't soft; it was like marble. I half expected her to open her eyes, to grab my hand and ask what I was doing, but she just lay there perfectly still. It wasn't Kim, not anymore. She'd become…empty. Afterward, she appeared again in my dreams. She reminded me that Ethan had the other half of the heart, as if I needed reminding, as if I'd forgotten. And that the two halves must be reunited, made whole. I don't know what's happened to Ethan, whether he's alive. I don't even know if I *want* to know anymore, because if he is… But *she* wants it. She always did. Now more than ever."

"Now more than ever?" Ray repeated. "What do you mean by that?"

"There's like this…urgency. She's always in my dreams, almost every night, always telling me to find Ethan, losing any patience she had. She just keeps…demanding."

Shady raised an eyebrow. As demanding as she'd been with her? Manifesting the way she had. Shady guessed not because, if so, Beth would be a jabbering wreck, surely?

"So, it's getting more urgent," Shady clarified, "and you found out about us at the Mason Town Museum because of Mandy, right?"

"Yeah, I saw an article online, then checked your website. There's a picture of her, and there's also one of you three standing next to the glass case, and then—" she eyed Shady in that way she did, isolating the others "—then I kept seeing your face as well. Even when I was awake, in my mind's eye. And I knew I had to bring the necklace to you, to this museum, so that you could help make sense of it all. I just…knew. Kinda."

There it was again, the caveat of "kinda," because maybe she didn't actually know what was going on. Maybe, like the necklace, she was being used as a channel too.

"Can you help me?" she asked, and her voice was small this time, uncertain.

"My dear," answered Annie, "if there's been a thorough search for Eth—"

"We'll help," Shady said. "I don't know what it is we can do, exactly, but we'll try."

Only briefly Shady glanced at Annie, noticing she'd pursed her lips slightly, but it was the expression she'd seen on Kim's face that affected her more. If it wasn't just latent energy attached to the necklace, if it was more than that, would Kim make good on her promise? Those hanging bodies, swinging into Shady's… She could feel the despair that rolled off them, their sorrow and fear. It became her own. Overwhelmed her. As Kanti had been overwhelmed. This gift, this strange, strange gift—more than that, a *legacy*—it could lead you down some dark paths. You had to take care not to linger too long, turning around only to find no way back. But if she could help toward solving the mystery of Ethan, bring closure to a family that had suffered enough, she'd give it a shot.

"Where did Kim die?" she asked.

"Just outside our hometown," Beth replied.

"Who was driving?"

"Her friend's mom," Beth confirmed.

"And who crashed into them?"

"Another woman, also with a kid in the car."

"And in that crash, only Kim died?"

"Only Kim."

Quiet for a moment, Shady continued. "What's the name of your hometown?"

"Wyatt. It's small. Real small. Closest big town is Rapid City, seventy miles away."

"Seventy miles?" Ray repeated.

"Uh-huh. We're in the backcountry. Close to the Badlands."

Shady echoed her this time. "The Badlands?"

Excitement grew in her at the prospect of visiting there. She'd ventured into the wilds of Canada before when trying to find out about Mandy's history, and she'd been to various other places too, including Oregon and California, but never had she been to South Dakota. Though situated in the Midwest, its roots were still in the *Old* West, the *Wild* West, the home of terrain both beautiful and hostile—and mysterious, it was that too. Full of myths and legends, of creatures that people thought were mythical, but myth was always rooted in truth, that which the Natives wouldn't talk about, and not just out of fear but respect.

The necklace, still glinting on the tabletop—weakly, though, like the overhead lights and a few of the spotlights by now—would only tell them so much. It was a lead, nothing more. To get to the bottom of it, she had to go with the girl to Wyatt. No way to calm the energy in the necklace otherwise, calm the spirit of Kim, not if they didn't find resolve. It was riding on Shady's shoulders to do so, with unknown consequences if she failed.

"Annie," she said, tearing her eyes from Beth and focusing on the older woman. Before she could continue, however, Annie held a hand up.

"You need time off?"

Shady nodded.

"For another road trip?"

"That's about the size of it."

Annie didn't hesitate. "Go. Absolutely. And take Ray."

"What about you, Annie? You coming along?" Ray asked.

"Someone has to run the museum, so I'll stay. But you know me..."

He grinned. "You'll be there if we need you."

Annie grinned as well, pushing her brown-rimmed spectacles farther up her nose. "In a heartbeat," she assured him, assured them all.

CHAPTER FIVE

They didn't all leave for South Dakota right away, only Beth. She'd grabbed a motel room on her way to Mason and planned to do the same on the return journey. Shady and Ray couldn't head out until Monday, so Beth said she'd go ahead to "pave the way."

"It's my folks," she elaborated. "They're, like, religious, you know?"

"So they won't agree with what we're doing?" Shady asked.

"They want to think Kim's in heaven," which didn't surprise the team. Of course they would; *anyone* would. No way they'd ever believe that God would allow their daughter to be grounded by distress. "As for Ethan, they won't talk about him. He's like that character in *Harry Potter*, 'He-Who-Must-Not-Be-Named.' They *blame* him for what happened."

"The black sheep of the family," Shady mused. "Was his relationship with your parents always bad?"

"Ever since I can remember," Beth admitted. "All Mom and Dad wanted was for him to do well, but he never really did. Dad got angrier about it than Mom, but Mom never goes against what Dad says. I don't think she knows how to. They're like…childhood sweethearts, you know? They've been together forever. They don't get it either, that not everyone wants to live in a place as small as Wyatt. That it can be…stifling."

"Do you like it?" asked Ray. "Living in a small town?"

How shyly she smiled. "I've got a boyfriend, so right now, yeah, it's okay, and I don't mind school too much. I may go elsewhere for college, though, who knows? First, I've got to get past all this stuff with Kim because…that can be stifling too."

"And you think finding out about Ethan will do it? Allow her to rest?"

Beth batted the question back at Shady. "Do you?"

She swallowed. "We can only hope."

On Monday, which was a state holiday—Indigenous Peoples' Day—she and Ray left Idaho Falls for Wyatt, South Dakota, stopping by the museum in Mason on the way. Annie had kept the necklace there all weekend, insisted on it, drenching it in love and light, trying to calm Kim and reason with her. "We'll do our best, we will," she'd said. "But if there's been a thorough investigation already…Kim, you mustn't make threats. And you never, *never*, make good those threats." She said she had no idea if Kim was listening, but again, it was worth a shot.

When Annie handed the necklace back to Shady to take with on their journey, she said she'd considered placing it in a lead-lined box first, just as they'd done with Mandy when they'd taken her on a road trip to trace her origins. They'd done so for protection, of course, their own. But then she'd thought better of it.

"Kim's not going to hinder your journey in any way. She *wants* you there. So, I've placed it in an ordinary cardboard box, but wrapped in white silk and with a tourmaline stone in there to soak up any residual negativity. Is that okay? Do you feel comfortable with that?"

Shady took the box, felt a frisson as her hands closed around it, but it was mild.

"That's fine," she said. "And we'll keep you updated."

"Please. Every step of the way."

In the Dodge, Ray tuned in to a country station as they pulled away, Annie on the steps of the museum behind them, waving.

"Seems appropriate," he said, "since we're heading to the Wild West."

"Never minded a little country," Shady told him and then winced as Ray burst into song. "Angel of the Morning" was playing, the Juice Newton version, Ray murdering it.

"Ray," she said, her voice raised to counteract the noise, "you are an angel, really, but your voice—whoa—it's something else."

"Devilish?" he asked, flashing her his best wicked grin.

"Well, yeah, kinda, as Beth would say. And let's hope it's the only thing devilish that comes our way this week."

They'd done some digging on Ethan, of course, to add to their knowledge about what Beth had told them had happened, and about Kim too.

There wasn't much coverage, not nationally, at least. This was small-town news, after all. There'd been an article about Kim's death in a local newspaper, which was also rather vague, lamenting the death of one of their own as tragic but also giving the impression it wanted to move on from it, not labor the point and bring everyone down. The article had carried a picture of Kim, though, freckle-nosed and hair loose rather than in braids, and shiny, like a halo surrounding her. It had been as hard for Shady to see her that way as it had in that other realm, hard*er*, in fact. There was an angel of the morning if ever there was one. In death, however, she'd chosen to present herself as something demonic. Stranger still to think she'd done that with good intent, not bad, because she so desperately wanted to find her brother. And yet…was she capable of bad too? That place she was in, the mist and dust, not something like the Badlands but a hinterland, as bleak.

The main photograph in circulation of Ethan was one from his high school days, in which he looked clean and smart. No doubt about it, though, there was a surly gleam in his eyes, a kind of "fuck you" vibe that sent shivers down Shady's spine. He'd gone missing, was either dead or alive, and if dead, by his own hand?

She'd reached out and touched his face, slowly tracing the contours of it. Nothing to feel from a computer screen, though, no connection.

Ethan Wick, 19, missing from his home of Wyatt, South Dakota, since August 25, 2021. He was last seen by his parents, Ed and Marion Wick, when he left the house during late morning. He gave no clue as to where he was going and didn't appear to take any clothes or bags with him. If you have any information on his whereabouts, please contact the sheriff's office in Wyatt. All information will be treated with strict confidence.

Continuing to stare at his photo, she tried to immerse herself in the darkness of his eyes. *Tell me where you went, Ethan. Your family wants to know. Kim does.* Kim, who might or might not have seen him on the day she'd died. Who'd seen *someone* or something. She'd unlocked her seatbelt, leaned closer to get a better look, lifted a hand and pointed.

All Ethan did was stare back at Shady in that cold but not unattractive way of his. He wasn't going to make this easy for them. Beth had already told her not to bother with social media—Kim hadn't yet been allowed to create a profile, and Ethan had never bothered with it—so they had to find other ways to connect. Through possessions of his, perhaps, and by experiencing his hometown, the feel and culture of it.

They'd set off early on the holiday Monday, been at the museum by eight, and were on their way again less than half an hour later. The journey was ten hours and twenty-two minutes, according to Google Maps, so no need to stop overnight anywhere, not if they took turns driving.

Having left Idaho, they crossed into Wyoming. Shady had been there before, as had Ray—to the Bridger-Teton National Forest, Cody for the rodeo, and Yellowstone National Park, which sprawled over several state lines, including Idaho itself and Montana. Wyoming, though, took the lion's share of Yellowstone and was surely one of the finest states in the USA, such little traffic on the road and such a vast expanse of land and sky. The deeper they went, the scarcer the traffic became, the two of them winding through valleys and mountains, which then opened onto flat, dry plains. Ray unfortunately kept singing, and she kept driving, all the way past Jackson and Dubois into Casper, where they stopped at the Little Shop of Burgers, Ray having a monstrous thing called "The Fester," with onion rings that later repeated on him. Finally, eight hours into the drive, with night falling, they entered South Dakota, Ray in the driver's seat now and Shady sitting back and admiring the scenery. A landscape that appeared untouched, just…left alone.

"Ray," she said, "how'd you like to live out here in a small town? Could you cope?"

"Tough question," he replied, briefly glancing at her. "It's beautiful for sure, great for hiking, getting back to nature, that kind of thing, even some whitewater rafting, I bet."

Shady screwed up her nose. "You like that sort of thing, the rapids?"

"I've been known to battle a few in my time," he declared, before adding jovially, "I'm quite the Channing Tatum when I want to be, you know, Shady. But...*living* out here...I'm not sure. You're such a long way from anything."

What *was* close by were reservations, plenty of them. They'd skirt the edges of Pine Ridge and Nebraska before reaching Wyatt, taking a series of smaller roads now rather than the main highway, as the GPS favored them as timesaving.

Those who lived in Pine Ridge didn't have the easiest of rides. Shady had made a point of reading about it on the journey, finding out some fascinating but tragic stuff.

"You heard of Walking Sam, Ray?"

"Walking who?"

"I was just looking up some urban legends for this part of the world."

"You were? Why?"

"To get to know it a bit better."

"From urban legends?"

Shady laughed. "It was interesting! So, on the Pine Ridge Reservation, we have Walking Sam. He's seven feet tall, with gangly limbs and no mouth. Thing is, Sam doesn't like to walk alone, so he feeds on the living, infecting their minds

49

and altering their thoughts."

"Jesus, Shady!"

"It's just a legend, but…I have a theory… Anyway, as Annie would say, I digress. He convinces the lost and the depressed—hormonal adolescents a particular favorite of his—that they aren't worthy of life and should therefore seek to end it." With the darkness settling and the sky cloudy rather than starry, there was, Shady felt, an eerie air of expectation, with Ray listening intently. "It's said that when he stretches out his arms, you can see the bodies of dozens of Lakota men and women hanging from them. Now, like I said, it's just a legend, okay? But this is where it gets interesting. Within only four months between 2014 and 2015, Pine Ridge had nine suicides and one *hundred* and three attempts. The youngest to die was twelve, Ray. Twelve! And the oldest only twenty-four. There've been several attempts at mass suicide on the grounds too, with, thankfully, a church leader discovering one of those plans and preventing it. When he did, though, he found teenagers already hanging from the trees, choking."

"And all this happened at the res?" Ray asked.

"Uh-huh."

"But we're not going there."

"No, we're going around it, to a small town in a big state that, as far as I can see, is full of nothing. I mean, you said you wanted to visit Wall Drug, right?"

"Yeah! It overshoots where we're going, but it looks so cool. You see the signs for it?"

"Couldn't miss 'em, Ray. They've been posted for around two hundred miles now. *Two hundred miles*! Because…that's *all* there is. A Wall Drug."

Ray's enthusiasm remained. "The Wall Drug isn't just

any store, Shady. While you were googling Walking Sam and other atrocities, I was finding out about it. It's got life-sized models of cowgirls and showgirls that you can pose with for a souvenir photo, a diner serving the best hot-beef sandwiches with mashed potatoes and gravy, an ice-cream parlor, an awesome gift shop, slot machines, the works." Then on a dime, from being excited, he became downcast. "Thing is, if it's past Wyatt, no way we'll catch it today."

Shady patted his arm. "We can visit on the way back. Take a detour."

"Hope so," he grumbled. "They say they do the best homemade donuts, maybe even better than the ones Mo sells. We've got to see, test it out."

"We'll make it our mission." Shady couldn't keep the sarcasm from her voice.

Again, he grumbled. "Yeah. Sure. Whatever. Anyway, back to the legend of Walking Sam, that less-than-salubrious character."

"*Salubrious*? You pick that word up from Annie?"

The grin was back on Ray's face. "Sure did!"

Shady grinned too. "So Walking Sam, as I keep saying, *is* just a legend. But what we know to be a fact about the reservation is that they have a lot of social problems. There's poverty, abuse, and a general sense of hopelessness. Those issues run like wildfire through it, not being able to see beyond the prejudice and hatred thrown at them. The criminal way they've been dealt with is just too big a hurdle to simply ignore."

Rather than the dark and empty road that lay ahead, she could see the bodies hanging from Sam's arms, albeit in her mind's eye; could see Kanti hanging too, the woman who used to hold her when she was a baby, *sing* to her, "pretty little Shady Grove"; and she could sense those she'd seen in that dust, courtesy of the necklace, also hanging, their bodies brushing against hers as she'd hanged right beside them. Victims, every one.

"And that's my point, Ray," she continued, distressed by the visions that remained so vivid, "there's *so much* hopelessness, don't you think? On the reservations and off, in big towns and small towns. So much injustice that people can't stand it. It's not Walking Sam who's collecting souls, it's the land itself that becomes infected. *That's* what collects souls around here, this hard, hard land, and it clings to them, refusing to let go, long after they're rotted in the ground."

She could tell Ray was shocked by what she'd said from the way he turned to her, the whites of his eyes clear in the gloom of the car.

"Ray…" Shady sat up straighter, her eyes also growing wide, getting a sense of something else, another glimpse… "Ray, the road. Keep your eyes on the road. Look, it's okay…I was just…I was musing, that's all. I know I sounded a bit crazy there, a bit…dramatic…but…RAY! SHIT! YOU GOTTA KEEP YOUR EYES ON THE ROAD!"

CHAPTER SIX

A beautiful autumnal night with no whisper of a breeze, and yet the darkness, just like the land, could be hostile too. They'd come off the main highway, the GPS having selected a shorter and lonelier route to Wyatt, a GPS that clearly had a unique sense of adventure, as they'd seen no other cars for miles. Shady had *forgotten* about cars, if she were honest, become preoccupied with something else: lost souls.

The car coming at them had quite literally come out of nowhere. She couldn't work out how that could have happened. The road was straight enough; it seemed to have no dips or twists and turns. If it had, that would explain its sudden appearance. Otherwise, they should've seen the headlights a mile off. But they hadn't. Shady had only spotted them when they'd been close, *too* close. The car not keeping to its side of the road but coming straight at them, swerving only at the last minute, just as Ray had swerved too.

"Fuck's sake!" Ray yelled as he slammed on the brake, the Dodge slithering to a halt and Shady thrown forward with such force her seatbelt locked.

After his shout, there was silence as both stared straight ahead, trying to catch their breath. "Fuck," Ray cursed again. "You okay, Shady?"

She nodded as he reached for the door handle. "What are you doing?"

"I need some air," he explained, climbing out.

"Ray? No! Don't!"

He was gone, though, before she could stop him, and so she reached for the door and went after him, only realizing her breath had hitched a second time when the chill night air forced its way into her lungs, causing her to exhale sharply.

Ray was checking over the car. No embankment at the side, which they could have slid down, and no trees to smash against. They were safe enough.

"Car's okay, Ray?"

He nodded and muttered, Shady only briefly taking her eyes off him to glance upward. The land was vast around them, but so was the sky, and because of cloud coverage, very few stars were glittering, the moon mostly hidden too.

"Ray?" she repeated. He'd bent down to examine a wheel arch, running his hand over it, but had now straightened. "Is it all okay?"

"Car seems fine. There was no contact," he finally answered, but then his voice exploded again. "Did you see it? What happened? Someone deliberately drove at us!"

Shady sighed. "That's what it seemed like to me, someone playing stupid games out here because...well, because they can, I suppose. Who's around to stop 'em?"

She'd been on enough lonely highways in her twenty-three years. America was full of them, but this one...it had to win the prize. Edging around the car, she came to stand by Ray. This close up, she could see his nostrils flaring.

"Calm down," she urged. "We're okay, and so's the car. That's what matters. Like I said, it was someone playing a game—kids, probably, from some small town around here. That's likely all they have to amuse themselves. Games of chicken, where they drive straight at you and pull away at the very last minute. But what I'm trying to say is, we're—"

"Shady, what's that? Just up ahead?"

Despite addressing her, Ray wasn't looking at her. His eyes were doing that thing Kim's had before her own crash, scanning the horizon, *trying to see*. But see what, exactly, in this darkness? Slowly, and with every nerve ending firing, she turned to where he was looking, his neck craned forward as he peered harder.

At first, it was only more darkness that met her gaze, the road ahead visible, but only just, soon swallowed by the night as if it were ravenous. She was reminded of what she'd said in the car, *how* she'd said it, about the land around here collecting souls. To do that, it would first have to collect bodies, *murder* people. Something it could easily achieve, because to survive in this wilderness, you not only had to be born to it, you'd need the blood of *generations* born to it running through your veins.

Still she peered ahead, breathing hard, wondering what the heck Ray had meant, when she finally saw it—lights. *Twin* lights. Red.

"Ray?" she said, she *whispered*. "Is…that a car?"

"Uh-huh." His voice was a whisper too. "I think it's *the* car. The one that tried to run us off the road. Correction: that *did* run us off."

"It's stopped."

"It has."

It had stopped a ways up and was now simply sitting there, idle.

Shady tried to search for reasons. "Maybe they've had a

few to drink and just didn't see us, not until we saw them, or they were chatting like we were, fooling around, got distracted like we did too. You didn't have your eyes on the road, Ray. *I* saw them first. You were too busy looking at me."

If she was being defensive, so was he. "Because of what you said, Shady!"

"Well…yeah…I…"

From glaring at her, he focused back on the red taillights—like demon's eyes, that's what Shady thought. Did Ray think the same? Not just red, but *blood* red.

"Idiots," he seethed. "Total fucking idiots."

To her horror, he moved forward, shaking his fist in the air and shouting.

"Ray…" she began, but he didn't hear her, was too busy listening to himself.

"Whoever the hell you are, whatever you think you were doing, you're an asshole, you hear? Keep to your side of the road. Turn your fucking lights on. You know, the basic things you gotta do when you're driving so you don't wind up killing anyone."

Shady rushed to catch up with him. "Come on, Ray, stop that. Don't. Not out here." Where they were alone, except for whoever drove Ole Devil Eyes.

There was a fair distance between Ray and the car, so no way he could be heard, something Ray realized too as he picked up pace, *determined* to be acknowledged.

Again, Shady tried to reason. Maybe he was right. If they were kids messing around, then they deserved a bawling out. The collision had very nearly happened. If Ray gave them a scare, maybe they'd think twice about goofing around behind the wheel in future.

Ray, with his red hair even more awry because he kept running his hand through it in aggravation, looked scary, to be honest. She'd cower if she saw him coming toward her. His anger was something else. Or was it actually fear? The same fear she felt as they both continued onward, the kind that got your adrenalin pumping, that could make you do something stupid, like confront another driver—a *crazy* driver—on a lonely road in a state you knew nothing about, where you were a stranger. No one else around should anything go wrong, should the occupants of the car step out and answer you back, waving a gun…

"RAY! STOP!" The beat of her heart was loud in her ears, her voice strangled as she continued to berate him. "RAY!"

He stopped. Finally. And he was panting too.

She caught up with him and grabbed his elbow. "What the hell do you think—"

He wasn't listening, wasn't even looking at her. His eyes remained fixed solely ahead. When she yanked his arm harder, he didn't budge his gaze one bit.

"Shit," she murmured, one half of her amazed that they'd ended up in a situation like this. She'd been on many a road trip in her time, and nothing like it had ever happened before. The other half of her, though, wasn't contemplating at all; it was busy steeling itself, getting ready to drag her eyes from Ray again, big Ray, crazy-haired Ray, dependable Ray, and back into the distance at something that only wanted trouble.

The car was still there, waiting. Oh-so patiently.

Except…it wasn't idle anymore. It was moving…*reversing*…slowly, slowly. So slow that it was like an illusion, almost; it made you question what you were seeing, think that you were imagining it, the game continuing and the darkness of the night in collusion.

Because that's what it felt like now, a game, one that had only just begun…

The car was still in the distance but closing the gap bit by bit, almost…*mockingly.*

She and Ray continued to stand there, her hand still on his arm, squeezing harder.

She found her voice again. "What are they doing?"

"Um…getting closer. That's what."

"But they're doing it so *slowly.* Why?"

"No idea."

Another thought occurred. "Do you think they heard you?"

"Heard me?"

"Yeah. D'you think they heard you, and now they're like…angry too?"

When he didn't answer, Shady scanned the horizon *beyond* the car, wishing, praying someone else would happen by, a friendly trucker, able to diffuse the situation and save them. The air was so tense, bearing down on them. A strange, strange land, *barren* land, and in the darkness even more alien than before. She had Native blood in her, courtesy of Kanti, but she didn't belong here, shouldn't have come. Right now…ah, right now she could be at home with her mom and dad, sitting across the dining table from them, feasting on chicken pot pie or some other heavenly delight, Bill's tostadas, perhaps, and listening to how Ellen had dealt with the late payers, the tactics she'd used. "Savage," Shady had called her. She wasn't, though. Ellen was as gentle as they came. But what was happening here had a savage feel, the person or persons in the car not those you should yell at.

So slowly they'd been reversing, speeding it up, sure, but

only a little at a time, stringing the game out, raising the tension. Now, though, there was a squeal of tires, a cloud of dust that gathered in the wake, rearing up to consume only the car's front half, Ole Devil Eyes at the back brighter than ever, *flashing* danger.

Run. A voice was in her head. Her own or Kanti's? The latter, possibly, because it remained so calm, so light, as soft as a whisper. If her own, it would have been a scream.

She screamed it now. "RUN! RAY, FOR FUCK'S SAKE, RUN!"

He didn't need telling. He'd already turned, grabbing her arm too, holding on to it as tightly as she held on to him and dragging her back to the beat-up Dodge, which just sat there, such a benign thing in contrast to the car coming at them, and yet it offered their only hope of salvation. Funny how such affection for it could fill her in such a terrible moment.

Just a few steps, that's all they'd managed, and the car behind kept getting faster.

Finally, they let go of each other to peel off in different directions, she to the passenger side and Ray to the driver's. She *flung* that door open, so hard she hit her shoulder with it, but the pain didn't register. Opposite, Ray was doing the same, diving into the vehicle. Once inside, they pulled the doors shut and locked them. Then, and only then, Shady risked looking back as Ray fired the engine, amazed at how close the other car was to them, something as fast as lightning now, preternatural.

"Ray! He's gonna smash into us again."

He?

She didn't know that. It could be a she. Yet what woman would take on two of them out there in the wilderness? Be that arrogant? That...*certain*? No, it was a man. A lone man. She could see him now, no others in the car, only his outline. A shadow man. Fearless.

"Ray!"

The Dodge's engine roared, and the tires squealed. More dust rose, so thick it was blinding. Ray floored the gas anyway, getting them out of there, keeping his eyes on the road ahead and, like her, hoping, praying, *willing* them to reach safety soon.

CHAPTER SEVEN

Shady didn't sleep well that night, and neither did Ray.

They *had* made it to safety, to a town just outside of Wyatt, if it could be called a town—a pit stop, more like, Ray tearing his way into the gas station there.

Whoever they'd encountered on the road behind them— a shadow of a man, who'd turned around in his seat as he'd kept on reversing, so competent at it, like he'd done it a thousand times before—he'd at some point stopped and given up. Shady imagined him having a little laugh to himself, just…chuckling, right there in the driver's seat, at the fun he'd had and that he might have again should more unfortunates happen by.

When they'd lost him, they had no idea. Ray had focused on the road ahead, and Shady couldn't bring herself to keep looking over her aching shoulder. She was sure she'd see a pair of eyes blazing as red as the taillights if she did, as devilish.

Whatever had happened, he was nowhere to be seen. And yet…

It *felt* like he was still there, watching, that they'd never be able to shake him off.

At the gas station they'd shrieked to a stop, no other cars but theirs there, plus an attendant in the store gazing out the window and looking pretty alarmed by their arrival.

"What do we do?" she'd asked Ray. "Go in there and get him to call the cops?"

Ray shrugged. "Whoever they were, they're gone."

"*He*," Shady corrected. "It was a man, and he was alone."

"You saw that?"

"Think so. Yeah. From what I could make out through the rear windshield."

He ran a hand through his hair. "He got that close?"

She nodded.

"Shit."

"Let's report it," she decided. "We'll go in there, into the store, but…Ray, what I could really use right now is a motel room. I want to get in there, lock the door, and sleep."

What had happened had drained everything from her, left her wiped out. They weren't going to see Beth today but tomorrow morning, heading on over to her house with a plan in mind, Shady putting her skills to good use. The way she felt now, though, power*less* instead of power*ful*, no way she'd be able to sense a thing unless she slept.

They entered the gas station store, the interior of which was neon bright against the darkness outside, nothing fancy about it. It was basic and old-fashioned, shelves stocked with a variety of goods whose packaging looked faded. The guy behind the counter, who'd been staring at them, was as young as they were, thin and pale too with dark, curly hair. He kept glancing nervously at them, and also at a security camera up high in the corner, no doubt hoping it was capturing everything. Shady didn't blame him for being jumpy. She would be too if she were him. His was a precarious job, the night shift in a gas station on the backroads. Other than them, someone a little quirky could stop by, a little…weird, a little fed up with life, perhaps, and then boom—it could all be over in a heartbeat. Why would he do it, Shady wondered. Put himself on the front line like this? Then again, did he have any choice? If you wanted more opportunities, better jobs, you'd have to move someplace else, and for some, for many reasons, that wasn't always an option.

He puffed his chest up a little as they approached, but Shady detected well enough the tremor in his voice. "Hey, can I help? You want gas?"

"We've got gas, thanks," Ray replied. "We wanted—"

Quickly, Shady interrupted him. "We wanted to know if there's a motel around here where we could stay overnight."

"Shady?" Ray turned to her, his expression quizzical, but she shook her head, shut him down further. The guy didn't just look nervous; he looked as if he was about to pee himself. He *knew* the dangers he faced well enough, didn't need reminding. If she truly thought the man who'd chased them down was out there somewhere, rather than imagining he was, she'd do it, get the attendant to call the cops and explain what had happened. But the man wasn't there. He'd gone. A good ole boy who'd had some good ole fun, going home to Momma.

She checked the clock on the wall behind the counter. It was nearly eight o' clock. They'd been on the road for hours, lunch a distant memory. She was tired and hungry. Perhaps they'd eat first, then collapse. Greet the morning in a better frame of mind.

"A motel?" she repeated as the guy continued to stare at her. "Is there one around here? And a diner of some sort where we can get some food?"

Such a benign question, and relief clearly flooded

through the guy that that was all they wanted, shoulders as straight as a broom handle becoming more slouched.

"Sure. Sure," he said, clearly eager to be rid of the strangers in town. "Go a little further up this road, turn right, and you'll see the sign for a Holiday Inn."

"A Holiday Inn?" Shady was relieved too. For a second she'd imagined some run-down old place, like those they'd stopped at on other trips, with plenty of *Psycho* vibes attached.

"Sure," he repeated. "And then a few minutes on from that is Buffalo Bar and Restaurant. They open late, do good steaks, wings, and a salad bar. You'll be all set."

"Thank you," Shady replied. "So we go up this road, turn right, and it'll all be there before our very eyes. Not a mirage but a miracle."

The guy frowned. "Yeah. What?"

She shook her head. Not only drained, she was becoming quite hysterical, talking nonsense. "Sorry. Never mind," she said, smiling. "It's just good to know. Ray, c'mon."

"No problem," the guy assured them. "You take care, now."

Shady swallowed. "And you. You take *good* care."

He seemed to notice the way she'd emphasized a certain word. Grew as pale as a corpse. Such a terrible metaphor, *macabre*, causing her to turn sharply from him, wanting to get out of such stark confines, into somewhere as familiar and comforting as a Holiday Inn where they'd be safe. Where they could barricade themselves in.

Before they left, though, Ray wanted to know something else.

"What's the name of this town?" They'd passed a sign, but neither had read it.

"Oh," the guy replied, his tone conversational again, "it's Murdoc. And by the way, make sure you take a right further up the road, okay? Don't get confused. *Don't* turn left."

* * *

It was a Holiday Inn, but like none that Shady had ever encountered. She'd stayed in hotels on family trips, Ellen and Bill often choosing Holiday Inns for their value, location, and warm welcome. The one in Murdoc had none of that. It was as basic as everything around there seemed to be, a reception at the front with the tiniest of breakfast areas and the accommodation in single-story motel chalets, shaped in a U around the parking lot.

Ray had googled the population of Murdoc: 452. He'd been amazed by that, wondering where the heck they all lived, because they'd passed very few houses on the way, and those they had seen were set way back as if out here, off the beaten path, people *wanted* to hide. The road the gas-station guy had told them to take had also gone on for longer than expected, no right turn evident, or left, and Shady—who'd been driving—began to wonder if he was playing games with them too? *Lying?*

Unease was edging its way back in when Ray spotted it, a crossroads. "There!" he said, pointing. "I think you turn left there."

"We turn right," Shady corrected.

"What? Oh yeah, sorry."

"Don't get us more lost than we already are!"

"Hey, we're not lost," Ray replied, trying to console her. "We're in a town now, no matter how small. And Wyatt seems to be the next town along, so we're fine. We're safe.

Look! There's the Holiday Inn. You see the sign for it?"

A sign that was hanging on rusted steel hooks, the parking lot practically empty. A light was on in reception, though, so it wasn't as abandoned as it first appeared.

Even so, having turned in there, she almost reversed out and headed on to Wyatt, no matter how weary she felt, where there had to be a better selection of places to stay. But she didn't. She drove the Dodge into a parking space, Ray's shoulders slouching too.

"Let's check in," he said, "then go eat. I'm starving."

He was out of the car before she could respond, which was probably just as well. So what if it was a little run-down? It was still a Holiday Inn. Minimum standards applied.

As she got out of the car, her hand traveled to her pocket to grab a piece of leather there, which had belonged to Kanti and which Ellen had given her, her grandmother's hand having carved stars upon it, more precious to Shady than anything. There was such softness to it, real comfort, a pertinent reminder that the stars were in the sky even when you couldn't see them, and that Kanti was too, protecting her from afar.

They checked in, and it was fine. The woman behind the desk, a name badge identifying her as Marsha, was middle-aged, as round as she was tall, and, if not exactly friendly, then courteous enough, handing them a key to room number eighty-two, telling them breakfast was served in reception—coffee and cereal only—between six and nine.

The room was okay—old-fashioned, sure, and smelling heavily of stale cigarette smoke despite a *No Smoking* sign fixed to the door. There was a cockroach on the faded carpet as they entered, but it was lying belly-up, dead, and the room had the twin beds they'd asked for.

Having dropped their bags, they hurried along the road to Buffalo Bar & Restaurant, the sign for that on rusted hooks too and creaking slightly as it caught the breeze. More a shed or barn than a restaurant, with no windows at all and built from corrugated iron, the roof black and the walls yellow, but inside it was well-equipped enough, a few people leaning against a long stretch of bar, not one of them bothering to turn as new blood entered.

A server approached them, of medium height, dark haired, buxom, and tattooed.

She cut straight to the chase. "Looking to eat?"

"Yes!" Ray replied enthusiastically, Shady merely nodding.

She indicated for them to follow her as she about-turned, seating them at a Formica-topped table, the windowless walls clad with fake wooden paneling that was threating to peel off in places. Although the bar area had a handful of people, in the restaurant was only one other couple, sitting across the central aisle. In their seventies, Shady guessed, the man wore faded denim dungarees and the woman a dark woolen dress. Whatever he'd eaten, he'd finished and was now just sitting, staring blankly at a plate scraped clean. The woman, however, had some salad and was picking at it, *nibbling* it, morsel by tiny morsel.

Shady tried hard not to stare, but, again and again, her gaze was drawn back to them. They were people, just like she and Ray were, like the server was, who'd strode off but was now returning, and like the guy at the gas station too, even the guy who'd almost run into them—*all* human. So why was she still feeling so afraid? So cold inside?

The server handed over menus, the laminate of which was predictably sticky.

"Want something to drink first?" she asked, her tone still curt, skulls on her arms and a crow's head with beady black eyes glaring every bit as much as its owner did.

Shady ordered water. Just that. Ray a Coors Light. As much as she envied him, would like something stronger too, she didn't tend to drink alcohol because of her ability; it could sometimes enhance it, but adversely. No way she wanted to add to her unease. When the drinks came, the server took their food order—steak for Ray and salad for her, which she had a feeling she'd only nibble at like the older woman across the way, any hunger she'd been feeling earlier on the wane.

As late as it was, they finished their food before that woman did, the man opposite—her husband?—still staring at his plate, not a word exchanged between them the whole time Shady and Ray had been there, all talking dispensed with years ago, it seemed.

They paid the check, left, and hurried back along an empty sidewalk to the Holiday Inn. Still no goddamned stars in the sky, only on the leather in her pocket.

After each taking a shower, they climbed into their respective beds, Ray immediately switching off his sidelight and asleep and snoring in seconds.

Again, she envied him his ability to do that, although later he'd tell Shady he kept waking too, was as disturbed through the night as she was, by nothing, by the silence.

Shady almost wished she'd spent the whole night awake. That would have been preferable. Because when she slept, she kept seeing red eyes, and not just one pair but *dozens*, hanging off the arms of a tall creature that collected souls. Walking Sam.

CHAPTER EIGHT

The sun rose at seven o'clock, and so did Shady and Ray, the pair of them deciding to skip the breakfast, check out, and get back on the road. They weren't going to meet Beth until ten, but they'd kick around in Wyatt rather than Murdoc. She got the impression *no one* kicked around in Murdoc.

Shady drove again, following the GPS on the main highway rather than taking the backroads. The town they'd found themselves in, if only for the night, didn't look as foreboding in the daylight. There was the Buffalo restaurant, no frills but good enough, and a few other businesses too—a laundromat, signs for an RV park, a pizzeria that the guy hadn't mentioned but which looked pretty much boarded up anyway, and also signs for a sports field, so there had to be a school around here as well, and likely a church of some denomination. Just an ordinary place. Isolated, but what of it?

They reached the crossroads, and she headed back toward the gas station, wondering if Mr. Nervous Guy was still there or if someone else worked the morning shift, and again it all seemed pretty normal as they passed by, a couple of cars at the pumps. Before she'd taken the turn, she'd glanced over at the road she'd been told specifically *not* to go down, the left turn off the crossroads. It looked like a gravel road, a bunch of spindly trees clumped on either side, but nothing much else. Most likely it led into more backcountry, endless plains. As forbidding as it seemed, she couldn't help but muse upon what it'd be like to travel that road, just…lose herself. Strangely, she felt *excited* by the prospect, pondering what it would *sound* like in such wilderness. Could silence be so loud it became deafening? So many places to hide if you wanted. So much…choice.

Unlike the evening before, the morning's journey passed uneventfully. Traffic on the highway was still pretty sparse around Murdoc but increasing the closer they got to Wyatt.

Wyatt Welcomes You! was the sign that greeted them as they entered city limits, the grass shoulders on either side of it a little unkempt. Buildings came into sight soon enough, the usual collection—mostly businesses, with a few houses scattered in among them, the bicycles and toys lying in their front yards evidence of the families who lived there.

She'd texted Beth, but so far, no reply. It being barely eight thirty, it could be she wasn't awake yet. She attended school but was on fall break this week, so the timing of their visit was perfect. Which school it was, Shady didn't know. In fact, she knew very little about Beth, but this visit, a deep dive into her family history, essentially, would rectify that. She was the middle child of the Wick family, and from what Shady had gleaned, had "middle child" syndrome. She knew Kim had felt close to Ethan, worshipped him, but when asked if she'd felt close to her brother and sister, Beth had chewed at her lip before replying.

"I love my family, but the truth is, I didn't feel especially close to anyone. Ethan got a lot of attention because Mom and Dad were always trying to nurture him, make him follow a certain path, then getting angry when he didn't. As for Kim, being the youngest and the cutest, she got a lot of attention anyway, but me…I think everyone used to forget about me. I was there and still am, the last one standing"— how bitter her laughter had been when she'd said this—"but I'm not sure I'm really seen. Even though they're gone now, Ethan and Kim still take up all their time. As usual, I'm left to get on with it."

Shady had wanted to reach out to Beth when she'd said that, to give her a hug, but she thought better of it, not sure the gesture would be welcome. Beth was *used* to her position in her family, saw it as something familiar. So instead, Shady had pointed out that her sister was taking notice now, wanting Beth to do something, even if it was about Ethan. And if she did, with the help of the Mason Town Museum posse, perhaps there'd be some kind of closure and the family, what was left of them, could grow strong again, rediscover each other, Beth finding her role at last as something of a hero, tragedy forcing her into it.

There was a coffee shop up ahead, and Ray suggested they could while away an hour there and then be on their way. If Beth didn't reply in that time, there could be a thousand reasons why. They had her address; that's what mattered.

The coffee shop—Bobby Jo's—was open but empty. Behind the counter stood a man—Bobby Jo himself?—who looked weathered, as if he worked outside rather than in. He lifted his head as they entered and climbed to his feet, no smile on his face but ready to offer service.

"What'll it be?" he asked as they approached the counter.

Ray gave him one of his wide smiles, Shady knowing what he was doing, trying to coax a smile back. He had a pretty high success rate, but not this time. The man simply continued to stare at them with watery eyes. There was something so *tired* about him, tired of life, she supposed, wondering if she was being dramatic but suspecting not.

She'd already taken in her surroundings, a mishmash of tables scattered around, some of them with plastic tablecloths in a shade of blue, others bare. There were condiments on every table, though, salt, pepper, and sauces, most bottles half filled. Beneath their feet, the linoleum was worn, and on the walls were posters of American movie stars and singers, including Elvis, Marilyn Monroe, and James Dean, but so faded they resembled ghosts.

Empty right now, but it would get some trade later, surely? Folks passing by, eager to sample the delights that Bobby Jo's offered? Shady couldn't imagine it'd be enough to fill these tables, just a trickle of customers. And yet still the shop remained valiantly open, because…what else was there to do? It passed the hours, no matter how slowly.

"Could we get two coffees and…" Ray hesitated. "Do you have any cinnamon buns? Or…donuts?"

The man shook his head. "Only what's in front of you."

A pallid selection of pastries, which Ray eyed with something like despair.

"Um…Shady?"

Shady left the choice to him.

"Okay, all righty," Ray continued, "two of your finest…chocolate chip cookies, please. Oh, actually, I see they're plain. So, yeah, two of your finest *plain* cookies."

The man turned, and so did they, heading toward a seat as far from the counter as possible, next to the window. It had begun to rain outside, Shady noticed, a fine drizzle that dampened the atmosphere further.

When their coffees arrived, they were lukewarm, and the cookies dry and brittle. No activity in the coffee shop, but outside, a sudden stream of cars was heading eastward.

"Wonder what's going on?" Ray said idly in between mouthfuls of cookie.

Shady was about to answer when another car *raced* by, a cop car.

She looked at Ray, and he looked at her. Both were frowning.

Even the man had stepped out from behind the counter, had gone to the door and, with one hand scratching at his head, peered outward.

An incident of some type had happened, drawing plenty of attention. Those cars before, who were they? Journalists or rubberneckers? Those who'd heard something was going down in Wyatt, where *nothing* went down, so wanted in on the action.

Ray stood. An abrupt gesture that surprised Shady.

"You okay?"

"Yeah…I…" He briefly scratched at his head too. "You know what? Think we'd better cut loose, get to Beth's, see what else we can find out about Ethan."

"Sure." Shady rose as well.

"It's just… Come on, Shady."

She followed him, glad to leave the confines of the coffee shop behind, squeezing past the man in the doorway, who grumbled something Shady couldn't quite catch but sounded like "Ain't what it used to be anymore." Whether he was referring to his business or the town, she had no idea and didn't wait around to find out.

Ray was walking at quite a pace, Shady having to hurry to catch up with him.

73

"You got the car key?" he said.

She nodded. "You want it?"

"Uh-huh," he replied, and on reaching the Dodge, she gently threw it his way.

As they climbed in out of the rain, another car raced past, more cops, the Wyatt SO in full force, maybe, Ray firing the engine and following them, the tires almost spinning.

She'd previously loaded Beth's address into Google Maps and now shouted directions, Ray duly going straight, taking a left or turning right as instructed.

They were at one end of Wyatt, and Beth appeared to live at the other end. As they drew nearer, Shady noticed more people on the street, some doing what the man in the coffee shop had and coming out of the premises they owned or worked at to stand on the streets, all staring ahead, puzzled.

"We nearly there?" Ray asked.

"It's right around this corner—"

He screeched to a stop.

Beth's house *was* right around the corner, but so were the cop cars, red and blue lights flashing, plus people on the sidewalk in groups. *Onlookers.*

Ray quickly parked. "Do you think that's—"

"Beth's house?"

He nodded. "What the fuck's happened?"

"We have to find out," Shady answered, already half out of the car.

As they headed toward the crowd, denial kept going around in her head. *Nothing* had happened to Beth. The Wicks had lost two children; they couldn't lose a third. And yet Ray had felt it, that something was wrong, and had rushed to get to Beth's address. And Shady? She'd felt

74

nothing. The intuitive one, the one with *ability*. She had to sharpen those senses.

A few cops were busy telling people to stand back and allow them space. Others had rushed toward the house a few yards away, just an ordinary house, much like the others that surrounded it, only the yard a little neater and the drapes closed in all rooms.

A house *not* like all the others, then. Not if such darkness had touched it.

Still having trouble believing it, Shady shook her head. "Doesn't mean it's Beth's house. Or that anything's happened to her."

Ray only glanced at her before joining the crowds.

"Terrible," someone was saying, a woman.

"I just...too terrible to fathom," another woman answered.

"This place has changed so much," said someone else, echoing the man from Bobby Jo's.

Someone else went further still. "Cursed," they said. "Not just the Wicks, all of us."

"Excuse me," Shady said, plucking up the courage to touch someone on the shoulder. "I'm new in town, and...what's happening?"

The woman didn't answer right away; she simply looked at Shady with eyes that reminded her of pebbles, cold, hard, and grey. She had a hard look about her overall, perhaps because she had to be, because out here life made you that way.

"Is it the Wick house?" Shady prompted when the silence continued.

"What do you know about the Wicks?" the woman fired back.

"Nothing. Well…I'm a friend of Beth's."

"Just blown into town?"

Shady shivered. There was an accusatory tone in the woman's voice she didn't like.

"Yeah," she said, pulling herself up to her full height, trying not to look defensive but suspecting she was failing. "Like I said, I'm a friend. Come to visit." Not someone who wished her harm, was the point she was trying to get across. Not someone…suspicious.

"Not sure what's going on, but good luck with that," the woman said, then turned away.

Ray had ventured deeper still. She could see his red hair from where she stood, so decided to try to reach him.

She heard more snippets as she did, people talking about "the family." Not using their last name anymore, almost as if trying to dehumanize them, a family that bad luck had followed, such terrible tragedy, none of which they wanted to rub off on them.

She got it. She did. She understood. But these people—the word *curse* being bandied around a bit more freely now as the situation continued—were doom-mongers.

"Ray!" Shady called. Although staring so hard at the house, he clearly heard her as he held up his hand to wave. "Ray—" she said again, finally by his side, but he interrupted.

"Look, Shady! Look!"

The front door to the Wick house was opening, a man leaving, not in uniform but with a sense of officialdom about him, a doctor, perhaps? She still had no clue what was going on, not until she heard it: a cry, a *howl*, like someone having the life choked out of them. A woman's cry. A mother's. And a man's joining it, as distraught. A father.

Quickly, the man shut the door behind him, wiping at his brow as if distraught too, then putting his head down and rushing to his car to speak to others there.

"This is about Beth," Ray said, stricken also as he finally turned to Shady. "That's why she wasn't returning your texts. Like Ethan, like Kim, she's gone."

Shady was staring at him, bewildered, completely, when she felt a vibration in her back pocket, a message notification on her cell.

Quickly she grabbed it, staring at the screen in amazement for a few seconds before hurriedly opening the message.

It was from her. Beth. *Just* sent, and only three words: *Find me. NOW.*

CHAPTER NINE

"What the hell are you thinking? We *have* to go to the cops."

Ray was right. Shady knew it, but still she hesitated.

"Shady!"

"Hold up, Ray, and listen, okay? Of *course* we go to the cops, but…the thing is, if we do, they'll hold us, question us. They may even take my phone away, and they'd be within their rights to do that, but the thing is, Beth's asked *me* to find her. Just like Kim asked me to find Ethan." Or rather threatened, more like. "Right now, we're below the radar. We can mess around with the rules, not get bound up in red tape. If Beth's missing, if she's been abducted, time is short. It always is in these circumstances, and that's why I think we do things our way. Just for a few hours. For today. Conduct some investigations of our own."

They were back on the outskirts of Wyatt. When people had dispersed, Shady and Ray had quickly gotten out of the neighborhood too, found a quiet road off the main street to park the car so she could tell him about the message. She hadn't done so while in the crowd, only returned the cell to her pocket as quickly as possible.

Of the Wick family, it wasn't only Ethan who was missing now; Beth was too. Although nothing official appeared to have been said yet, further rumors in the crowd confirmed it. The story went that she hadn't been seen since the previous night. When her mom had checked on her first thing this morning, she'd found her bed hadn't even been slept in.

Right away, Ray wanted to see Shady's cell. "When was it sent, exactly?" he asked.

"About nine twenty this morning. Which could be hours after she disappeared."

"Weird. But maybe good weird. It means she's still alive."

He studied the phone as intently as she had in the crowd. "This text. Where is it?"

Shady didn't reply, not right away. Before Beth had left the Mason Town Museum and returned home to Wyatt, they had of course exchanged contact details and Beth's address. They hadn't texted each other much since, though, as there was no need; Beth knew Shady and Ray were following on in a couple of days and was satisfied with that. Before this latest text, however, she'd messaged to say she'd arrived home safely, and Shady had replied that she was relieved and would see her Tuesday. *This* Tuesday, the morning of. She and Ray were to go to her house and be introduced to her parents, who didn't approve of the kind of approach Shady would take, but whom Beth was hoping could be persuaded once they'd met her, desperation making them more open-minded. If not, if she and Ray got thrown out of the Wick household, they'd find someplace else to stay where Beth could visit with some of Ethan's possessions, Shady sitting with those items, holding them, and tuning in to see if any more information could be extracted concerning his whereabouts, like where he'd intended to go that day. Although she admired Beth for wanting to be honest with her parents, Shady had fully expected the latter to happen. Never, though, had she imagined she'd be hunting for *two* missing persons.

The text. She'd seen it. The *latest* text. She'd stood in the crowd, felt the cell vibrate in her jeans pocket, retrieved her phone, and read it. *Find me. NOW.* And it had vanished?

Taking her cell back, she examined it closely, read the older, more benign texts. *Shook* the cell, as if miraculously that'd make the message reappear. Placing the phone on her lap, she then rubbed at her eyes. Picking up the phone again, she stared at the conversation thread, all the while trying to work it out—what had happened? In the crowd, when she'd returned the cell to her pocket, had she swiped something she shouldn't have, somehow deleted it?

Determined that was the case, she quickly googled how to retrieve a deleted message. Ray asked her what she was doing, but she hushed him, wanting to concentrate. Going back to the conversation thread, she tapped on *Edit* in the top left corner, then selected *Show Recently Deleted*. A bunch of messages duly appeared, complete with the time they'd been deleted, but there was nothing from Beth Wick.

"Shady? What's going on?"

"It's gone," she replied, having no choice but to agree with him. "It was there, though, Ray, I swear. I *saw* it. But…now it's gone. How?" She turned to him, looked straight into his green eyes. "I'm not making this up, hallucinating. I know what I saw."

"Well…call her. Maybe she'll answer."

Shady did just that, cursing when it went straight to voicemail. After trying several more times, she left a message, begging Beth to call back.

Ray sighed. "At least I don't feel so guilty about not going to the cops."

Shady was as frustrated as he was. "You do believe me, don't you?"

He turned to look at her. "Ain't never known Shady Groves to lie."

"And I'm not lying this time either."

"So what the hell's happening?"

Although they were a way off from the Wick house, they could hear it, another cop siren in the distance, the case now a *bona fide* one, being taken seriously. Wyatt would be crawling with cops and investigators, all as puzzled as they themselves were.

How could one family be hit so badly so many times?

Ray started speaking again. "No way we have a hope in hell of getting into the Wick household now. Without Beth to introduce us, we can't just turn up, two out-of-towners suddenly on the scene. We'd be taken straight down to the sheriff's office."

"The cops may still come looking for us," Shady pointed out, "if her messages are backed up on the cloud. They'll see she's been in touch with us. Two *strangers*."

"So what do we do? Go home, wait to see what their investigation turns up?"

Shady shook her head. "I stand by what I said earlier. We do some investigation of our own. While we can. Sure, we have to keep our heads down, especially in a small town like this where it's obvious we don't belong, but we do what we can, because that message—and I'm going to say it again, Ray, I want it to hit home—I *did* receive it. They were Beth's words, and somehow, someway, they came through on my phone and then…weirdly disappeared. I have to find Ethan, and I have to find her." Or she'd hang, and it didn't matter if Kim was metaphorically speaking or meant it literally. Hanging was hanging; there was still a noose around her neck, being tightened. Time was running out. For her as well as Beth. Kim's face remained vivid in her mind, her eyes burning. Shady would find them for her own sake, *their* sake, and for their parents'. *No one* should have to suffer as much as they were right now, having had everything they loved cruelly taken from them.

After a few moments' silence, Shady said, "Remember when we were back at the museum with Beth, downstairs in the basement?"

"Uh-huh." Ray's eyes narrowed, clearly trying to second-guess Shady.

"Remember she received a phone call and left the basement to answer it?"

"Yeah. That's right. She did."

"And when she came back downstairs, she told us who it was from."

Ray nodded. "She said it was her boyfriend."

"That he was checking up on her."

"Okay. So?"

"We can't go to her parents' now, agreed. This is a sensitive case. We have to tread carefully. Wisely. Quickly."

"So what you're saying is—"

"We find out who her boyfriend is. Go after him instead."

* * *

If they were going to hang around in Wyatt, they'd need to find accommodation. In a town of just under seven thousand, Shady still worried they'd stick out like corncobs in a hedgerow. They were strangers at a time when the town was closing ranks. If they wound up in a jail cell, her parents and Ray's would have a fit about it.

Murdoc, therefore, seemed like the best option, somewhere slightly removed from Wyatt. They could head back to the Holiday Inn, endure it for another night, remain out of sight and out of mind. But today, they'd need to hang surreptitiously around Wyatt, in more coffee shops, bars, and stores, anywhere people might be discussing latest developments with the Wyatt family. Eavesdrop, basically— or as Shady preferred to call it, "information gathering"— looking also for any opportunity to get involved and ask some questions of their own. To *pretend* they knew Beth too. Kinda. Shady casually throwing in something like "Jeez, her boyfriend must be *so* upset," and hoping to invite a name that way, someone slipping up and saying, "Sure, Paul, Aaron," or whoever he happened to be, was crushed. One thing she'd make sure to do was keep her cell well charged and always at hand, in case there was a return phone call or another message…

Driving back toward the main street, they parked just beyond Bobby Jo's and started walking back along the street together.

Ray was nervous, still fearful of being thought of as involved in the Wick case. Shady had to point out they already were. Beth had reached out to her, just as Kim had reached out to Beth. They were in as deep as they could be.

On the outskirts of town, it had been quiet, barely a soul around, but as they approached the main hub, there was more life, people going about their business after the excitement of the morning but with a new weight on their shoulders, downcast.

It was mainly older people, the young out of school yet likely kept indoors after what had happened. Shady and Ray were interested in groups of people, gathered together and gossiping.

Beth Wick was missing. Either abducted or she'd taken off by herself without a word to anyone, leaving no forwarding address. That's what it became clear some people thought.

Three women outside a grocery store caught Shady's interest, one of the trio in particular, her arms folded over a tan-colored coat and lips pursed. Shady sidled up to them, Ray heading inside the store to see if anyone was in the aisles instead.

Thankfully, a few stalls were outside filled with produce, giving Shady an excuse to hover, grabbing a paper bag so she could fill it with zucchini she'd later empty out.

If she looked surreptitious hanging around, the women didn't seem to notice. They were, as she'd hoped, too engrossed in chat, Shady correct in presuming the topic.

"…terrible news…so shocked…poor Marion…coping, do you think?"

"That's the hard line, is it? Beth…abducted?"

"Ed…and Marion…insisting."

"So…*not* the hard line?"

"Not yet."

"Overreacting?"

The pursed-lip lady nodded vigorously.

"Can't…blame them." Her friend was clearly more sympathetic.

"No…can't, but…Ethan…"

At Beth's brother's name, Shady edged closer.

"Missing…own decision, though. Selfish."

The third lady, who hadn't said much of anything yet, seemed to protest, if not about Ethan, then about Beth and the danger of tarring her with the same brush.

"She's a good kid," she said, Shady able to hear better now. "As sweet as Kim was."

"Quiet, though," Pursed-Lip Lady said. "Sulky."

"Sulky?" questioned the lady who'd been quiet herself.

"Depressed, maybe?" Pursed-Lip Lady suggested. "Angry. Because of what's happened to her family. How…unlucky they've been. So she's taken off too. Is just as selfish."

"No," Quiet Lady continued to protest. "She wouldn't devastate her ma and pa that way."

"And yet it seems she has." Not once did Pursed-Lip Lady unfold her arms. "She's done exactly that. They've had bad luck for sure, the Wicks, but you have to wonder."

"Wonder what?" the more sympathetic one said, her voice noticeably aghast.

"What they've done to *deserve* it. You never see them at church on Sunday, do you? And they don't mingle much. Never have, Ed and Marion, since they got together in school. God, so many years ago! Do they keep themselves to themselves for a reason?"

"Jesus!" The word was out of Shady's mouth before she could stop it. And it was louder than she'd expected, *way* louder, all three women turning her way.

"Excuse me?" said Pursed-Lip Lady, clearly unhappy at hearing the Lord's name taken in vain.

"Sorry," Shady said. "I…um…I thought I saw something moving, you know, among the zucchini. A spider or something."

"A spider?" Once again, the more sympathetic woman

sounded aghast.

Shady pointed. "Yes. In there. Which is why I said what I did." But what she wanted to know was why they'd said what *they* had, and so she chanced it. "I heard you talking."

"Oh?" Ah, she wished the other two would say something, not just Pursed-Lip Lady.

"About Beth," Shady continued. "Awful, isn't it? That she's been abducted."

"Or she's run off," Pursed-Lip Lady reminded her.

·Shady shrugged. "Looks like the cops are taking it pretty seriously."

"Of course!" Quiet Lady joined in again. "Considering the family's history. *Very* seriously."

As she clung to the zucchinis in the brown paper bag, Shady tried to look interested but not *overly* interested. "I mean…if she was abducted, by who? Wyatt's just an ordinary place. Who'd do that? Her parents must be so worried, and what about her boyfriend? He must be out of his mind too, right?"

Pursed-Lip Lady bristled. "Just who are you? How do you know Beth?"

No way the woman could know everyone who lived in the town, surely? No matter how much of a busybody.

"I'm a friend," she chanced. "I'm from…um…Murdoc, nearby. You know it?"

"Murdoc?" Now she screwed up her nose. "Of course." She eyed her even more curiously. "So you live there?"

"Uh-huh. Just came to Wyatt today to run some errands. It's my…younger sister who knows Beth, actually. They go to school together."

"Your sister doesn't go to the school in Murdoc?"

"Um…they're in the same grade, I mean, and met

86

through some friends… So, did Beth have a boyfriend? I think my sister said she did, that they were real sweet on each other, but I can't remember his name. Like I said, he must be awfully upset—"

"Norma, honey, I have to go."

It was the quiet lady, clearly tiring of Shady's babble. The sympathetic lady took advantage of the interruption, also having had enough of a discussion for today, saying goodbye to Pursed-Lip Lady, whose name turned out to be Norma, and hurrying away. It was just Norma and Shady standing there now, the former's lips pressed so hard together they'd turned white. *What's her beef?* Shady wondered. It was as though she had X-ray vision, knew that Shady was lying. Maybe she had a job, or maybe she was a housewife, but with her suspicious mind, she'd missed her vocation: spearheading the Wyatt SO.

"Well," said Shady, holding up the brown paper bag, "I'd better pay for these."

"Yes, perhaps you should."

Eager to escape her glare, Shady turned. No point in pursuing the matter of Beth's boyfriend further with her. Nothing more was going to spill from those flattened lips.

"Nice talking to you," she muttered, continuing to put space between them, when Ray appeared in the doorway, as pleased as a bee sipping on sugar water.

"Jesus, Shady," he said, Shady wincing, wondering if Pursed-Lip Lady had heard. "I didn't think it was going to be this easy, but guess what?"

"Ray," Shady said, appealing with her eyes for him to save it.

It didn't work. He remained oblivious to her expression—and to the woman standing a little behind her.

"I found out the name of Beth's boyfriend! Two women inside were talking about what happened earlier, so I got talking to them too. Ah, Shady," he said, shaking his head somewhat dramatically, "he's either revered or feared around here. I think it's feared, actually, because the way they said his name was, like, in low whispers, you know? Kind of hush-hush and furtive."

"Ray—" Shady tried again.

"It's okay, don't worry. The women are nowhere near. They're still inside."

"But, Ray—"

"So we got a name, at least, to go on. And it's Johnny. Johnny Latham."

It wasn't Shady who gasped at the information but purse-lipped Norma, who'd closed whatever gap Shady had put between them.

"Johnny?" she echoed. "*My* Johnny?"

CHAPTER TEN

There was a burst of silence, so awkward it set Shady's teeth on edge, and then Pursed-Lip Lady, Norma, *Mrs.* Latham, her hand traveling to her other hand and twisting a wedding ring there, shook her head furiously.

"My Johnny," she repeated, "is *not* seeing that Wick girl, let me assure you. Who said that? Who's in the store? People are...*afraid* of him? Let me see who said that!"

Ray, remaining in the doorway of the store, began to stutter. "Oh...well...they're not afraid, not really. I didn't mean that. Honestly, they weren't gossiping or implying—"

Mrs. Latham looked more horrified still. "They have no right to imply anything!" she retorted, so agitated, so affronted, she paled, even staggered a little. "My boy's a *good* boy."

Shady's hand shot out. "Mrs. Latham, hey, it's okay. I think Ray here got a little carried away with himself. Look, do you need to sit down?" She looked over the road at, thankfully, another coffee bar and tried to steer her there, shocked when the woman allowed her to. Just seconds before, Mrs. Latham had been in fighting mode, wanting to know who had talked ill of her son. Before that still, she'd as good as accused Beth's family of attracting ill luck because they weren't good folks, citing the missing Ethan as the bad seed around here. And now, so easily, she'd crumbled. Why?

Ray took her other arm, couldn't get her across the street fast enough, and once inside the coffee shop, seated her as far from the window as possible.

There was no conversation, not until coffee was ordered and the cup was in front of the woman. "They say things about him," she spat, "some people around here. But they're wrong. When he was younger…" She waved an agitated hand. "Oh, it's all in the past now, but when he was younger, he was wild, as young boys can sometimes be. It's only natural, isn't it? They have so much *life* running through their veins. But he's different now. He's changed. He has a steady job, a *wonderful* job, and makes good money. Helps me out at home. Any wild days are long gone, but people in a small town…they never seem to want to forget. He's a *God*-fearing boy," she added, the coffee cup now in her hands shaking a little. "If he *was* dating Beth Wick, he had nothing to do with her disappearance."

Her eyes were misty, although any tears remained unshed, plus there'd been a slight crack in her voice toward the end. If he'd been a bad boy but had changed, why the sorrow?

Ray was mortified. "Mrs. Latham," he said, his own voice not altogether steady, "I really am so sorry to have upset you. I didn't mean to."

Shady tried to catch his eye, to convey it was okay, that this wasn't his fault. *He* was a good guy, Ray, always had been through school and beyond. Didn't use testosterone surges as an excuse for being otherwise. His eyes remained solely on the woman, though, and Mrs. Latham returned that gaze. "You come from Murdoc too?" she asked him.

"Huh? What?"

Shady kicked him under the table.

"Oh," he said, glaring at Shady, but only briefly. "Yeah. The outskirts. You know it?"

"It's the next town along," she barked. "Of course I know it!" And then more softly, "It's where my boy works, at Gilcrest Pharmaceuticals. Nine till six, five days a week. But he's on his way up, will be a part of management before you know it."

"That's great, really great," Ray enthused, Shady nodding her head and smiling too.

Johnny Latham, despite what Ray had said, sounded pretty ordinary, at least *now* he did. So who was to be believed here, the women Ray had talked to in the store, who'd named him as Beth's boyfriend, or Johnny's own mother, who denied it? They had to remember too that Beth hadn't said her boyfriend's name, only mentioned he was checking up on her.

"He's at work now, I suppose?" Shady said.

"Of course."

"Like you said, nine till six." But *after* six, what did he get up to then? She could see Ray was also thinking that. Beth had gone missing yesterday. They didn't know when exactly, but it could well have been during the hours Johnny *hadn't* been at work. It could have been last night—when they'd been almost run off the road too, just before Murdoc. *That's* what they should report to the cops, although neither had registered the make or model of the car. It had happened a few miles out of town but might still be of significance.

They'd do it, she decided. Straight after their encounter with Mrs. Latham. The text was something else; it could have gotten them into trouble, made suspects of them, but reporting a car incident was different. They had to help the cops in the search for Beth, not hinder it.

"Mrs. Latham, you knew Ethan, didn't you? I heard you mention him earlier."

"I knew of him, yes," she replied, taking a sip of coffee at last. "For a while he was friendly with Johnny. There were several of them, forming something of a group."

A double whammy for Johnny, then, if he'd lost both a friend and a possible girlfriend.

"Terrible what happened to him, wasn't it? His disappearance."

She pursed her lips again, a hint of froth from the coffee on her upper lip. "If you heard me talking earlier, if you were...*listening*, you'd have heard me say he could have gone missing of his own accord. Just taken off, away from here."

"Yeah, yeah, I did hear you say that. But...his family have always believed different." By that, she meant Kim, glossing over what his parents had thought.

"Families *always* believe different about their own," she said, pushing the coffee cup away from her, some of the liquid spilling over the edges. "Let me tell you," she continued, "since you're so keen to know a few things. Ethan and Johnny ran around together, they did. They got into trouble some. Also true. It's not been an easy ride with Johnny, not since his father died when he was twelve. He's our only child, and I tried hard to keep him in line. But like I say, through his formative years, it wasn't always easy. And him running with Ethan Wick made my job harder. *He* was the bad influence, Ethan. *He* talked him into doing all sorts of things. The rumors..." She pursed her lips tight again, one hand clutching at the nape of her coat. "Rumors is rumors, is all. And baseless. He talked about Ethan, you know. He'd come home after a night of drinking. I'd always be awake, waiting, and he'd sit in front of me and take my hands." Her eyes, far from piercing now, had become almost glazed, and her voice lowered to a whisper, causing Ray and Shady to lean in slightly. "He'd say, 'Momma, Ethan has a darkness about him. There's something…wrong.' And he'd shudder when he'd say it, not once, not twice, but several times. And I'd tell him right back, 'Don't you go near him now, son. You leave him well alone. He's *bad* for you, Johnny. All he'll do is drag you down.' He'd nod. Promise me he'd break all ties."

"And did he?" Ray asked, practically agog at all Mrs. Latham was saying.

"Not until the day Ethan disappeared. Want to know what I think? I think the boy simply got too big for this town. He liked the darkness. It attracted him, as Johnny said, and out there, beyond this town, there is *so* much darkness. So he took off without a word. Broke his momma's heart and his dad's too. And that little sister of his, that poor little sister—"

"And Beth?" Shady was at pains to point out. "It broke Beth's heart as well."

"Beth?" Mrs. Latham looked confused, as if she no longer remembered a Beth, and then her lip curled. "I told my son to stay away from Ethan, from the entire Wick family. Those stupid women in the grocery store don't know what they're talking about. They're wrong. Beth's too young for Johnny! She's just a girl. Johnny needs a woman. He had nothing to do with Ethan's disappearance and nothing to do with Beth's either. Don't you dare even think it, you hear? Don't you dare!" The table rocked, and more coffee spilled from her cup as she abruptly stood up. "I have to go back to the grocery store, buy something nice for Johnny's dinner like I always do. *Always.*"

She was so damned agitated again, Ray reaching out and still appearing so mortified, thinking up ways to calm her. "That's great. It sounds like you're a great—"

She balked at his touch, shrugged it off, raising her voice as she interrupted him, the young woman behind the counter finally lifting her eyes from her cell phone and frowning.

"He comes home for dinner. You understand? Every night." She swung around to address the girl behind the counter. "You were at school with Johnny, weren't you?"

The girl colored.

"I said you were at school with Johnny?" Mrs. Latham all but shouted.

Ray had risen, and so had Shady. "Mrs. Latham, please. None of us meant anything—"

No way she'd let Shady speak; instead, she continued to harass the girl.

"He was a good boy, wasn't he? What's your name? What is it? You're familiar."

"Leonora," the girl replied, such confusion in her voice—and, Shady had to admit, fear.

"Mrs. Latham," Shady said, louder this time. "I think you need to calm down."

But already she was heading toward the counter, leaning over it as Leonora backed away as far as she could, pressing her own body into another counter behind her.

"Tell them, go on," she demanded, "about Johnny, about *my boy*. And while you're at it, tell them about Ethan Wick too. You remember him? The bad influence that he was? Arrogant. Cocksure. Swaggering around the school like

94

he owned it. When he bothered to turn up, that was. Starting fights. *Threatening.* And not just students but teachers as well. And those rumors…do you know about the rumors? Do you?"

Leonora shook her head. "Miss…I never had much to do with Johnny."

"But you know about the rumors?"

"Well…yeah."

"THEY'RE NOT TRUE!" Mrs. Latham all but screamed. "NONE OF IT'S TRUE!"

Shady and Ray reached her, determined to pull her away from the counter if need be, poor Leonora dissolving into tears in the face of Mrs. Latham's aggression, clutching at her neck, pale amber eyes on Ray, pleading with him: *Get her away from me. She's crazy.*

As Shady gripped the woman's arm, Ray taking the other, visions filled her head, images of this woman indeed sitting up at all hours. That much was true, waiting…waiting…waiting… *Praying.* That's what she did, her hands clasped so tightly together as she stared at the clock, as she listened to it counting down the seconds, the minutes, and the hours. *Bring him back safe. Bring my boy back safe.* A desperate mother who loved her son, who was just so scared for him, all the time.

"Oh, Mrs. Latham," she whispered. Perhaps she was telling the truth here. She was a victim, and so was Johnny, of someone like Ethan. Ethan, who'd loved the darkness…

Her voice was drowned out, however, and so were the visions by the sound of something else—a siren, not belonging to a cop car but an ambulance, speeding past the coffee shop and the sound echoing long after the vehicle had gone.

She was busy staring after it, wondering where it was going. To the Wick house? Had something happened to one of the parents? To both of them? *More* tragedy?

So busy staring, in fact, it took a moment to register that Mrs. Latham, who'd also turned toward the sound of the ambulance, was now adding further to the cacophony, not with more shouting but something much worse: a strangled cry that faded to a whimper. And then she was falling, Ray trying to keep her upright, but she was as heavy as a stone statue, clutching not at her neck, like Leonora was, but at her chest.

At her heart.

A *cracked* heart.

Another one.

CHAPTER ELEVEN

Mrs. Latham was rushed to the hospital, Shady and Ray allowed to accompany her but in their own vehicle, following on. The ambulance arrived at the Saint John of God at the same time as another did, that one carrying a woman laid out on a trolley, accompanied by a man with his head in his hands, weeping. The Wicks, it had to be, the couple rushed deep into the building as Mrs. Latham was too—two mothers who could take no more.

In the waiting room of the ICU, Shady leaned on Ray for support, his arm readily coming around her shoulders. "Will she be all right?" she asked him. "Will *they* be?"

Of course Ray had no answer. All they could do was wait and see.

Taking a seat, Shady reached for her cell, deciding to text Beth again, Beth who didn't know her mother had collapsed and—from the look of him—that her father was at breaking point too. With Ray looking on, she stabbed at her phone, sent message after message:

Beth, where are you?

Are you okay?

We need to talk. Urgently.

Can you communicate with me again?

Find a way.

Beth, please. Where'd you go?

Finally, her finger hovered over the screen before deciding to go ahead.

Your mom's in the hospital.

If she *was* on the other end of the line, able to text, that should get a response.

It didn't.

"Shit," breathed Shady before turning to Ray. "What do we do now?"

He asked a question in return. "Where's the necklace?"

"Safe, in my pocket." Though Annie had wrapped it in white silk with a tourmaline stone for protection, Shady had taken it from its cardboard box and nestled it in Kanti's scrap of star-etched leather instead, which she'd transferred into her jeans pocket, not wanting to wear it but have it near at all times. "I've tried letting Beth know about her mom, but what about Johnny? What if he doesn't know about Norma yet?"

"Hospital staff will sort that out," Ray said confidently.

Shady rose. "Let's check that out, huh? Make sure."

The nurse station ahead had several people behind it, looking extremely busy and somewhat harried. They waited patiently until someone at last looked their way, a woman in her mid to late thirties with dark hair coming loose from a bun.

"Can I help you?" she said.

"Hi," Shady replied. "We came in with Norma Latham. We were in a coffee shop with her in town when she collapsed."

"Norma Latham?" she repeated, now glancing at a computer screen. "Ah, yes. I see."

Ray cut straight to the chase. "Is it a heart attack?"

The woman eyed him for a few seconds. "A *suspected* heart attack. She's with doctors now, being assessed."

"Mrs. Wick also came in at the same time," Shady said. "She collapsed."

"Marion Wick?" The nurse shook her head and sighed. "A crying shame. All of it."

"Did she have a heart attack too?" Shady pressed.

"*Suspected* heart attack," the nurse amended, just as she'd done with Norma Latham. "Again, tests will be run to confirm it either way." She seemed to relax her shoulders a little. "Look, they're in the best hands, okay? That's all I can say for now. Are you"—she frowned—"family of Mrs. Latham or Mrs. Wick? Friends?"

"Friends of Mrs. Latham's," Shady confirmed. "Haven't seen her in the longest time, though."

"You're visiting?"

"Uh-huh. For a couple of days. Her son, I'm concerned he doesn't know what's happened to his mom. Is there—"

"Johnny Latham?" The nurse's face hardened. "I'm sure someone called him, but the strange thing is, he's due here soon anyway to deliver supplies."

Shady nodded, as though knowledgeable. "That's right, he works in pharmaceuticals."

"Oh, he does," the nurse replied like Norma herself, pursing her lips slightly. "He works at Gilcrest, over in Murdoc. They must pay 'em well there, that's all I can say. Look, if you want to wait for more news on Mrs. Latham or see Johnny when he comes in, take a seat. There's coffee in the machine over there, and, actually, it's pretty good."

"Is there any chance we could see Mrs. Latham too? Later, I mean?"

"Not if you're not family. Sorry."

"Johnny it is, then," Shady muttered to Ray as they wandered over to the coffee machine, grabbed a coffee each, and retook their seats.

She was less than halfway through hers when there was a flurry of activity farther down the corridor as someone entered. Not just entered, they *breezed* in.

A man. *Just* a man. Young, around Shady and Ray's age, but he had such an air about him, a magnetism. In the corridor, *all* heads turned toward him, but perhaps it was only her jaw that fell open, Shady quickly clamping it shut again, trying to remain cool.

The man was greeting everyone as he passed, and they were greeting him right back, the women especially. Cries of "Hi, Johnny, how are you today?"

So this was him, Johnny Latham, Norma's son, clearly unaware of what had happened to his mom if he was acting like this, so chirpy. Strange way to act too if he was Beth's boyfriend. Her predicament he had to know about. In his arms he held some boxes, the supplies the nurse had mentioned, perhaps, and he continued to blaze a trail, swaggering to the nurse's station, where only one looked unimpressed: the nurse they'd talked to.

"Helen!" he said, greeting that particular nurse with such enthusiasm she was forced to offer a smile, no matter how tight. "Can you sign for these little beauties, please?"

Offering the boxes for her to take, he then produced a folded sheet of paper and, with one flick of the wrist, unfolded it.

Suave. Sophisticated. *Handsome.* He was all those things. He had dark hair, smoothed back, and was skinny but muscular too, the silvery suit he wore clinging perfectly.

Shady! Will you stop staring!

She berated herself but didn't obey. It was as though she *couldn't*. This man, this vision, she'd never seen anyone like him before, certainly not in her hometown of Idaho Falls. There were plenty of nice guys there, of course, that she'd liked in the past, and dated, but they were all pretty down-to-earth, regular guys. There was nothing regular about Johnny Latham. If Beth *had* been seeing him, could Shady blame her?

She found she was drifting toward him.

"Shady?" Ray said, behind her. "What are you doing?"

"It's Johnny Latham," was the only reply she could muster.

"Yeah, I know, but…"

His voice faded into the background as the nurse, having signed the paper and placed the goods on the desk, pushing them a good distance from herself, started speaking again.

"Unfortunately, Johnny, I've got something to tell you. Your mother—"

Shady had arrived beside him, and, not knowing what possessed her, she interjected.

"She's had a heart attack," she said. "Your mother has had a heart attack."

"Excuse me!" the nurse said, clearly outraged and rightly so. No matter how much she herself might dislike Johnny, you didn't break bad news in such a blunt way.

Johnny, though, simply turned to Shady.

"Well. Well. Well," he said. "Who do we have here?"

His eyes…they were darker than hers, even, *fierce*.

"Johnny. Mr. Latham." The nurse was still trying to secure his attention, as Ray was trying to secure Shady's. She was sure she heard him calling out her name, as puzzled.

Again, they were voices that faded. Quickly. Easily. It

was as though she were in a vacuum instead, just her and Johnny Latham. A man who was both feared and revered. Whom there were *rumors* about. And yet, in that moment, none of it mattered, not even the fact his mom was lying beyond the doors of the waiting area on a gurney, her cracked heart being tended to. Shady was entrapped. *Dazzled*. Wanting to stare into those eyes and keep staring, discover what it was that hid in his soul. *Excitement. That's* what was fierce about him, his lust for life, or for something. Maybe it was for her? Because she could tell he wanted the same thing, to keep on staring, to see through her façade too.

"Mr. Latham! Did you really not hear what the girl said?"

Finally, the spell was broken, the nurse practically shouting at them.

Realizing what she'd done, how she'd blurted out about his mother, Shady reddened. "I'm sorry. Really sorry. It's just we were with her—"

The nurse wasn't behind the counter anymore. She'd come around to stand between them, busy glaring at both.

Shady tore her eyes away to glance at Ray, whose puzzled expression was almost comical. Or did it simply reflect her own, as she was feeling stunned too?

Johnny had also averted his gaze, his attention back on the nurse, and instead of appearing shocked, he simply raised an eyebrow.

"Yeah, she's taken ill. Poor Mom." He then shrugged. "So can I go see her?"

"You can go into the IC area, yes. The waiting room for that is through those doors," the nurse explained. "And it's a *suspected* heart attack she's had. Tests are being run."

"Poor Mom," he repeated, but he was smiling, didn't

look concerned at all.

A warning sign. A *huge* red flag. As her only son, he should be distraught. Shady should despise him for the way he was acting, as much as the nurse clearly did, and yet…

The nurse was beckoning for him to follow, which he did, Shady fighting back feelings of being left bereft by the prospect of his absence, knowing it was wrong, that she was acting weird, but it remained anyway, an ache. Bad boys, *if* he was one, she'd never really had a weakness for. Some of her friends did—Sam Hope, in particular, and even Josie'd had her moments, but never really Shady. And now here she was…falling.

Falling?

He and the nurse were some distance from her and Ray, just about to head through to the IC unit, when he not only turned but whirled around on his feet.

"I didn't get your name," he called, addressing Shady.

Ray bumped her arm, a warning against telling him, maybe.

"It's Shady. Shady Groves."

"Shady Groves? Nice, I like it. You new in town?"

"I'm not from Wyatt," she told him.

"So where you staying?"

Beside him, the nurse was fuming, her arms crossed and nostrils flaring.

"Murdoc."

He smiled widely. "Ah, Murdoc. I know it well. I work there."

"I know," she breathed, couldn't stop herself.

Again, he raised an eyebrow. "You do, do you? Okay, all right. Well, Shady Groves, let's get this over and done with, then. I'll come find you, okay? I'll *definitely* come find you."

CHAPTER TWELVE

"Let's get this over and done with."

They were outside the hospital now, heading back to the Dodge, and Ray was repeating what Johnny Latham had said, *incredulously* repeating it. "That's his mom he's talking about! And what was with all the flirting between you two? Isn't he supposed to be seeing Beth Wick? You know, Shady, the *missing* Beth Wick?"

"Look, Ray, I know. I'm kinda shocked too, okay, by his reaction," and by her own, but she ignored that for now. "But about Beth, we don't know for sure he was seeing her. That was just talk in a grocery store. His mom told us otherwise, remember?"

"His mom who he's so incredibly fond of."

"Ray! We don't know anything about his relationship with her either, okay? Despite what she's said so far, and what he's said, we can't presume it's a positive one."

Shady came to a standstill, and so did Ray.

"I'll tell you what I *can* presume," he said, his expression sterner than she'd ever seen it, "is that he's a slippery snake. No one, but no one, should react that way to news of their mother having a heart attack. He, like…wasn't bothered."

Faced with Ray's indignance, she relented. "I agree. It's odd. This whole situation is. Beth's missing, her mother's in the hospital, and little wonder, and now Mrs. Latham has collapsed too, the mother of Beth's supposed boyfriend. I don't know where we go from here, what we're supposed to do with it all."

"We go to Beth's house."

"What?"

"We go to Beth's house because that's where her things are. And you touch things, Shady. Because that's what you do. We focus on Beth rather than Ethan, and we find out where she's gone." He glanced back at the hospital. "If she's been taken by someone."

Shady didn't miss the accusatory note in his voice. "You think he did it? Johnny?"

"Her *boyfriend*? Gotta be a prime suspect, don't you think?"

"Her *suspected* boyfriend." God, she sounded like the nurse now, religiously repeating that one word. "If he was, if the sheriff thought so, you really think he'd be moseying around a hospital, delivering supplies? They'd have pulled him in for questioning already."

"Then we go to the sheriff's office, either before or after Beth's house, and we tell them we think she was seeing him, that she was seeing someone, anyway. Maybe the gossip girls of Wyatt know Johnny was her boyfriend, but what if the deputies still have no clue?"

She sighed. "Okay, okay. You win. I was thinking we have to tell them about the car incident last night as well."

"Really?" He scratched at his head. "Yeah, maybe we should. And the text?"

"We don't have the text, remember?"

"Yeah, but—"

"No, Ray, it'll muddy the waters. Make them think I'm

a freak or something."

He rolled his eyes but relented too. "It won't, but...okay."

"You know, her house might be crawling with deputies still."

"And it might not be," he countered. "This is a small town. Her parents have reported Beth missing, and given the family history, they're all over it, but they could be all over it in the wider community. Thing is, we're never gonna know unless we check it out for ourselves. And meanwhile"—he looked pointedly at this watch—"the clock keeps ticking."

When he said that, she could almost hear the second hand counting down, the hollow beat of it. As already surmised, time was of the essence in a missing person's case, as far as Beth was concerned, anyway. Ethan not so much...he'd gone missing *years* before.

"So we go to the sheriff's office *and* the Wick house? Which one first?"

"The Wick house," Ray replied, already on the move. "Definitely."

Shady followed him, unable to resist a last glance at the hospital.

* * *

The sun was low in the sky as they approached the Wick house, the darkness like a cloak and Shady grateful for it. It was pretty quiet on the street, the drapes of most houses closed against what was an even greyer day than ever in October, with news of a missing Beth having broken. Had she been abducted, Shady wondered as they scurried along the sidewalk, Ray with his hoodie covering his red hair and she hunched so deep inside her jacket she'd almost disappeared. Or had Beth just taken off? They were the very same questions that applied to her brother. He'd been nineteen, she was eighteen, both dangerous ages sometimes. And it wasn't as if Beth wasn't capable. She'd driven over twelve hundred miles round trip just a few days beforehand by her lonesome. What did her folks think of that? If she was going to introduce Shady and Ray to them this morning, then surely she hadn't told them her true destination. So what story had she made up? So much confusion, and possibly a heap of lies too.

If Beth *had* taken off, she hadn't done so in her car, because there it was, still parked in her parents' driveway, the one she'd driven to Mason, a Ford. So how had she disappeared? On foot? By bus? In someone else's car?

Shady shuddered as they drew close to the vehicle, Ray doing the honors and scanning the area to see if anyone was on the street or drapes were twitching.

"It's all clear," he told her, Shady running her hands along the car, trying not to look as though she might be stealing it.

It was merely a cold piece of metal. No sensation from it whatsoever. Just an everyday, ordinary object. If it had a story to tell, it was holding on to it.

"The house'll be locked up," she said, turning her attention toward it.

"And it might not be," he countered. "There'd have been a lot of commotion when they wheeled Mrs. Wick into the ambulance. They might have forgotten."

She was the one looking around now. "We can't just break in!"

"Not even if it's for the greater good? If it helps to find Beth? Look, you go and wait by the side of the house, where you can't be seen. I'll check the door."

She obeyed, stamping her feet when she got there and blowing into her hands to keep warm. This job of theirs, the things it required them to do…but Ray was right. They *were* required to do this. Beth had come to them for help, not for herself, admitted, but for her brother, and now this—she'd gone missing too. If they didn't help…then what? Their sister, the only one of the three they knew was dead for certain, how threatening could she get? Would she haunt Shady forever in dreams if they failed to find a resolution?

She was mulling over the prospect, shivering harder, when Ray arrived by her side.

"So?" she said.

"They didn't forget. The front door's locked. We could go around the back, though? Don't seem to be any houses overlooking it."

"Okay, come on," she said, the pair of them scurrying again.

They accessed the small yard at the back through a latched wooden side gate. As well as grass, there was a paved area where the family could sit on sunny afternoons with a glass of something cold, patio doors leading into an open-plan kitchen, also locked.

Shady did the only thing she could, cupping her hands around her eyes to peer in through the glass. It was neat inside, everything in its place. *Sterile.* Once a family home, she guessed it hadn't seen so much action in recent years, no hordes of teenagers to mess it up, just one.

"And she kept mainly to her bedroom."

"Huh? What was that, Shady?"

108

She spoke louder. "I said Beth kept mainly to her bedroom." How she knew that, she didn't know, but she went with the insight, encouraged it. "And after Kim's death, so did her mother, lying on her bed in the dark, always in the dark. Having been forced apart, the final three scattered too. Being together was painful. There was just too few of them."

"Okay," Ray said. "Go on."

"And…and…there's *such* darkness in this house, Ray. Can you feel it? See it?"

"See it?" he repeated, doing what she was, cupping his hands and looking in. "I mean…there are no lights on in there…"

Shady shook her head. "That's not what I meant. It's not just the darkness of night, it's a *cloud* of darkness, one that's been kicked up, rising high, that…transports you, takes you somewhere you never wanted to go, but once there, you can't escape either. These people are trapped, Ray. And it's a horror they're trapped in. A relentless, unending horror, digging its claws deeper till it reaches your heart, your soul, and…*savages* them."

"Shit!" Ray breathed. "Really?"

"And it's through no fault of their own. They're victims. Innocent. Ordinary people, like you and me. And…and…look! Look at how deep the darkness is! Surely, you realize it too? It's *consumed* this family and wants to keep on doing that, to take more and more. Kim knew. Was it the darkness she was pointing at just before the car crash? She *still* knows about the darkness. How greedy it is, how it lies in wait. Remember what I said, Ray? That energy doesn't just soak objects, it soaks the very ground we walk on too. *Infects* it. Like a Native burial ground in a fucking

109

Stephen King novel, you know? That shit is real. *This* shit is real. I don't know if Beth was abducted or took off, but you're right, she's in danger. Real danger. She's almost out of time. And if she is, then so's her mother, so's her father. I can see him, her dad, sitting at the counter in there, with both Beth and her mom gone too, and there's a shotgun in his hand. All the darkness has to do is nudge him that little bit further. Then it's on to the next victim, and the next, an infection that keeps on spreading. Oh, Ray, what's happened here…it's terrible."

A noise distracted her—thankfully or fearfully, she couldn't yet tell—the crunching of leaves beneath feet. She turned around, saw something to her right before she noticed what was in front of her…a shadow retreating into the bushes. Then it was gone, and her attention was *fully* on the man in front. A cop.

"Turn around," he said, his hands stretched out before him, holding a gun. "I said turn around! Slowly. And place your hands on the back of your head."

Shady blinked. What was going on here? They were being…*arrested*?

Ray was turning, his hands coming up as instructed.

"I said put your hands on your head!" the cop screamed at Shady, a young man as nervous as the gas-station guy, his hands, and subsequently the weapon, shaking a little.

Just as it would be for Beth's father, it'd be so easy for him to use it.

CHAPTER THIRTEEN

It had taken plenty of pleading, but eventually the deputy sheriff lowered his gun, although only a fraction, both Shady and Ray desperately trying to explain they weren't burglars.

"We're friends of Beth's," Shady said. "We were looking for her. Wondering if she'd heard about her mother, if she'd come home."

"So you use the back door to do that?"

Ray nodded, somewhat ruefully. "We tried the front, but…there was no reply."

"The house is in darkness," the deputy said, "*complete* darkness. You didn't register that?"

Oh, Shady'd registered it all right. When she'd stood at the window, looking into the kitchen, it was as though she'd been transported into the cloud of darkness that had descended on this house, devouring the occupants, not satisfied until it had them all. Was that where Beth was? In the darkness somewhere? Had she been *put* there by someone? This poisoned ground beneath her feet, how far did it extend?

The deputy was on his phone, calling for backup, no doubt.

Shady took a step forward, her hands still on her head, but the deputy yelled at her to stop.

"Can I just take my phone out, please?" she pleaded. "I

can show you we know Beth. There've been texts between us. Look." When the deputy raised his gun again, she told him he could take the phone out of her pocket himself if he wanted to.

He shook his head. "You do it. Slowly. Or I'll blow your damned head off."

"Jeez," Ray muttered. "They make Idaho Falls police look like puppies, huh?"

Shady ignored Ray, doing what the deputy had told her and removing the cell from her pocket as slowly as she could. "You see," she said once she had it in her hand, "it's a cell phone, just that, nothing more. We're not armed. We're friends. Of course, I'm sure you already know this," she continued, "but her brother went missing a couple of years back. Ethan. Beth wanted to find out what had happened to him, and…well…she thought we could help. I know this sounds weird, but I can explain if you'll let me. Everything."

The sound of a text coming through stopped her in her tracks. Tearing her gaze from the deputy, she looked at who it was from, her legs almost giving way when she saw.

It was Beth again. And one word: *Don't.*

"Shady?" Ray clearly sensed something was wrong.

What did Beth mean? Don't what? Shady was so stunned, she struggled to remember what she'd just been saying. And then it *flew* back at her. She'd said she'd tell the cops everything, how they'd come to be there, the truth. And she'd meant it. *That's* when the text had come through. She now raised her head. Should she tell him about this? *Prove* she and Ray weren't lying?

Another sound filled the air. Sirens. Backup coming indeed. Shit! They were going to be arrested and taken down to the sheriff's office. Shady was torn, the deputy and Ray still looking at her.

"What is it?" Ray pressed. "Did someone just text you?"

"Show me that," the deputy said, stepping closer and holding his hand out.

Don't. Don't tell them anything. That's what the text had meant. From Beth herself. But how did she know what was happening? Shady looked around her. Was she in the house somewhere? In all that darkness? Hiding. She'd also seen a shadow in the garden, retreating…or thought she had. *Beth?*

The deputy had taken her cell and was looking at it, his expression puzzled.

"Open the messages from Beth," he demanded.

She frowned. Open them? The latest was there on her home screen. Blazing away.

When he handed the cell back, waving his gun at her for good measure, she was about to point that out, didn't see how she could get out of it. *See? It's there. In black and white.* Except it wasn't. The home screen had nothing but a photo of her and Ellen and Bill, a holiday pic taken in Florida, plus the date and time. No message notification.

She quickly unlocked it, went straight to messages, and checked the string from Beth. Just like that other message, it had gone. All there was were those that had been sent historically and all benign, simply Beth telling her she'd reached Wyatt safely from Idaho Falls and that she looked forward to seeing them again, to "getting things sorted."

"What the hell?"

Swallowing hard, she shook her head. Couldn't fathom it at all.

As more deputies arrived, intent on arresting them for sure, realization dawned.

It wasn't just the land that was infected around here.

113

People were.

Including those in the sheriff's office.

She could tell them nothing.

* * *

Shady and Ray *were* released, but it was hours later, Annie on the phone having to vouch for them. That Beth wanted them to help find her missing brother had been played down, Annie knowing instinctively to do that, clearly testing the waters before she spoke and deciding to dial it way back. She'd told them they did a spot of investigation on the side, a hobby more than anything, gathering material for YouTube and other social media, and the deputy sheriffs had told her, Ray, and Shady in no uncertain terms to leave well enough alone, that what had happened in Wyatt, and was happening still, was "none of their damned business." It was an ongoing matter for law enforcement. If any material was found, they'd be prosecuted.

Going one step further, they also told them to get out of town and not come back. They had their home addresses and, if need be, would get in touch in the future for further questioning. On their way out, they bypassed an office, partially glass-fronted, belonging to the star of the show, the sheriff himself. He hadn't spoken to them personally, left that to his deputies, but there he was at his desk, just sitting there, feet up, drinking coffee. A big man, his belly hung over his trousers, and his cheeks were red as though he were doing something strenuous. Shady's eyes caught his, just for a few seconds, their color indefinable. The warning in them was clear, though:

Stay away.

They owed Annie an explanation, of course, and, once back in the Dodge, they FaceTimed her. She was someone Shady could confess all to, which she did, everything except the texts, keeping her eyes averted from Ray, feeling his gaze on her as he no doubt wondered why. Truth was, she wanted more time to mull it all over. Used to weird, this was something she couldn't grasp, having to remind herself that Ray, like the deputy who'd arrested them, didn't yet *know* what the second text had said.

"If you're not welcome in Wyatt anymore," Annie said, wearing a very grave expression indeed, "then what are you going to do? Come home?"

"Beth's still missing," Shady pointed out.

"Yes, but as they've said, it's a matter for law enforcement, and perhaps, for now, that's what it should stay. Beth recruited you to help with Ethan's whereabouts, not her own. A historical case is one thing, a current ongoing case something quite different."

"We can't come home tonight, whatever we decide," Shady replied. "It's too late."

Ray disagreed. "I can drive, Shady. I don't mind. I can't *wait* to quit this joint."

"No." Shady was adamant. "Not tonight. We'll go back to Murdoc, to the Holiday Inn."

How downcast he looked. "For real?"

"For real," she confirmed, surreptitiously nudging his arm just as she'd done at the sheriff's office, a sign to follow her lead. Another thing Annie didn't know was what had happened to them on the road coming here, the mysterious driver behind the wheel who'd seemed to enjoy taunting them. Both she and Ray had agreed on silence about that, not wanting to worry her overly. Because she *would* worry,

Annie. She'd be in the car, driving to South Dakota on increasingly lonely roads and putting herself in danger too.

Danger… There seemed to be so much of it suddenly. A historical missing persons case with more depth to it than they could have possibly realized. The necklace in her pocket, even wrapped in Kanti's star-etched leather, felt as if it were burning a hole.

It was agreed. They'd leave Wyatt as they'd been told and go back to the Holiday Inn, hoping the journey there would be an uneventful one. They'd had enough for one day.

Twenty miles was all it was, so they could be there within the hour. Such a lonely stretch of road, though, even on the highway at that time of night, Shady driving and both her and Ray glancing nervously around, wondering who'd emerge from the darkness.

No one did.

Just before the turn onto Murdoc's Main Street, Shady once again glanced toward the road to the left of the crossroads. No sign of life down there at all, sparking such curiosity about it. Curiosity about everything, to be honest, her head at bursting point.

Buffalo's looked to be closed, as did everything else on the strip, only the bright lights of the Holiday Inn offering any beacon of hope.

They turned into the parking lot to see it wasn't as empty as before. Outside one of the motel rooms at the far end was a group of men sitting on stools, construction workers, it looked like, having themselves a little party, no matter the hour and their neighbors.

"Shit," said Ray. "We gotta endure that? Seriously?"

"It'll be okay. I'm sure we won't be put anywhere near them."

116

Turned out they were placed right next door, only discovering that *after* they'd gotten their key and were heading toward their room. Marsha, who was still on duty behind reception, sure had herself a sick sense of humor.

There were three of them—big and burly, still wearing hi-vis vests over padded jackets. Latino, they looked like, with a penchant for rap. *Loud* rap.

Once it had clicked where they were, Shady wondered whether to double back to reception and ask for another room or scoot on out of there, and to hell with the fact they'd already paid cold hard cash for the accommodation. The latter was an attractive prospect but for the worry concerning Beth.

Ray adopted what he clearly hoped was his most winning smile, aimed right at the partying construction workers.

"Hey there," he greeted. "How's it going? Um…we're next door. And boy, has it been quite the day. We're done!"

If he was hinting, they didn't seem to get it. Also, not one of them smiled back.

"Ray, open the door," Shady whispered, eager to escape their glare.

He did so, chancing a wave at them before disappearing. Still no response. This room was every bit as gloomy as the other they'd occupied, and, lo and behold, there on the floor was a dead cockroach, Shady wondering if whoever cleaned the rooms was responsible for carefully placing one in each room as a kind of "welcome to hell" gift.

She'd scooped it up before, so Ray did the honors this time and flushed it down the toilet. He then proceeded to take a shower while having a singsong of his own in there. That, alongside the rap blaring outside, made Shady's head pound.

She lay on her bed, fully clothed, waiting for him to finish in there so she could go shower too, pondering so much, not least who it was texting her. Beth or someone else? And if so, ghostly or alive? She recalled Kim's face, the way she'd dragged herself so determinedly toward her, the threat she'd issued. Now it doubly applied. Shady had to find both Ethan *and* Beth. But where could they be? Close by? Thing is, all that was out there was wilderness. There was too much to consider, especially after a long and somewhat harrowing day, her eyelids so heavy despite the assault on her ears from all directions.

She yawned and turned on her side and tried not to think at all. She needed to have herself some respite, *glorious* respite, in a motel room off the beaten path.

The beaten path… Those words repeated as she closed her eyes. Or rather, the *not*-so-beaten path…a place where no one goes. Bad lands. *Hard* lands. Not beautiful, not really. She should empty her mind, not continue to dwell, but it was as though she couldn't resist, her mind pulling her toward such thoughts, something magnetic in the air again, placing her on a road. A backroad. The dust kicking up as you wandered down it.

And lining it, hanging bodies.

CHAPTER FOURTEEN

Shady woke with a jolt. The room was dark, and she was cold despite a blanket over her—not one she'd placed there, she was certain. She'd lain on top of the bed. So who had covered her? And why was it so dark? That place she'd been in her dreams had been dark too...or...misty? That was it. Full of swirling mist, as blinding as darkness could be. A silent place she'd been drawn to, as she'd been drawn to something else today, *someone.*

Fuzzy-headed, disoriented, and so tired still.

Where the hell was she?

As for silence, there was no longer that.

Voices traveled toward her, muffled but growing louder the more conscious she became. There was loud music too, although bursts of laughter rose above it.

She was in the motel room, of course, in the middle of nowhere or as good as, surrounded by the small town of Murdoc, having now been banished from nearby Wyatt. Ray had been in the shower, and she'd been waiting to take her turn but must have, in the interim, passed out. Ray had clearly gotten out of the shower, seen her sleeping, and covered her with a blanket. Was he in the twin bed next to her? The noise didn't matter, not for Ray. He could sleep through a frat party.

"Ray?" she whispered, repeating herself when there was no answer. "Ray!"

Still he didn't reply, and so, with a sigh, she pushed herself upward, swinging her legs over the bed and onto a thin strip of carpet. She'd tiptoe across and prod him awake. It was so cold still, *she* was, that dreamlike place she'd woken from utterly bleak and disturbingly familiar as well. It was similar to that place in which she'd seen Kim, she of the vengeful face and bloodcurdling threats. *A child, Shady. She's just a child!* Or rather, she had been. Death, however, might have crafted her into something else.

Taking a couple of steps to the other bed, Shady patted nothing more than flat bedsheets on an empty mattress. In that same moment, another burst of laughter erupted outside. *Ray's.* She'd recognize it anywhere. He wasn't there; he was with them!

"Jesus, Ray! What the fuck?"

And how long had she been asleep?

She'd put her phone on the bedside table, so in the darkness she felt around for it, almost sending it crashing to the floor.

The suddenly blindingly bright screen told her it was nearly 2:00 a.m., which meant she'd been out a good couple of hours. And still their neighbors were having themselves a whole heap of fun, Ray thinking he might as well join them.

Continuing to stand there, she wondered whether to return to bed and pull the pillows over her head, try to get more sleep. She could really use it. She felt not just weary, but *bone* weary. They were making one hell of a racket, but she'd slept through it before.

She put the plan into action, slipping beneath the covers fully clothed, trying to ignore a slight smell of muskiness and smothering her head with the pillows, which turned out to be as thin as the carpet, offering no barrier at all.

"Shit!" she swore, seething, actually seething. Why the hell was management allowing this to continue? Other guests, even. There *were* other guests, weren't there?

She tried to remember. Certainly, there'd been other cars in the lot, but staff cars, perhaps? Or even other construction workers, working the night shift out there in the wild, fixing telephone lines or potholes in the roads or something, and not due back until the early hours. There was no recreation or tourist trade in Murdoc, that was for sure; this was a stop only for those who *had* to be there, like them, construction workers away from home, their rooms probably block-booked by the company.

If she was right, no one would complain. As for Marsha at reception, if she slept at the motel, she probably kept a good supply of earplugs.

If the three men were construction workers, why weren't they busy working? Could be they were surplus to requirements tonight, and so a little parking-lot party was in order.

She sighed. *If you can't beat 'em, join 'em.* Should she make like Ray and do it?

What if…Ray got a little carried away? They'd had liquor with them, the workers. What if they were offering it around, asked him what he did for a living, and, his tongue having loosened a little, he told them—everything. What if they didn't *like* what they heard?

"Shit the bed, Ray!"

She threw the pillows off and sat up, attempting to smooth down her hair. What must she look like? Eyes no doubt rimmed with dark shadows and skin inclined more toward sallow than olive, a couple of zits having broken out on her chin too. A wreck. And yet earlier, someone had looked at her with nothing but desire in his eyes. Johnny Latham. She could see him now, his movie-star looks, enough to turn any poor girl's head. Working in a deadbeat town like Murdoc, but a good job, apparently, at a pharmaceutical company where you could forge your way to the top. He'd looked deep into her eyes, the man who might or might not have hooked up with Beth Wick, and she'd looked back into his, everything else ceasing to exist. Drawn to him. *Inexorably*. Her breath hitching to think of it, stuff around her fading again, even the noise. That was the power he had. *Such* power.

"Oh, Johnny." Her tone was much softer whispering his name than Ray's.

Johnny, whom she'd told about his mother suffering a heart attack, suspected or not, and who hadn't seemed to care at all…

Shady shook her head, hard.

She was sliding again into another world, comprised of nothing but fantasy. And she wanted to stay there, but she mustn't. There was something about him, something that was just so…different. But was it good different? Or bad?

She unclenched her fists. Hadn't realized until she'd done so how hard she'd been squeezing them. *White-knuckle* hard.

Another burst of laughter. Ray having such a good time out there with the three strangers, and she inside this room, riddled with angst.

Already the pillows had been cast aside, and now it was the sheets' turn, Shady once more back on her feet and striding Kim-like toward the door.

"Fuck it," she breathed, yanking it open.

* * *

They had tequila and rum. They had a few hand-rolled, under-the-counter cigarettes too.

Shady refused them all, much to their surprise, especially as Ray was digging in, as relaxed as if he were at the Golden Crown back home in Idaho Falls with Brett, Teddy, and the gang, as if he'd known these three all his goddamned life. It didn't matter, though, that she was stone-cold sober, because Shady found she was enjoying herself. *Really* enjoying herself. The three men from down New Mexico way, despite their initial lack of smiles, were certainly all smiles now, the liquor having loosened them up as well.

"Why don't you drink?" one of them had initially asked her, as if it was the greatest mystery in the world, also shaking the tequila bottle at her in a determined manner.

"Doesn't agree with me," Shady had replied, shaking her head.

"Oh," another said with a sly grin. "What does it do? Make you a little jigga-jigga?"

"Jigga what?" she said as all of them, including Ray, fell about laughing.

"You know." He wiggled his body and hands dramatically. "Jigga-jigga!"

Shady remained unsmiling. In fact, she got herself quite worked up.

"If you're gonna insist on acting like...like idiots," she said, also rising to her feet, "like...children, then you know what? Forget it. I'll go back inside. And turn the volume down, okay? That goes for your mouths as well as the music."

Four faces, including Ray's, stared up at her. The man proffering the tequila quickly retracted his hand, his companions swallowing, looking every bit as sheepish as he did.

"Shady," Ray began, "I don't think—"

He didn't get any further. The tequila-pusher shot up, turned the music down as requested, and then offered something other than a liquor bottle: his hand.

After introducing himself as Oscar, he apologized, Shady taking his hand eventually, noticing in his eyes something other than mirth and the effects of too much alcohol: respect. His two friends followed suit, also rising to introduce themselves properly, Luis and Juan, and then afterward, with everyone sitting again, Shady smiled to show there were no hard feelings, wishing she could have a toke on a cigarette, just to…ease things.

Further conversation did a pretty good job of that, though.

It was conversation she found fascinating, and the men clearly did too, the night growing deeper and darker, befitting the subject.

Ghost roads.

Apparently, they'd touched on it with Ray before Shady had joined them, but then got sidetracked. Now, though, they picked up the threads.

"We do the road repairs around here," Oscar explained. "On the night shift."

"*Always* the night shift," Juan added wryly, sipping from the bottle he held.

"But not tonight?" Shady said.

"Not tonight," Luis confirmed. "The city-water boys are

in. We hit a water pipe, so we have the night off."

"First night in an age," Oscar explained, raising big bushy eyebrows, "so why not party?"

Shady could have told them why not. *Because this is a motel, and people are trying to sleep.* But being as she was seemingly the only one trying to do that, she remained quiet, too intrigued by what they had to say to worry any more about getting some rest.

Big guys, all three of them, strong-looking, like they lifted weights at the gym. A long way from home but making themselves comfortable on the porch of their motel, beneath a yellowed porch light. They sent money back to their families in "Duke City," as they called it, but didn't get back there themselves too often. It was hard on the families, Luis pointed out, and Shady could imagine what a tough choice it must be, born of necessity. They didn't labor the point, however, not when they had the ghost roads to discuss.

"They're roads so far out," Oscar said with something of a gleam in his eyes, "glorified dirt tracks, really, that start in the middle of nowhere and end in the middle of nowhere too. You'll find them in the Dakotas, Wyoming, and Montana especially. Man, that state is just so vast and so, so empty. Out there, you really do forget civilization exists."

"If only," Luis said, then snorted, the other two *and* Ray agreeing heartily, raising their glasses or bottles and drinking some more.

"You don't come from here, do you?" Juan asked. "Ray said."

"No. No. We're...um...here on business."

Again, Oscar raised his eyebrows. "Business? In Murdoc? A place like this?"

"Nearby Wyatt, actually," Shady said, omitting the fact they'd been banned from the place and hoping Ray hadn't shared that particular gem too.

"Ah, I see, I see," Oscar murmured, wiping at his lips in an almost thoughtful manner. "You work in a museum, our amigo told us," he continued, referring to Ray. "Interesting place, it sounds like. Very interesting, with an eclectic mix of objects, but the ghost roads, they're interesting too. Urban culture, that's what they're a part of, legend and myth. Allegedly. But when you're on one, especially at night and there's just the three of you, you feel something, you know? Something…otherworldly."

All eyes remained on Oscar while he took a breath, even Luis's and Juan's, their fascination for such places clearly not dimmed by something like mere experience.

"Okay, let's talk about famous ghost roads first," Oscar continued. "In Colorado, there's the Riverdale Road. You heard of it?"

"Not sure," Shady replied. "It sounds familiar, but…"

"Well, they have a lady in white there, and she wanders along it in the dead of night." He laughed suddenly. "Ha! The dead of night. I get why it's called that now! Sheesh, it's never clicked before." Wiping at his mouth, he resumed his tale. "There's supposed to be a mansion there off the road somewhere, though when we worked it, there was no sign of it. Just as well, huh?" he said, turning to Luis and Juan and laughing again as they clinked glass against glass. "They say the mansion was, and maybe still is, home to satanists, you know? And that the gate to hell is there too. Beneath a chicken coop!"

There were more riotous bursts of laughter, with Ray banging his hands hard against his legs. *How much has he had to drink?* Shady wondered.

"A damned chicken coop," Ray repeated. "Crazy."

Oscar took another swig of tequila and grew serious again. "So, that's the famous Riverdale Road in Colorado. Perhaps if we're ever back down that way, we may need some finer colitas than we have tonight to find our way to the mansion."

"If you're going to the mansion, bro," Juan answered, "let's get one thing straight: you're going alone."

Oscar grinned. "Okay. All right. I hear ya."

"What about the Zombie Road in Missouri?" Luis said. "All those dark shadows?"

"Yeah, yeah," Oscar nodded. "There are shadows everywhere at night, man. *Everywhere.* But none more so than on Missouri's Zombie Road. Stories about it go way back, to Native times." He looked at Shady specifically when he said this and nodded, perhaps recognizing her heritage. "There were drownings in a river nearby, *executions*, more like, the Native Americans always a target, with those that had perished coming back and walking the road, searching, always searching for something…their families, probably, lost loved ones. Seen as dark shadows out the corner of your eye, they creep up on you, getting closer and closer. If they can't find their families, know what they'll do instead?"

"What?" Ray said, having brought his glass halfway up to his lips.

"Grab anyone!"

Oscar muttered those two words so dramatically that all four men were in hysterics again, only Shady perhaps noticing that the porch light above their heads had grown significantly dimmer while he'd been relating the tale, no stars in the sky either, the clouds still hanging heavy and the temperature, cold to begin with, dropping a little more.

Oscar resumed speaking, sweeping his arm around in a wide arc. "So much land out here, and so many roads that you think lead nowhere, but actually, it's not true. They go to places you don't want to go, not anymore, that you shouldn't. There's no light, yet they draw you onward as if they were a flame and you were a moth, your wings all of a flutter. It's only shadows that exist there, so do me a favor, okay? If you get stuck on a road like that and something approaches you, don't turn around, don't stare at it. Don't get caught."

Again, dramatic words, but there was no laughter this time. Even the song playing in the background was more subdued.

"There are famous ghost roads," Oscar continued, "and not-so-famous ones, ones more…obscure. There's a reason some roads aren't much talked about. You know why?"

No one answered, but all were rapt.

"Survival. Life is hard enough, and certain knowledge…it makes life harder. So they intentionally ignore those ones. Not their business. Bury their heads in the sand."

"They avoid them," Shady said.

Oscar nodded. "Like I said, some you talk about, and some you just don't."

That night, more tequila and rum were drank, and the chatting continued, ghostly or otherwise, and just as Shady was growing sleepy again, deciding to head back to bed, it was Juan, not Oscar, who turned to her, looked her in the eyes, and said, "Of course you know there's supposed to be a ghost road around here, don't you? The Spook Road."

CHAPTER FIFTEEN

"It's there. Up ahead."

"So it's the left turn off the crossroads," Shady said when she saw Ray pointing. "The one the guy at the gas station told us specifically *not* to take."

"To be fair," Ray replied, coming to a halt at the yield sign, "he told us not to take it 'cause there's nothing down there. The town, the Holiday Inn, everything, is to the right of it."

"True," Shady conceded, but the way he'd said it had felt more like a warning.

Ray exhaled. "So, are we going down it or what?"

"Sure."

"Really?"

"It'll be fine! It's daylight."

That one point perhaps the only consolation she could offer. The previous night had finally ended, she and Ray getting to bed some time after four and subsequently waking late, way past checkout time. But that was okay because they *weren't* checking out, not now with the Spook Road to explore, as Juan called it, a road that went on forever, apparently, straight into the Badlands, across five bridges. *Five.* A legend about those bridges too.

Ray had needed to double-check that story, the rum and

tequila he'd drunk and the cigarettes he'd smoked making everything just a little too hazy for him to recall reliably.

She'd told him, their stomachs grumbling from a lack of Lucky Charms, that South Dakota no doubt had *many* ghost roads, but the Spook Road was Murdoc's very own.

From their viewpoint currently, it looked like any other road, leading toward a disrupted horizon, trees on either side of the road huddled together, their boughs hanging precariously low in places. It led *out* of Murdoc, away from civilization, or what civilization there was.

Five bridges and a legend, Shady repeating what Juan had said.

"The road is straight to begin with, then it winds this way and that, twists and turns all the damned time for miles and miles. The locals don't really use it, apparently. It leads to the Badlands, but the 'ass end of it'—Juan's words, not mine—where no one really goes, nothing out there but scrubland and rattlers. Certainly, no one seems to travel the road at night. Again, not according to Juan, anyway. It's unlit, and it's barely maintained."

Shady remembered asking Juan—seemingly the font of all knowledge when it came to the Spook Road—if he'd been down it.

"Only so far," he'd said, indicating his two hombres, "and with them, not alone." He gave a wry laugh before adding, "Like I said, the road twists and turns, and Luis here, like the little princesa he is, started feeling sick, so we turned back. After that…well, after that, we've had no time to go exploring, either too busy working or sleeping." *Or even drinking*, thought Shady, but with a smile. "One thing I did think, though," he'd continued, "driving down it, it's like you're on your own out there, even if there are others sitting right beside you. It's like…you've left one realm and entered another. Crazy, man." He'd paused, then cleared his throat. "As I said, there are five bridges. One way."

Shady had frowned. "What do you mean? Wouldn't there be five bridges *both* ways?"

Juan shook his head. "You'd think so, huh? People report that they feel *watched* as they travel further along the road, from the trees. They've even reported catching sight of shadowy figures, some in between the trees, but others…others are hanging."

"Hanging?" Shady gasped.

"Uh-huh. Either murdered or suicides. Or maybe a mixture of both."

"A black spot," Shady continued.

"What's that?" Juan asked.

"A black spot," she repeated. "We were talking about it on the way here, me and Ray, about parts of the land being…infected, you know? Bad stuff having happened there, like you say, suicides or murders, and the land becoming tainted because of it. Not only that, it becomes magnetic, almost, drawing more and more bad stuff to it, compounding it."

Juan nodded thoughtfully, although his companions, Oscar and Luis, appeared slightly glazed, what they'd imbibed taking its toll. What she'd just said was something Juan could get behind, though, or so he claimed, also asking about her heritage.

"You have Native blood?"

"On my mother's side."

"So, the land, you're attuned to it? More sensitive than most?"

How could she answer? She *was* more sensitive than most

131

when it came to reading objects, but the land, especially out here, did she feel a part of it? In tune? Certainly, she loved nature, hiking and fishing with her folks, her dad mostly. And there were times she *had* sensed a heartbeat, the rhythm of the world around her. But it was only at times. Not being brought up with Native traditions, that side of her needed developing still.

Having only provided him with a vague answer, he nonetheless seemed happy, checking his watch and deciding to get to the point of the matter: the legend that surrounded the Spook Road. There were bridges along it. Five. One way. But on the way back, one disappeared. It could be any one, anywhere along the route. It just…vanished.

Shady had frowned. "How?"

"No one knows how," Juan had replied. "That's the thing. But there it is. That's the legend. Five one way. Four on the way back. Sometimes. A discovery only some have survived to talk about. Because"—how low his voice had become, barely above a whisper—"most don't get to. If there's only four on the way back, then what it means is you've lost your way, despite being on the same road as before. And you'll never be found again."

In the car, Shady having relayed all this to Ray, the pair of them continued to sit there.

"I've googled it," she said after a while, "while you had your head down the toilet this morning, barfing. There's not a lot on the Spook Road, nothing like there is for the Riverdale and Zombie Roads, but there is some stuff, and, as Juan told us, it has that myth attached to it. And whaddya know? There it is, Ray. Et voila. Before our very eyes."

"People go missing there?"

She nodded. "Didn't find any evidence of that, not

online. *Un*officially, though…"

"And that's why we're exploring it? Because of Beth?"

Shady pondered this, but only for a second. "Because of Beth *and* Ethan."

Ray turned to her, and, oh, he looked pale, and not just because of what he'd consumed a mere few hours ago. He was nervous. Real nervous. And Shady had to ask herself this: Was she nervous too? Maybe. Slightly. Deep down. But she was also excited, because this road led to a wilderness that she wanted to see, no matter if it was the ass end of it. The Badlands. A land that belonged to the First Peoples. That felt almost mythical too.

"It's worth a shot," she continued brightly. "We have to find them. Sorry to use a cliché, but explore all avenues. So should we do it? Should we go?"

Ray pressed down on the gas. "Here goes nothing!"

* * *

A long, long road, as Juan had said, that twisted and turned. On some stretches, it was as if the trees on either side were reaching out to each other, their limbs like lovers, seeking to entwine. In other areas it was sparser, and what land they could see was indeed the barren kind, no sign of any grazing cattle, and the mountains visible but only in the far distance, although it dipped and swelled some on the foothills.

A colder day than yesterday, and the light rain was back, washing away all colors, if there'd been any in the first place, any golds or varying shades of green. It was a dull land and a dull day, Shady shivering in the passenger seat before turning the heat up, wondering if that might combat the chill or if it would sink deeper still, into her marrow.

"There's the first bridge," Ray said. "Coming right up."

A bridge they traveled over rather than under, a creek beneath them that had run dry long ago, trees now growing where presumably water had once flowed.

The road twisted again, Ray hugging the shoulder as it narrowed in places, as it was difficult to see anything oncoming until it was practically too late.

Nothing *was* oncoming, though. The road was clear. Uncommonly clear. Or perhaps that was the way of it out here. These really were the roads people avoided.

Luis had felt sick on this road, and Shady was getting nauseous too. That could be the real reason people didn't choose this route but stuck to more developed roads. Even Ole Devil Eyes, and a blessing if so. No way they wanted to run into him again.

"Hey," said Shady, scanning the horizon, "there's the second bridge."

"Two down," agreed Ray. "Three to go."

"No problem this way, apparently. It's on the return journey the funny stuff starts."

"We'll see about that," he said, not as nervous now, relaxing into what they were doing, maybe even enjoying himself, considering it a bit of a challenge.

Another twist, first to the right, then back to the left, more trees huddled, and more glimpses of land in between, Shady admiring the mountains when she could, a fine layer of mist at their base, the *only* thing to admire around here, it seemed.

They hauled tire over the third bridge, the car rattling slightly as if they were traveling over stony ground. Again, more trees, no shadows in them, no one *swinging*. Not in daylight. *Beautiful* daylight, no matter how weak.

A few more miles and more of the same scenery, and the fourth bridge was there, seemingly a distance of seven to eight miles between each, but as there were no markers on the road, it was hard to tell. On the way back, they could monitor it more carefully.

Along with the absence of markers, there weren't even telephone or power lines dotted along the road, just trees and scrub and nothing more.

"Like it would have been in the old days."

"What's that, Shady?"

"Oh, I was just thinking, this is what it would have been like way back when, everything natural, with no modern life to interrupt it. You know, if we stopped the car now and took a hike from here, it'd be such a throwback, having to survive with nothing but what we have."

"No way I'm stopping the car out here," Ray told her.

"You getting scared again?"

He glanced briefly at her. "Not scared, but…can you feel it? It's not just lonely, or isolated, it's kinda…sad. I don't think anything could exist."

"Not even ghosts?"

He gave a laugh. "Why would you linger here? If you were a ghost?"

"There's a Badlands Banshee, you know," she said. "I read about it. A creature in a white shift, with long black hair that wanders along shrieking and howling at the moon."

"Charming," quipped Ray. "You know what I heard the Badlands compared to?"

"What?"

"Hell with the fires out."

"Really?"

135

"Uh-huh. So that's where you're dragging me, Shady, all the way to hell."

She smiled. "C'mon, you wouldn't have me going alone now, would you?"

They were joking. Trying to lighten the mood. The bends, though—sharp, some of them, the road slithering like a snake—ensured her nausea would get worse. The fifth bridge must be up ahead soon, but if so, it wasn't at as regular an interval as the other four.

They fell quiet, Ray focusing on negotiating the bends, and Shady glad there were no Lucky Charms sloshing about in her stomach. It was as if an age had passed, each minute of the drive dragging now and no improvement on the vistas, just the same old, same old. *Once you've seen one group of huddled trees, you've seen 'em all,* she thought, feeling tired now as well as nauseous, beginning to close her eyes, sliding into sleep but still seeing the road in her mind, still traveling down it, *eternally* traveling. If this was hell, as well as the Badlands, then whose hell? Those in the trees who watched you? And if they existed, were they watching them right now? She could easily imagine it, their arms rising, their hands reaching out from either side of the road, just like the boughs of the trees did, but not for each other, for her. Shady. Calling her name. *Screaming* it.

How did they know it? How could they possibly know it?

Asleep. She must be. But if so, she was still aware of the shiver that wracked her body, also that she was trying to make herself smaller in the seat, curling into a ball, it seemed, not wanting anyone to watch or touch her, the hands of the damned, for surely their flesh would not just be putrid but icy cold, able to freeze her blood and turn her heart to stone.

How did they know her, and who were they? Something else was happening now in the dream, *only* the dream, someone striding out of the trees—a girl, a young girl, and in her eyes a familiar gleam, the savagery of it. *Find him. Find her*, she said, not mouthing the words, but Shady heard them anyway, the threat they contained.

Heard something else too, something that both chilled and confused her further.

Find me as well.

I've told you, you have to.

CHAPTER SIXTEEN

"The fifth bridge… All done, Shady, every one of 'em. Shady?"

"What? Huh? Sorry, you say something? We're over the fifth bridge?"

"We are. Did you fall asleep?"

"Um…not sure. Did I?"

Ray was clearly bemused. "You should know!"

"Yeah," she said, sitting up and wiping at her mouth, some drool having gathered in the corners. "Think I did for a few minutes. Surprised you didn't notice."

"Sweet dreams?"

A shudder passed through her as what dreams she'd had returned, the shades of them, at least, quickly fading. They had *not* been sweet but nightmarish. And at the end of them, coming out of the trees, had been Kim. Her blond hair red with blood, and blood on her face too, dripping onto the dress she wore until she was soaked in it, her eyes bulging like those of a hanged person, telling her she had to do something…*had to*. Find not just Ethan and Beth but her as well. And yet…why was she lost? Her body must be in a cemetery in her hometown. So what did she mean by it?

Shady shook her head. She had no idea what any of it meant, a way to help any of the Wick family still a mystery to her for now. "Mileage," she said instead, much to Ray's confusion. "How many miles was it between the fourth and fifth bridge? It kind of dragged."

"Oh, okay, I get you. It *did* drag, but actually it was around the usual, eight or nine."

She frowned. "Really? Oh, okay, so we've done them, then? No more bridges."

"No more, and all were present and accounted for on the outgoing journey. There's just more road facing us, so dull, so bor—"

He stopped mid-sentence, Shady sitting up straighter too.

It had been a long, long road, given the distance to the first bridge from Murdoc had been around fifty miles, one heck of a stretch. Shady had supposed they'd just turn the car around once completed and head back, start counting the bridges again all the way to the crossroads. Then what? Stay another night and delve deeper into this mystery?

She reckoned so. Had accounted for it. What she hadn't accounted for was *this*.

The road, if it could be called that, the dirt track, no longer twisted and turned but had straightened out, this time promising nothing less than gloriousness.

The Badlands. The *fabled* Badlands, which she'd heard about but never seen, the jewel of South Dakota. Plain, barren, unyielding landscape had now been replaced by quite another, a horizon of mountainous spires and pinnacles that rose and fell, an endless ridge as jagged as shards of ice, perhaps as lethal too but the most beautiful of colors, even on this, the greyest of days—*striped* with colors, all the reds, yellows, blues, and purples, white as well. Imperfect, some peaks rising taller than others, but because of that, perfect. Created by nature on a good day, when she was feeling at her most inspired, just wanting to give some relief to the land, a reason for being. And this was it: reason enough.

"Wow, Shady," Ray said. "Just...wow."

She herself was speechless, "wow" not really cutting it.

It was perhaps the most beautiful sight she'd ever seen, despite the surly sky.

As she continued to stare, something shifted at the very core of her.

"Can we go closer?" she asked.

"What? Yeah. Sure."

They carried on along the dwindling road, which either petered out at the foot of the closest rock formation or forked off in another direction, and they did so in silence. That Ray felt something too was obvious. He radiated awe.

The road did fade out, but another one started right up, running along the base of the rocks before disappearing into more strange lands.

Ray stopped the car, and Shady quickly climbed out— she *ran* to the peaks, her high-tops kicking up miniature dust clouds. Some peaks were low enough to climb, and so she did it, held her hands out and connected with the stone, felt the cool hardness of it beneath her palms and dragged herself upward, greedy all of a sudden, *ravenous*, determined to see over them, wanting more and more, to feast her eyes.

And it didn't disappoint; there *was* more, stretching into the distance as far and as wide as the eye could see, canyons both great and small, the buttes and gullies in among them too harsh for humans to exist there, but they couldn't be erased either, for they were mightier, more enduring. This was the world before mankind existed, and it would be the world when mankind was gone. All anyone could do was the same as her: stand there, reverent. She was just so grateful there was something on earth her kind couldn't destroy.

"Got ya," Ray said, huffing and puffing as he came to a standstill beside her. "Honestly, Shady, you scampered up those rocks like a mountain goat."

She only smiled in response, kept gazing straight ahead, couldn't tear her eyes away.

"You okay?" he asked, this time reaching out and touching her shoulder. "You're crying!"

Was she? If so, she had no idea. She raised a hand and touched her cheek. It was wet.

"Happy tears," she whispered, dropping her hand and patting at her pocket instead, Kanti's star-etched leather scrap in there, Kim's chain inside it. "Really, they're happy tears." She turned to him, felt now as if words were bursting from her. "This land...this...*incredible* land. Do you feel it like I feel it? A connection? A *true* connection. It's like...like I belong here, was born to it." She took a breath, but only because her lungs would explode if she didn't, then rushed on. "Inside me, there's like...memories of another time. Memories that aren't mine. I know they're not, at least nothing I've experienced personally. It's more a *collective* memory, when times were better, and yet time doesn't exist at all out here; it's a place that defies time. Oh shit, Ray, I'm probably not explaining myself very well. I'm overwhelmed, clearly, by this, by what we're seeing, but if I'm crying, don't worry, just don't worry, okay? I'm so fucking happy."

More tears came, Ray reaching out to hold her.

She went into his arms willingly enough, but turned her head to the side so she could still see the Badlands. It was a name given to them by the Lakota people, a translation of *mako sica*, she'd read, due to extreme temperatures in summer, a lack of water, and being hard to navigate. In winter, the rain would make the wet clay slick and sticky, almost impossible to traverse, and if water collected, it'd be muddy and unsafe to drink. Yet despite it being so formidable, it was still a wonder, a sight to behold. It drew people to it to marvel at its splendor. A national park, established in the seventies, but the way she and Ray had come, there wasn't another soul around. They had it to themselves.

At last, she drew away from him, clearing the ground beneath them of stones with her sneakers. "Can we sit? Just for a while?"

"'Course," he said.

Again, silence ensued, Shady listening to it, thinking it *did* have a sound, like the tinkling of bells, a rhythm as the earth itself had if she were to press her palm hard against it, a heartbeat. Badlands. Both an apt name *and* a misnomer. And they'd traversed a bad land to get there, the twisting, turning road, the one with five bridges. A road to avoid, allegedly haunted, but if it led to this, she'd take it anytime. Wouldn't be afraid to. Right now, fear was a foreign concept. There was peace, only that.

Blessed peace.

She laid her head on Ray's shoulder, and he leaned his head against hers. How long they stayed that way, she didn't know, or care, anything other than the land losing all relevance.

* * *

The drive back to Murdoc had been uneventful, Shady downcast, though, at having to leave the Badlands behind her, twisting in her seat as Ray once again drove, and staring back at them until they disappeared from sight.

Five bridges on the way there, those same five bridges on the way back. Nothing untoward at all, despite what legend dictated. And soon, *too* soon, they were back at the crossroads, and Murdoc was ahead, Ray pulling over before he went any farther.

Hours had passed on the ridge. It was now late afternoon, growing dusky, too late to do anything except head back to the Holiday Inn, freshen up, and go grab something to eat at not just the town's finest diner, it's *only* one, Buffalo's.

"So that's what we do?" Ray said. "Spend a third night here?"

"Looks like it," Shady said, not wanting to leave at all anymore, and not just because of the mystery they hadn't solved yet. She'd fallen in love with the land. It was as simple as that. This was no holiday, and she was mindful of Annie being alone at the museum, but Annie had also given them her blessing to stay a while longer, to see if they could find out anything more that was relevant. And during that time, hopefully, maybe, they could head to the Badlands for another visit, even if only for an hour, half an hour, even, because she had to see it again, had to *feel* the way she had, that sense of belonging to something whole.

Before Ray could start up the car, Shady stopped him.

"Actually, hang on. I want to google something."

"What?" he asked, curious.

"I'll tell you in a minute."

As she stabbed at the screen, he remained quiet yet looked around him, she noticed, as the dusk took hold. They were on the edge of the Spook Road, in truth an unnamed road, as far as they could tell, anyway; certainly no signage gave any clue to what it was otherwise, and there were no houses along it, no damned mansion with a chicken coop disguising a gateway to hell. A shiver ran through Ray—she also noticed that, despite her researching. And she knew why. This road was okay by day, but by night it could take on a different personality, *earn* its nickname. All the shadows…

"Here it is," she said at last, holding up her phone for him to see. "What I've been looking for. The Heavenly Haven Cemetery."

Ray frowned. "The what?"

"The Heavenly Haven Cemetery, Wyatt's *only* cemetery."

"Wyatt? Shady, we've been warned to keep out of Wyatt. Plus…" he hesitated. "It's late. It's likely the cemetery will be locked."

"There'll be walls around it."

"So?"

"We can climb over!"

He stared at her, aghast. "For real? Break into a cemetery, in a town we've been as good as banned from? For what?"

"For Kim," Shady said. "To find her grave."

He continued to look nervous. "In the dark?"

"The dark is our friend," Shady said. "In this instance, anyway. It'll cloak us."

"What if they've got CCTV?"

"In a town like Wyatt? In a cemetery? For real? Come on, Ray, we have to do it!"

"*Have* to?" he said. "Why?"

"To see if I can connect with her!"

"You've got her necklace!"

He made a good point. Shady realized she hadn't taken

it out of Kanti's leather scrap since they'd left Bingham County, keeping it contained, the memory of Kim's vengeful tone still prominent. When they got back to the Holiday Inn, she'd do it, sit with it again. Hopefully all would be quiet there tonight, Oscar, Juan, and Luis on shift, and Ray by her side to keep an eye on her. She'd definitely do that, it was time, but the girl's grave was something they could explore too. Just a girl. A kid. So often Shady had to remind herself of this, clinging to the truth of it. A kid who wanted to be found too, alongside her brother and sister. And so that's what she'd attempt to do in the only place she knew where—the spot where her body rested in the ground.

She explained all this to Ray, and, eventually, he conceded.

"You got the zip code?" he said, tapping at the GPS.

CHAPTER SEVENTEEN

The cops didn't know their car, so there was no need to feel paranoid. Even so, Shady found herself hunched low in her seat as they traveled the distance from Murdoc to the Heavenly Haven Cemetery. Ray was a little hunched too, forever glancing left and right, no doubt hoping, like she was, that they not only wouldn't get caught, but that the cemetery lived up to its name and wouldn't scare the living daylights out of them.

Turned out, it was on the outskirts of Wyatt; they didn't have to venture too far in, both of them also wondering whether they could at some stage find out about Mrs. Latham and Mrs. Wick, how each were doing. But that was a worry for another day, for tomorrow, maybe. Right now, Shady was steeling herself for another possible encounter with Kim.

They left the Dodge a short distance away and walked toward the cemetery, again hunched, this time against the cold, a hint of drizzle in the air, *forever* in the air, it seemed.

"Gates are locked," Ray pointed out, as was expected.

Shady took a step back and studied the wall. "Think we can get over?"

"I think so, just about, but let's go around the back. There seems to be more trees there, maybe some overhanging branches too. We can use them for leverage."

They did exactly that, a bit of huffing and puffing, an "ouch" from Shady when she banged her knees hard against the wall, and then they were on the other side. Somehow. Someway. Determination really the thing driving them on, Shady especially.

It seemed a degree or two darker on this side, the night congealing like molasses. She put such an observation down to nerves and, of course, an ever-ripe imagination. Walking in graveyards was peaceful during the day, but as she suspected with the Spook Road, they could take on a different identity at night. The question to ponder was which was truer to their nature, the benign or the less so?

They only had the light from their cell phones to see by, and that which a crescent moon cast above them, the pair of them squinting in the dark, a sea of headstones before them.

"How big is this place?" Ray asked, scratching at his head.

"Big," Shady said. "Clearly. So we'd best get started. And don't say it."

"Say what?" he replied innocently enough.

"That it'll be like looking for a needle in a haystack. I don't need the reminder."

"No intention of saying anything like it," he retorted, holding his hands up.

Shady had previously looked on the *Find a Grave* website, so had confirmed Kim's grave was there, had a general idea of location too, but it would still prove a difficult task.

They replaced the gravel path beneath their feet with wet grass, drawing closer to the memorials, the outline of a small chapel ahead giving a further point of reference.

As they shined the lights from their phones and began

reading the epitaphs of those in Wyatt who had come and gone, in body and hopefully in spirit too, Shady tried to tune in to the atmosphere rather than the cold, hard stone.

Loneliness. There was that. And, inevitably, sadness too, the tears shed saturating the ground as much as rain ever could. The cold was simply the chill of an autumnal night rather than anything preternatural. It was normal. All normal. And although trepidatious at first, as Ray had been, she settled into the task of finding Kim.

Rows and rows of headstones, some plain, others fancier. So many names, so many dates, and messages bequeathed from loved ones, "*Until we meet again*" the dominant cry. Such hope in such few words, possibly the only hope that could carry some through.

What did happen to people when they died, Shady wondered. Where did they go? What other realms existed aside from this one? Were they better, the same, or, for some, worse? Despite her abilities, she had no answer. All she knew was that some didn't go anywhere; they stayed right here on this plane, the dead, reaching out, trying to make contact with those like her who'd take notice of them, who'd go the extra mile and help.

Kim, where are you? You've guided us this far, so guide us now.

A sound from up ahead, like that of a stone being thrown, then hitting the ground.

Shady's head came up.

"You hear that?" she called to Ray.

"What?" he answered.

"Like someone's thrown a stone."

He shook his head. "It's so quiet in here, as quiet as the—"

"Ray! Don't say that either!"

"Sorry." A flash of teeth showed he was grinning at the joke he'd almost made, but it quickly faded. "You think there's someone else in here with us?"

"No! I don't know. Or maybe I just got an answer to a silent prayer."

She picked her way through more headstones, somewhat squeamishly. Scenes from that old Stephen King film *Carrie* sprang to mind as fresh as if she'd only just watched it rather than an age ago—a vengeful hand reaching up through the earth to grab at her ankle. *Nothing* like that was going to happen at Heavenly Haven. But, oh, her heart was beating hard.

Another sound: a scamper.

She turned swiftly around. Was it Ray, so light on his feet suddenly?

It wasn't. He was still a couple of rows behind her, reading another headstone, absorbed in the words, it looked like, eventually heaving a sigh.

"You okay?" she called again to him.

"Yeah, sure. It's just this headstone," he called back, pointing to it. "This was a kid younger than Kim, and the epitaph, it's just…it's sad, Shady. Really sad."

She nodded in sympathy. "What's it say?"

"It says, '*In our hearts you're bigger than the Dakota sky, sweeter than a meadow in springtime, more constant than the moon and stars.*'"

"Always there," Shady said, also choked by the sentiment.

"Yeah," Ray replied. "That's what it says. '*You're always there.*'"

Shady turned back around, swallowing hard. It was easy to get caught up in tragedy in a place like this, but they had a job to do. Where had that stone landed? Just up ahead, she was certain. Where the sound of scampering had come from too.

Placing one foot in the front of the other, moving forward again, there was another noise, a *hiss* in her ear, suddenly and out of nowhere, making her catch her breath.

Coming to a halt, she tugged at her ear. "What the hell was that?"

Seeking out Ray, *needing* to see him again, she couldn't. Where he'd been standing was now nothing. She blinked hard, expecting him to reappear. Willed it.

People didn't just disappear!

Except they did. She knew that. All the time. They vanished as if they'd been vaporized. Then you had to go look for them, try to find them, dead or alive.

Where the heck was he?

She called out, "Ray!"

Grew angrier too, and so quickly. Why would he do that, up and leave her? Someone she trusted with her life. He'd let her down, disappointed her.

"Ray, what the fuck?"

Another slight thud behind her, like more stones being thrown. Again, she whirled around. "Is that you, Ray? Is it? Stop goofing! This isn't the time. *Who* is that there?"

A shadow. That was what. Tall and wide and looming.

"Ray." She muttered his name this time as she strode forward, not so careful to pick her way through the maze. She'd give him a piece of her mind when she reached him!

A prankster at school, the class clown, making everyone laugh. That was Ray. He'd made *her* laugh too, on plenty of occasions. Working with him could be a ball, but as she'd said, this wasn't the time. Certainly, it wasn't the place.

What was he thinking?

And why, oh why, was the shadow static, not responding to her at all?

"If this is your idea of a joke—"

A word flashed in her mind, like it had flashed on her phone the day before.

Don't.

Simple but powerful, able to halt her again.

Don't what? Don't get angry? Don't call Ray out for what he'd done? Laugh it off?

Don't.

Or did it have another meaning entirely? Don't trust the cops. That's what she'd taken it to mean yesterday. And don't trust what was in the shadows right now. Get any closer.

It wasn't Ray.

Whoever it was wasn't fooling either.

Not someone at all. Some*thing.*

Attracted to this land because… Shady tried to think, to stop panic from clouding her mind. Why would it be attracted to this land? *Because of grief, that's why. Because of sadness. Because of death. It's attracted to* all *land like this.*

Shadows…there was something about them, something that one of the construction workers had said. If you saw one, don't stare at it, don't get caught; it was something like that. He'd been referring to the shadows on ghost roads way out in the backcountry, but he hadn't said *why* not to do it. Was it because shadows like this fed off all things negative? Or was it more than that? They could…*absorb* you somehow?

Was that truly the fate of those who were never found?

The cemetery, benign by day, was not so at night. Was

never so at night.

Perhaps nowhere was.

She'd come here because she'd wanted to find Kim Wick's grave, but it was a mistake. One of monumental proportions.

She turned so quickly that she slipped, her hands coming out and only the hard stone of a memorial saving her from falling. Quickly, she straightened and ran, seeking to put as much distance as she could between herself and the shadow, but certain, absolutely certain, that it was coming after her, was amused, even, by her attempts to escape, because once seen, you couldn't unsee. And once it had seen you, you were marked.

Her heart pounded in her chest as she continued, her breathing becoming more erratic. Where was Ray? Where the hell was he? She was running, trying to escape, but what if he was still here somewhere? She couldn't just leave him!

There came the sound of scampering again beside her. But when she looked, she could see no one. Someone was keeping pace, though. Someone…*guiding* her?

Ray, where the hell are you?

She was going so fast, and the ground in places was so uneven. *Full of mounds. Full of hands, reaching up, not wanting to be left here either, not with what's behind you.*

"Aargh!"

Shady screamed as she toppled over. Because of a hand around her ankle, someone dragging her down, wanting a little company? Some comfort? Someone to hold them in their cold, cold grave. The shadow could easily overwhelm her now, Shady sucking in a breath and wondering if she'd ever have a chance to expel it. Closing her eyes. Waiting.

"Shady? Where'd you go? Come on, stop messing

around, will ya? Where are you?"

Messing around? *Her?*

The only thing to assault her was a voice belonging to Ray. How mystified he sounded. And a little grumpy too.

She pushed herself upward, onto her knees. Nothing skeletal preventing her. Her foot had caught on a grave marker, that was all. And if the shadow was behind her, it had come no closer. Ray was the only one who did.

"What are you doing down there?" he asked, most bemused again, as if she loved it on the ground, scrabbling about on rain-soaked grass, as though she'd done it deliberately.

"Ray! For God's sake, help me up, would you?"

"Oh. Sure! Sure!"

Once hauled to her feet, Shady dusted herself down. "Where'd you go?"

"Me?"

"Yeah! You!"

"Where'd *you* go?" he countered. "I couldn't find you."

"I was here the whole time! But I turned around, and you were gone. Jesus, Ray, I thought…I thought…"

His hands came out to hold her like he had on the ridge, so warm and so familiar. In that moment, and as angry as she was, she wanted him to hold her forever.

Still soothing her, he stroked her hair now, like a parent with a child, eventually taking a step back so he could explain.

"I had to take a leak. See that tree there? I went behind it."

"Oh," Shady breathed. "That's why I couldn't see you!"

"Yeah, then when I came out, I heard something to the right of me, similar to what you said, like a stone being

153

thrown. So I headed over there. And guess what?"

"What?"

"I found her grave, Kim's, like I was...led to it, you know? Want to come see?"

That was the reason they'd come here, but even so, she had to ask herself that question too. Did she want to see it or scram, get out of there?

"Ray," she said, wishing she didn't sound so pitiful, "is there, like...anything behind me?"

"Anything behind you? Like what? Gravestones, you mean?"

She shook her head. "No! Something other than gravestones. Like...a shadow."

"A shadow?" He did as she'd asked and peered into the distance. "There are shadows everywhere, Shady. But...there would be. It's what happens. It never gets totally dark, and what light there is refracts, producing a dozen shades of grey."

Not totally dark, and yet the shadow had been. *Dense* with darkness.

She had to do it, turn and see for herself. Be brave.

There *were* shadows. Ray was right. A multitude. But there wasn't *that* shadow, tall and wide and menacing. It had gone. Vanished. Perhaps *she'd* been the one to absorb it, straight into an imagination she'd allowed it to break free of.

She turned back to Ray.

"You want to go see Kim's grave?" he repeated.

"Uh-huh," she said, and he took her hand, explaining something else along the way.

"You know that sound we heard, like someone throwing stones?"

154

"Yeah?"

"There's an apple tree with ripe fruit on it. Can you imagine that, Shady? An apple tree in a cemetery? Bizarre. Anyway, I reckon it was the sound of apples falling. Maybe we should grab a couple each on the way out. It'll take care of dinner."

CHAPTER EIGHTEEN

Two apples—two *bitter* apples—hadn't taken care of dinner. And so they'd wound up back at Buffalo's, the same tattooed, surly server approaching them, seating them at the same table, and, wouldn't you know it, the same couple were across the aisle, the old lady picking at a fresh plate of salad, the old man still in dungarees and digging into steak with a side of breaded shrimp, soup, and gravy, no doubt intent on clearing his plate like last time.

Groundhog Day. At its worst.

Kim hadn't been at the graveyard, not in spirit, at least. Shady and Ray had reached her headstone, Ray shining the light from his cell phone to see what was inscribed there.

Kim Wick, it read. *Our angel. Beloved daughter, sister, and friend.*

Below that were the dates of birth and death.

As Shady had touched the headstone, tears pricked at her eyes like when Ray had read aloud the epitaph for another child, someone taken too soon. Or were they? Was that just something people thought? Maybe it was true, what others believed, that you came here for a purpose, no matter how big or small, and once fulfilled, there was simply no need to stay any longer. You left and went elsewhere. It was an intricate plan instead of chaos, decided upon before you took your first breath. If so, if you did believe that, would you find comfort in it if you lost a child or someone so beloved, had had them torn from you? Mr. and Mrs. Wick had suffered so much. Surely no one would choose that amount of grief to endure, pop their hand up in a pre-life meeting and take not one for the team, but three.

They had to find Beth, find them all, and in doing so, save another life—that of their mother, who was lying in a hospital bed, having collapsed because she *couldn't* endure it.

As her hands had connected with the granite, so beautifully carved, an angel upon it sitting with her hands in her lap, her eyes cast downward, Shady hadn't known what to expect. An image of Kim as she'd seen her, dark and savage and demanding? Or Kim as she'd truly been, a kid with blond hair in pigtails and freckles, who'd brought such joy to her family and who'd clearly loved them back, fiercely, the black sheep especially. *Please, please let it be that Kim*, she'd prayed, feeling shaky enough already. What she perhaps hadn't expected was to feel nothing, just the cold hardness of the stone. Wherever the spirit of Kim was, it wasn't there. *Find me.* And yet there'd been that scampering earlier, someone whom she'd felt was guiding her, away from the shadow…

On the way out of the cemetery, Shady despondent, more confused than ever, Ray had pointed to a jackrabbit darting between the headstones.

"Loads of them here," he'd said. "Did you notice? Scampering about."

That was the very word he'd used, *scampering*. Jackrabbits had been responsible for what she'd heard, and apples thudding against the ground as they fell from the trees, not stones being thrown. Logical, all perfectly logical. The shadow a product of imagination too. And yet as they'd climbed back over the wall and landed with a thud themselves on the other side of it, relief had flooded through her at leaving the dead to themselves. To rest in peace. Some of them. Because that scampering…she'd turned her head to the side, and nothing like a jackrabbit had darted out of sight. There were shadows in there, *innocent* shadows, and there were shadows that had more life to them.

They'd gone back to the motel before Buffalo's. No sign of the construction workers, although a few more cars were in the lot, those passing through but placed in rooms a distance from theirs, and they were quiet, a light peeping out from some but no other signs of life.

Which was good, something she took advantage of, the peaceful atmosphere, sitting cross-legged on her bed while Ray sat on the edge of his, only a sidelight on beside her. The necklace was already in her hand, having been released from the leather scrap, and she was handling it gently as she closed her eyes…

Mist. Like last time, she saw it immediately. Rising upward. A swirl. A frenzy, actually, more agitated than before. She was in the mist, and she was searching, but because it was swirling, she felt unsteady on her feet, nauseous, as if she was about to tip over any minute and fall. If that happened, would she hit the ground, which was as hard and unyielding as Kim's headstone, or would she just keep falling? Into what, an abyss? If that was the case, it would be dark, completely. Ray was wrong when he'd said nothing ever was. That shadow was, and the pit would be, and she'd choke in there, her mouth wide open and swallowing more darkness. A terrible place to be, horrifying, and no way to escape it or climb out. With her hands before her, she continued to search for Kim. Couldn't understand why she wasn't there, why she didn't come striding out of the mist with her blood-rimmed eyes blazing. *Find us! I've told you! Find us!* Although Kim hadn't appeared or said any such thing, Shady screamed back, *I'm trying to! I'm doing all I can to help.* You *help* me. *Make it clearer what I have to do. For* her *sake, Beth's. She's in danger.*

She was spat out of the mist, back into the motel room, Ray staring at her.

"Shady?"

The chain was still in her hand, almost burning her palm.

She leaned forward to grab Kanti's scrap of leather and hurriedly wrapped it in there.

"What's wrong?" he pressed. "What happened?"

Shady shook her head, took a little more time to compose herself before answering. "I don't know. Nothing. Just a mist, a swirling mist. That's all I saw. And I felt…I felt like I could fall if I wasn't careful, into a pit of some kind, and if I did, I'd stay there, never rise again. Oh, Ray," she said, his name bursting from her, she was so frustrated, "why do the dead speak in riddles? Why can't they say what they mean? Spell it out!"

He sighed. "Perhaps they're doing their best. Perhaps…you know, it's not that easy communicating across the great divide. I don't know. Just my thoughts on it."

Just his thoughts, but he could be right. It *wasn't* easy to communicate; even the living had trouble doing that.

It had been such a wonderful day, and it had been a strange and frustrating one too, the combination of which made her feel not just tired but exhausted, and yet she was hungry, needed some fuel and then sleep, plenty of sleep. And so, it was to Buffalo's they'd gone, the pair of them ordering the daily special, sirloin with ham-and-bean soup, and Shady even chancing a Lone Star beer, keeping Ray company, clinking bottles with him when they arrived, relishing the cold liquid as it slid down her throat, the hit it would give.

There were a few people in the diner other than the old couple, some of them eating too, but no one spoke much, and neither did they, their food arriving and set down before them, Ray picking up his flatware and delving in. So tired, so confused, and so hungry, yet Shady at first only toyed with hers, pushing food around the plate and bowl rather than eating it. The question seemed to torment her: Kim wanted to be found as well, but if she wasn't at the cemetery, where was she? How could they ever hope to find out, especially if they were now banished from Wyatt? Wasn't like they could go around questioning everybody or sneak into Mrs. Wick's room at the hospital to question her. If they were caught, it'd be a one-way ticket to the county jail for sure.

Kim's death, her *tragic* death, must have been reported in news bulletins other than what Shady had already found online, which gave no real details at all, just a mention of it. Perhaps a visit to the local library back in Wyatt would yield more information. She could check the archives there, *all* the local papers, disguise herself sufficiently enough.

She was thinking that when Angie the sullen server turned friendly, suddenly, like a switch had been thrown, replenishing Ray's beer, then lingering at their table instead of scurrying off—eager for a chat, it seemed, a local girl who'd also be a fount of information. The same person as before but different, so different.

Almost as if someone had possessed her…

* * *

Where ya from? Why are you here? How long you planning to stay? Those were the questions Angie had initially fired at them, not just standing by their table now—she'd asked Ray to scoot over so she could sit down, Ray eagerly obeying.

Although older than them, it was hard to tell if she was at the beginning of her thirties or the end. Shady had visited plenty of small towns in plenty of states and often felt as if the people there had a look about them. As if their features had hardened somewhat, or at least the look in their eyes. There were many ghost roads in America and many ghost towns. Some of the latter looked as if they were functioning okay, still people there, but many, *many* were run-down like Murdoc—rurally placed pit stops, if anyone ever bothered to stop there at all. They were struggling just to survive, holding on by their fingertips, still in existence only because a road ran through them. Murdoc looked like it was struggling, despite a big pharmaceutical company having apparently based itself there. If it had, which would be odd in a place so remote, it must be on the outskirts. There was a main street of sorts, but the businesses there were almost always closed, as far as Shady could tell. It was a town to feel some sympathy for, and perhaps the people who struggled to keep it alive deserved sympathy too—like Angie, so sullen before but now in a different mood entirely, lively, taking her hair down and letting it fall to her shoulders, the ends wavy but dry. Even so, she was pretty enough in her own way, just tired, the dark circles under her eyes rivaling

Shady's own.

They answered her questions, or rather Ray did, telling her they were on a road trip but without giving the reasons.

When he finished his beer, Angie got him another, brought a bottle of Jim Beam over too. Setting the bottle down, she nodded at it. "Duty done. We're closing in a while. No more customers for tonight, so yeah," she continued, eyeing Shady, "a little treat for myself for getting through another day in good old Murdoc. Want some?"

Shady shook her head. She'd finished her beer and would stick to water from now on.

"Okay, suit yourself," Angie declared, pouring herself a shot, and Ray too.

There were so many tattoos on her arms, skulls and crows, hearts and flowers, an eclectic, somewhat heady mix. Shady noticed a snake too, winding its way up from her elbow, the tight short-sleeved T-shirt she wore obscuring its final destination.

Angie raised her shot glass. "Here's to new blood. We don't get a lot of it 'round here."

Shady frowned. "This is a thriving business, though? Seems to be."

Angie glanced briefly at the old couple across the aisle. "The locals come often enough," she said. "Someone has to cater to them, offer another set of walls to look at."

"You own this place?" Ray asked.

A burst of laughter escaped her. "Me? No! I just work here. The owner's nice, though. She pays us every week on time. That's what matters."

"And you live locally?" Shady also inquired.

"Sure. About ten minutes' drive. It's handy."

"Do you ever…think of leaving?" The words were out of

Shady's mouth before she could stop them, Angie looking at her slightly askance and even Ray appearing puzzled. What an insensitive thing to say! Just because she thought of Murdoc as a kind of deadbeat town, it didn't mean the residents did. Even the old couple had turned their heads, maybe having caught what she'd said.

"Sorry," Shady continued, so glad she hadn't accepted another drink, wondering what she'd be like if she had, even more of a liability. "Of course you haven't. It's wonderful around here, truly beautiful. I mean it. The Badlands, I've never seen anything so…*good.*"

More silence from Angie, and then another burst of laughter, Shady relieved to hear it.

"Yeah," she said eventually, when Shady thought it'd be an indignant *no.* "I think about it every day, cutting loose while I still can, heading off into that big old yonder while I'm young enough." She'd lowered her voice at this, maybe aware the old couple were listening too, and leaned farther across the table. "But…I don't know. I was born here, my parents were, my grandma and grandpa. I have a kid, no husband, but a kid. Got roots, you know, and it's not so easy to yank 'em up. My momma looks after Lily when I'm at work. In a big city, would I find someone to do the same? Would I even be able to afford it? Okay, it's not Vegas around here, nothing glamorous about it, but it's down-to-earth, at least. It's honest." She sat back before adding, "Most of the time."

"Most of the time?" Ray asked.

Angie nodded, her sullen look reappearing; seemed she had to work hard to chase it away, resurrecting a smile.

"You got Lakota blood?" she asked Shady instead, similar to what she'd been asked outside their motel room during

163

party time.

She shook her head. "My grandmother was Cree."

"Cree, huh? Think I've got some Native blood running through my veins too, but diluted, you know, which I guess makes me a hybrid. So, you like the Badlands, which is Lakota land?"

This time, Shady nodded. "We visited them today. They're amazing.

"They sure are," she agreed. "You see buffalo?"

"Buffalo? No."

"Oh, they're there. Sometimes. Which route you take?"

Shady swallowed slightly, gave Ray a brief look. "The road straight out of Murdoc."

Angie cocked her head slightly. "The Spook Road?"

"Uh-huh. I believe that's what it's called."

"You crossed all five bridges? There and back?"

"We did."

"You know about the legend?"

"Something of it," Shady replied.

There was more laughter from Angie but a little different from before, more…forced. "That stuff, it's nonsense. Someone, somewhere, made up a story, and it stuck. Hey, Grace, Jack," she continued, now addressing the couple next to them, their heads turning her way, but slowly, "that stuff about the Spook Road, it's nonsense, huh? About the bridges. Been up and down it a few times. Never had one disappear on me yet."

No smiles appeared on their faces at being included in the chat; rather, they continued to look weary, the steak on Jack's plate now finished even if plenty of salad remained on Grace's. She'd piled that plate high, so high that merely nibbling at it, birdlike, would take an age. Thinking they

164

were going to continue to stare, then look away and ignore them, Shady was stunned when the woman suddenly opened her mouth and spoke.

"Just a myth," she said, her voice cracking slightly as though from disuse, as though she and her husband didn't talk much, even on dinner dates. "Plenty of myths 'round here."

There was a whisper of something from the husband, who'd turned his head away, his eyes back on his empty dinner plate.

"Pardon?" Angie said. "What was that, Jack? Didn't quite catch it." When he didn't reply, she pressed him further. "Jack?"

It was Grace who answered. "Don't mind him. He's just playin' with ya."

Angie laughed as if Grace had cracked the greatest joke, but she didn't let it go.

"Just tell us what you said," she continued, Shady wondering whether to intervene, to deflect, somehow change the subject. "Jack? C'mon."

"Look, I—" Shady began, but Jack finally spoke up too.

"Don't drive it by night, is what I said." How defensive he sounded. How...pained. "Keep away from it then. Things *don't* get a reputation for nothing. Least not in Murdoc, they don't, so don't make light of it. Don't think you're...*above* it. Just stay away." He stood up, an abrupt gesture for an old man. "Grace, get the check. We're going."

"But my salad!" she protested.

"You never eat the damned salad! Now come on. I'll wait in the truck."

As he headed off, Grace fished about in her purse, retrieved some dollars, and slammed them down—the exact

165

amount, no doubt.

Angie rose. "You want a box for your salad, honey?"

Grace raised a hand. "Leave it. Leave it. And ignore him, okay? He…thinks things. Up here," she said, tapping at her skull. "Listens to rumors. Believes 'em. But rumors is rumors, is all." A crack in her voice again, more defined, as she added, "They have to be."

"Okay, Grace." Angie's voice was gentler now, appeasing. "See you Friday?"

"Oh yeah. You sure will. We'll be here Friday. G'night." She then eyed Shady specifically. "G'night and…goodbye."

"Bye," Shady replied, surprised to find her voice was little more than a whisper. Such a strange place, and she and Ray strangers in it, understanding so little. The Spook Road, though, she was beginning to understand *that*; whether a bridge disappeared or not, it was somewhere that divided people, and yet look what lay at the end of it: heaven.

Grace and Jack left, along with some stragglers at the bar, featureless people with their backs to them, no women, just men. A chef also emerged from the kitchen, still in whites, and shouted goodbye to Angie. The place was now empty but for the three of them.

"If you want to lock up…" Shady said, but Angie had no intention of it.

"Lock up? When we've got bourbon to finish? You and me, Ray, at least."

"You're not driving?" Shady said, knowing how prim she sounded.

"Uh-huh," Angie responded. She was. "There's no one on the roads at this time."

Shady didn't like it, but she didn't argue it either. In a place like this, the rules *were* different; she was learning that

166

much. Their entire way of life was.

"What do you do?" was Angie's next question.

Although aimed squarely at Shady, Ray told her, "We work in a museum."

Angie raised an eyebrow. "Oh? Fancy! Where? In Idaho Falls?"

"Just outside it," Shady said, "in a town called Mason. A small town."

"Ha! You imagine a museum in *this* small town? What the heck would you stuff it with?"

You'd be surprised, Shady felt like telling her. The necklace in her pocket, for one, charged with energy of the strangest kind.

"The pharmaceutical company…" Shady said instead.

"Oh yeah. Gilcrest."

"I imagine they're a big employer of people around here?"

Angie pulled a face. "A few people I know work there."

"Some great opportunities going on," Shady persisted.

"For some, sure. Not so much the people I know. They're in admin, that kinda thing. Tell you what, though, no way I'd want to spend my days in an office. This place suits me just fine. I can wear what I like, and while I may not own it, I feel at home."

Shady took a deep breath. "You know a Johnny Latham? He works there."

"Johnny Latham?" She shook her head. "No, 'fraid not. Although…" She frowned. "The name rings a bell." She thought further. "No, can't recall who he is, not right now, anyway. Tell you one thing I do know, though." Again, she leaned in as if Buffalo's wasn't empty after all, as if the walls had ears. "Gilcrest may be a big shot around here, occupy a building as tall as it's wide, employ a good few people, but I don't see much of the money they're making being plowed back into Murdoc, you know? I mean, you've been here a couple of days, right? You've seen how depressed it is? If they've set up shop here, you'd think they'd maybe want to invest here too, huh?"

Not only talking, Angie was growing agitated, knocking back more bourbon almost absentmindedly, urging Ray to do the same, not wanting to drink alone. Shady thought she did, though, drank alone, that if she took her hand and connected, she'd find the town wasn't the only thing depressed. Angie had roots here, but just because you were born somewhere, did it mean you had to die there? She felt trapped, as many did in towns like Murdoc and Wyatt, places that, far from being a tight-knit, loving community, ate away at despair instead.

"Sorry about that," Shady muttered, too lost in thought again to check her words.

"What was that? What did you say?" Angie said, and Shady winced inwardly. She knew from experience Angie let nothing go.

"I'm sorry about Gilcrest. Not pumping money back into Murdoc. *Lifting* it. They should."

Angie attacked the bottle, filling her shot glass and Ray's, the contents of the bottle running perilously low. "*You're* sorry," she said eventually, Shady gulping a little, seeing a fierceness in Angie's eyes, a sullenness returning, that hint of anger. It lingered there, then dissipated, the woman *fighting* to conceal it. Oh, if only Shady could take her hand, see what truly lay behind the façade, of people like Grace and Jack too, the secrets they concealed.

Because they did, kept secrets, no physical connection

needed to confirm that.

And so came another strange thought landing in Shady's head: they kept secrets because it was *dangerous* not to, to expose them, the rumors.

In towns like Murdoc and neighboring Wyatt, you minded your own business.

CHAPTER NINETEEN

Ray was as sick as a dog. Beer and bourbon in copious quantities had not agreed with him. Angie, though, didn't even seem fazed. Finally getting up from the table, she walked straight as a shooting arrow to the door to let them out. Ray, however, staggered all over the place, Shady having to hold on to his arm and guide him all the way out of the bar and restaurant, then down the street to the Holiday Inn, Angie driving past a few minutes later, blasting the horn.

"What a woman!" Ray kept saying. "What a…*glorious* woman."

He'd seen what he'd wanted to, someone glorious indeed, and she, Shady, had seen someone else a little more desperate. Perhaps both versions were true.

Again, with no sign of the construction workers and no rooms illuminated, not at that late hour, they let themselves into their home for the night. Shady flicked the light switch, and there it was, a cockroach upturned on the carpet in front of her.

Ray headed straight to the bathroom to begin what was to prove a long night's barfing, swearing at intervals that it was *not* the drink, that it must have been the food.

"Denial ain't just a river in Egypt," Shady kept telling him, torn between amusement and despair. It had been another long day, and she'd love to grab some sleep, but with Ray busy on the big white telephone to God, that looked a ways off yet.

Eventually, she slept, they both did, sometime in the early hours of Thursday morning, Ray on his back and snoring so hard Shady was sure he'd blow the roof off. Even so, she managed to nap throughout it, dreamed also, with an assortment of people in those dreams. There was Angie, Grace, Jack, Johnny, and Mrs. Latham, all going around on some kind of crazy carousel, smiling at her and laughing, Grace's mouth wide open and various teeth either missing or blackened stumps. *The rumors. Ah, the rumors. Find out about the rumors*, she kept saying. *What damned rumors?* Shady felt like screaming back, but too late. The carousel had turned, *his* face reappearing, Johnny's, Shady now praying the carousel would slow so she could look into his eyes. *What are the rumors about you, Johnny? And will you find me like you promised? Or is it up to me to find you?*

She woke with a start, a yawn on her lips as she turned to see Ray in the twin bed beside her, still passed out. Grabbing her phone from the bedside table, she was stunned to see it was later than she'd expected—past ten, so again, no chance of breakfast.

She showered and dressed, and all the while Ray slept. Should she wake him or just leave a note? Plans had formed in her head, and she was eager to make progress.

In the end, she left a note, telling Ray to call her when he could, adding also that she was *not* going near the Spook Road alone, so not to worry on that score.

Quietly, she slipped out the door, heading to the Dodge and firing it up.

Reaching for the dead was something she did for a living, but today was about reaching for those still living, trying to find out more information, anything relevant to Ethan's and Beth's disappearance, and to Kim too. She was the one who'd involved them in all this, who'd guided Beth to the Mason Town Museum from a coffin in which only her body resided.

As she drove, Shady looked around her at crumbling businesses and tired homes, nothing upscale here, not in Murdoc. And yet something was: the premises of a thriving business that should benefit a community, but which apparently did not. A large business whose presence was not immediately obvious, almost as if it were hiding, but in plain sight. Because there it was, the Gilcrest Pharmaceuticals office building on the farthest outskirts of Murdoc, once a warehouse, perhaps, yet now converted, all shiny and new and so, so promising. Johnny Latham was on a career path there and doing well, according to his mom, not stuck in an administration job but climbing high.

A golden boy to suit a golden company, his smile golden too.

She could pinch herself. Why was she still obsessing about his charms? She had to rein herself in. But boys like him, *men*, you didn't find their kind in places like Idaho Falls or in places like this. He was brimming with confidence, or was it arrogance? Would that be more of an apt description? Although she suspected it might be the case, she hoped it wasn't. Wondered too if he'd leave one day, head to New York on the east coast or Chicago, somewhere that could accommodate a personality like him. Like Angie, he had roots in this area, in Wyatt, but if his mother was ill… Or perhaps being a big fish in a small pond suited him. In big cities, highflyers were common, and he'd fade out completely.

Regarding Mrs. Latham, she'd find out today how she was doing, and Mrs. Wick too. If she couldn't go to the hospital, she could at least call. There'd been no real news on Beth locally. She remained missing, and although there were some media updates, there wasn't a lot of coverage, not as much as Shady and Ray had expected. Nationally, it was no surprise there was no mention. People went missing every day in a country like America. A kid from a small town who might or might not have run off wouldn't ordinarily make wider news.

Shady was busy thinking about this as she walked across the Gilcrest parking lot to the lobby. An airy, perfectly temperature-controlled area, it proved as shiny on the inside as it was on the outside, the tiles beneath her feet so polished you could see yourself in them.

There was a reception desk, the woman sitting behind it impeccably presented, her hair like a waterfall, speaking into a phone as she checked the computer screen in front of her.

Taking advantage of the fact she was busy, Shady scanned her surroundings, just as she'd scanned the streets of Murdoc on her way to Gilcrest. The walls were tiled also, again sparkling but cold and clinical—apt, really, considering where she was, the desired effect. What she saw to her left drew her closer.

It was a portrait gallery, featuring several gilt-framed photographs of different faces, all of whom were beaming for the camera, looking delighted to be alive, to be working there at Gilcrest, *such* a prestigious company. Smug shots. That's what Shady christened them, everyone so damned pleased with themselves. Closer now, she stopped in her tracks, noticing within the sea of faces—about ten or eleven of them, an assortment of men and women—*his* face,

Johnny Latham's, smiling the hardest of all. *So* confident. *So* self-assured. A man with the world in the palm of his hand, it seemed. She checked: Did the smile reach his eyes? It did. It was genuine. Whatever his role at Gilcrest, he adored it.

Having to work hard to drag her eyes from him, she also noticed a plaque beneath his photograph: *Employee of the Year, 2023*. The pride of Gilcrest, then. Held in high esteem, except by the nurse at the hospital, Helen, who'd *bristled* in his company.

So where is he? she wondered. Inside this building too, just yards away, or out on the road, delivering supplies? What was his job description? And what plans did management have for him? If he was important enough to have his photo on the wall of the lobby, *why* was he doing deliveries? And did any of it really matter? Because he was allegedly Beth's boyfriend? Mrs. Latham had said he wasn't. It was gossip. Idle gossip. *Rumors.*

Perhaps if she reached out…if she could touch the photograph…read it.

She couldn't stop herself, forgetting, if she were honest, where she was, her eyes back on Johnny and the same happening as before, drowning in his gaze.

He was just so…magnetic. As beautiful as the Badlands. A part of it…

"Miss? Miss? Excuse me? Could I ask you what you think you're doing?"

Shady snapped back into the moment, quickly dropping her hands to her side, having not yet made contact. She swung around to face who'd spoken to her.

It was the receptionist, who'd risen from her seat, such a frown on her face as she primly sidestepped the counter and hurried toward her.

"You can't touch those," she continued. "You can't touch him. I'm not sure what you're doing here, but if I can help... Have you come to see someone?"

Shady could only stutter in reply. *You can't touch him.* Those words rang in her head.

"Johnny," she said at last, having to force his name through her teeth. "He works here?"

"Johnny Latham? He certainly does," the woman replied, a name badge identifying her as Paige. Mention of him softened her. She was proud of the company's rising star too.

"I've got an appointment with him," Shady continued, the lie flying from her.

Paige's frown returned. "Today? This morning?"

"Uh-huh." Shady had to work hard to keep the tremble out of her voice. "Yes."

"You couldn't."

When she said it, Shady almost doubled over with relief. What the heck would she do if she *could* have an appointment? Be shown to his office for him to do what...stare at her, aghast?

Paige was shaking her silky mane. "Mr. Latham is out right now and isn't expected back until later, when he does indeed have a variety of meetings, but with management. I'm sorry, I didn't get your name?"

"Lucy," Shady said, plucking the first one she could think of. "Lucy Clarke."

"Oh, okay, Miss *Clarke*," she said as if she knew Shady was lying. "I don't have you scheduled in. I'm sorry. Perhaps you've made a mistake."

"Me?"

"Yes," Paige said firmly, the intimation being that no way the golden boy could have.

"His mother," Shady continued. "She's ill. In the hospital." Why, oh why, she was saying this, she didn't know, except she was desperate to make sense of something around here, certain ideas niggling at the back of her mind, but none of them sliding into place to form a bigger picture. When the woman didn't reply, Shady added, "A suspected heart attack."

How confused Paige looked, disbelieving. "Is she? Johnny and his mother are very close, I believe. I'm sure he would—"

Whatever else she'd been about to say was lost as the doors to the lobby opened again, a burst of laughter and chatter in the air as a group of people entered, both men and women.

Immediately, Paige was flustered, flattening further her waterfall hair and brushing at her clothes to make sure there were no offending creases.

She walked toward them, the smile on her face as wide as any of those in the photographs, as fixed, Shady well and truly forgotten. *Insignificant.*

Shady studied the group more closely, although she'd noticed right away that Johnny wasn't there. Someone she *did* know was there, though, or that she at least recognized, causing her to turn away sharply and examine them no more.

Someone else was rushing toward them, perhaps having emerged from another set of doors behind the reception desk, a greeting on their lips filled with enthusiasm.

"Welcome! Welcome! We've *so* much to talk about. Paige, coffee, please, and then no disturbances, none."

"Of course, sir. Or course," Paige enthused right back.

The county sheriff was who Shady recognized. When she

and Ray had been taken to the sheriff's office in Wyatt, she'd spotted him, made note of the warning in his eyes as he'd uttered no words but simply stared back at her through the glass partition of his office. *Stay away.* Thank goodness she was insignificant, as the group breezed past her, and no one called out, asked her who she was or what she was doing. The real question, though, was what was *he* doing there, so friendly with everyone, so…*in their pockets.*

The loud chatter, the back-patting, laughter that sounded more like braying, was gone, everyone having disappeared behind those other doors. On a deep and somewhat shaky breath, she retraced her footsteps toward the entrance and stumbled out into fresh air.

While she stood there, inhaling deeply as if trying to cleanse herself from the outside in, Paige's words kept resounding: *You can't touch him.* She was wrong, though, because stashed inside Shady's jacket was Johnny Latham's photograph.

She could touch him in that way, at least.

CHAPTER TWENTY

"Ray, don't worry. I'm fine. I'm just out and about, doing a little digging. Yes, I'm being careful, and no, stay where you are. For now, anyway. I'm not surprised you're feeling rough! You know how much you drank last night? A lot! Angie was nice, sure, but she was only being friendly, so let's see about a return visit tonight, okay? Let's just…see. No, I won't be long. A couple of hours. Yes, I'll have lots to tell. Hopefully. You really do sound terrible. Maybe it was a little food poisoning too, who knows? Grab some more sleep. Feel better. Oh, hang on, hang on, I've got another call coming in. It's Annie. Okay, gotta go. I'll speak to you soon. In an hour? Sure. Now go on, get more sleep."

Shady ended the call with Ray—a Ray who could barely speak, his voice was so hoarse from all the hurling he'd done—and answered Annie instead.

"Shady, dear, how is everything? Are you both okay?"

"We're fine," Shady insisted. "How about you?"

"Busy keeping the ship afloat in Bingham County. But if you need me—"

"We know, we know, all we have to do is call."

A slight sigh preceded Annie's next question. "Are you any closer, dear, to discovering Ethan's whereabouts and, of course, poor, poor Beth's?"

"Yes…and no," Shady replied, an enigmatic answer, but the truth.

She'd escaped the lobby of Gilcrest Pharmaceuticals with Johnny's photograph, climbed back in the Dodge, and gotten the heck out of there, driving along another road that was as good as a dirt track, not one that headed west, though, as the Spook Road did, but east toward Wyatt instead. Not that she'd gotten far. When Ray had called her cell, she'd pulled over to answer it, noticing how lonely this road was too, as much as the one with five bridges, everything so far from civilization here, both a comfort in that and a sadness. To be this alone was fine for a short while, useful, actually, to do what she had to, but to be alone for too long—*undiscovered*—that wasn't a good thing.

"Shady?" Annie prompted, as she'd fallen quiet, and so Shady told her the latest developments, mentioning the Spook Road, their drive in both directions that had proved uneventful, touching on the Badlands too and how beautiful they were, unable to resist describing them to Annie as a way to relive the experience again. She also mentioned Johnny, that she'd gone to where he worked and stolen his employee-of-the-year photo.

"To do what?" Annie asked. "Tune in?"

"Uh-huh." The Natives believed that having your photograph taken captured something of your soul, entrapped it, so who was she to argue?

"Then do so while I'm on the phone. Just in case."

"In case of what?"

"You tell me," Annie batted back. "What exactly do you suspect this man of?"

"I...I don't know. There's speculation he's Beth's boyfriend, as I've said. Certainly, he was Ethan's friend. Used to run with him."

"But not his only friend, I'm assuming. Wasn't there a

gang of them?"

"That's right. Beth said Ethan was with a gang of some sort."

"But regarding Beth, you think Johnny might have kidnapped her?"

"Someone seems to have."

Annie wasn't as certain. "Maybe. Maybe," she murmured, now the enigmatic one. "As I've said, I'll stay on the phone if you want to handle the photograph now."

Shady agreed, placing the cell on the passenger seat, on loudspeaker, and picking up the photograph.

She didn't close her eyes right away, just stared at him. *So handsome. So charming.* Strange how she could feel this connection to him, but only physically. She had to forge something *mentally*, which proved more challenging than she'd thought.

There was nothing there, not initially, that she could get a handle on. No memory ingrained from when he'd had this photograph taken, perhaps, been *asked* to, the pride he had felt. Certainly, pride was stamped all over his face. He was pleased with himself, spectacularly, so why wasn't a hint of it still attached to the end product, a lingering emotion? He must have studied his own photograph, *approved* it, reached out and touched it, as she was doing, tracing the contours of his face, but she could detect nothing.

All there was, was a void. An emptiness.

Come on, Johnny. Who are you? What's your story here? You're a small-town boy made good. On the rise. That meeting you have later, is it with him, the county sheriff, perhaps some local politicians among them, all the head honchos. Are you a favorite son or something, one of the inner circle, freely admitted? What for? Why?

Nothing still, and Shady grew frustrated. The gilt frame and the glass that protected his image felt so cold in her hands as she continued to run them over it. If she had the real him before her, flesh and blood, he'd be warm to the touch, firing up something inside her, a spark that could easily become something else: a *blaze*.

Shady almost threw the picture from her.

An image of someone screaming had appeared in her mind, and it had done so at the very moment her desire for him had increased. No way she could tell who it was. It had been too brief, but they were screaming so hard it had split their face in two.

Was it Johnny? Or someone screaming *at* him?

As shaken as she was by it, as surprised, she held fast. *If it isn't you, Johnny, who is it? Were they on your mind at the time you had this picture taken? The* only *thing on your mind. Is that why you're grinning so hard? Nothing to do with a promotion at all. It was because of them. Because of how...terrified they were. Oh, Johnny, what have you done?*

No use. Whatever feelings or sensations there'd been, they'd gone, far too tenuous to keep hold of, Shady having to admit to Annie that she sensed nothing, *almost* nothing. Whoever had screamed, she'd keep it to herself for now because if she let on, Annie might panic and insist she return home. "It's in the hands of the authorities now," she'd reiterate. "We've done what we can. We've tried." And they might well be sensible words, but the one who'd screamed...could it have been Beth? Beth, who'd warned them *not* to go to the sheriff. Somehow, someway, she'd fought to get through to her. Guide her. Maybe Kim was guiding her too, Shady remembering again the scampering of feet in the cemetery that had led her away from the shadow, *not* jackrabbits at play, despite what Ray had said.

"Annie, another phone call's coming in. My mom…"

"Oh, right, of course, yes, yes, take it. But we'll check in soon. This evening?"

"This evening sounds great."

"Okay. Perhaps best not to get too hung up on Johnny, you know. If you felt nothing…"

"Sure. I understand, Annie. Speak to you in a while."

With the call ended, Shady continued to sit there, staring outward along the dirt track, wondering how much it twisted and turned on its way to Wyatt. Ellen hadn't called, not yet, although there'd been several texts between them. Shady, of course, assured her that she was fine and all was going well in South Dakota. She'd *love* to hear her voice right now, the reassuring tone of it, a mother who trusted her child, who gave her free rein, refrained from asking too many questions, but—like Annie, like Kanti—she'd be there if she was needed. Shady's friend Josie had also sent a text, asking if she and Ray would be back by the weekend, the crowd meeting downtown at the Golden Crown for another friend's birthday. Shady smiled to think of the gathering; the gang *she* belonged to was full of good people.

Whereas gangs out here, Wyatt way, perhaps were not.

She studied the photograph again, traced Johnny's features *again*, the smile on his face and in his eyes genuine, but for what reasons? Something had clearly thrilled him. This beautiful, dark, empty man that everyone loved. Everyone except…

The cell back in her hand, she conducted a brief Google search, then held it to her ear.

* * *

"Yes, yes, I remember you. You're inquiring after Mrs. Latham?"

"That's right, is she okay? Was it a heart attack?"

The nurse that Shady had spoken to before, Helen, paused.

"I know I'm not family," Shady pressed, trying to strike the right balance of concern, "but I'd really like to know if she's okay. We were having coffee with her when she collapsed."

"So you'd class yourselves as friends?"

"Yes," Shady replied, hoping that relationship was enough to extract some information.

The nurse relented. "It *was* a heart attack. She's had surgery and is still in the ICU. Right now, we're taking it day by day."

"I see." Shady's voice was dutifully solemn. "And could I inquire about Mrs. Wick too? She's…kind of a friend as well."

"Mrs. Wick is still in the hospital, I believe."

"Also still in the ICU?"

Again, a slight pause. "I've been told she's been moved elsewhere."

"So, she didn't have a heart attack, at least?"

"Look, I really can't—"

Shady gave in. "No, of course you can't. Sorry." She changed tack, desperate to keep her on the phone. "When we were there, Mrs. Latham's son came in, Johnny."

Shady could almost see the frown develop on Helen's face. "And?"

"And…" She closed her eyes, plunged right in. "It must have been such a shock for him, when it hit home his mother was so ill. I assume…he's visiting regularly. I know they're close, that…that…she thinks the world of him. She's very…*proud*. The rising star."

She'd been too obvious, gushing over Johnny. From here on out, it could go two ways: Helen could slam the phone down, thinking the girl on the other end was as deluded as everyone else in town, or stay on the line, out of morbid curiosity if nothing else.

Miraculously, she stayed.

"Who are you?" she said. "Who are you…*really*?"

"Helen, I—"

"At reception, it seemed like you'd only just met him."

"I had—"

"And you were staring at him," Helen interrupted yet again. "Doe-eyed."

She couldn't deny it, only address the crux of the matter. "You don't like Johnny. It seems everyone does except you. Why?"

How stern Helen's voice became, nothing nurse-like about it at all. "Tell me who you are. As you may have guessed, it's not easy to pull the wool over my eyes, so I think you'd better tell me the truth. Now. I mean it."

Shady stalled this time, as if waiting for something. A text to come through, perhaps? One word written: *Don't*. But no such thing happened.

"I'm a friend of Beth Wicks," she answered finally. "Not that I knew her very well, but I've come to Wyatt to see her because…she asked me to, because…we had stuff we needed to discuss about her older brother, Ethan. I arrived only to find she was missing too."

No hesitation now from Helen. "Have you told the sheriff's office this?"

"I've been in contact with them, yes."

"But have you told them you had things you needed to discuss with her?"

Shady paused. "Not in so many words, no. I'm worried that if I do, they'll think I had something to do with her disappearance."

"And you don't?"

"No! I was trying to help her!"

A couple of minutes before, while they'd been talking, she'd heard others in the background, colleagues chatting to one another, conversation punctuated with laughter and the beeping of machines, but now the background was absolutely quiet, the woman clearly having moved from the nurses' station and gone somewhere more private.

"Tell me more about you and Beth," she said. "What she wanted you to do."

"She wanted me to find out about her brother," Shady repeated, "who went missing—"

"Two years ago, yes, I know."

"She wants to know what happened to him."

"Via what methods? Are you an investigator of some sort?"

It wasn't far from the truth, not really. That role seemed to be written more and more into her job description. "Yes," she said, "of sorts. Working privately. I wanted to come to the hospital to see you, only my time with the deputies…it was more of a run-in with them, and they've made it clear they don't want to see me in Wyatt again, *warned* me."

"I'll bet," was the nurse's wry reply.

"I heard Beth might have been seeing Johnny. Romantically, I mean."

"I wouldn't know about that," Helen said. "Although if she was, I can't imagine him as the faithful kind."

"He's a bit of a lady's man?"

"Truth? I don't know *what* he is."

Shady frowned. "It's just, if he was seeing Beth and now she's disappeared…I wonder if he was involved?"

As she uttered those words, she could barely breathe. From what she could understand from local news, law enforcement was no closer to finding Beth. Who they suspected, though, she had no idea, but surely he'd have been among the first to be brought in, not free to deliver medical supplies and attend meetings. What would Helen say in response? Had Shady pushed the boundaries too far? The answer, when it came, rocked her.

"If he is, you can't touch him. You can't touch *any* of them. Turn around."

"Turn around?" Shady repeated. "I don't understand. What do you mean?"

"Turn around and do as the deputies say. Leave Wyatt."

"I'm not in Wyatt. I told you, the cops don't want me there. But…I am close by."

Exasperation in the nurse's voice now, and something else pushed its way in too…fear. "Turn around and leave! You're a private investigator, a woman on your own—"

"There's two of us," Shady said.

"That red-haired guy you were with?"

"Uh-huh."

"You're young! Both of you. Too young. You wanted to get information out of me, but the thing is…I *can't* tell you anything other than what I have. I can't because what happens here, it's…*unseen*. Don't get me wrong, there are good people in Wyatt, many, many good people, but there are also plenty that aren't. Ethan Wick going missing, now Beth…maybe that's just the start of it. Something bad has been planted, and it'll keep growing, expand. I don't know if Beth was seeing Johnny or if he took her, and I don't know what happened to her brother either... *I don't know*. But I know this, if you voice any suspicions, even indirectly, even to those you think you can trust, stuff can happen, *bad* stuff. You might not go missing, but you can be ruined easily enough, taken down. And no one's ever held accountable. Strange, don't you think? That the sheriff pursues matters only so far."

The sheriff she'd been warned about via a message from Beth's phone.

"Johnny," the nurse continued, "is too good to be true. *Too* confident. You know?"

Shady did. She'd thought so too.

"Two-bit Johnny," the nurse added.

"Two-bit Johnny?"

"Yeah, I have twins that went to school with him. He disrupted every class, never took a test, got his way by bullying, not brains. And yet look at him now, raised so high."

"Two-bit Johnny," Shady said again, almost *breathed* the words, somewhat mournfully. It didn't suit him. At least now it didn't. But she had to see him more clearly, not remain so dazzled. "If he was so bad, why's it the opposite now? He seems really popular."

"Because people are easily led, that's why," Helen declared angrily. "Blinded."

"You don't think he's changed?"

"Johnny? I have twins, like I said, twin girls. He liked one of 'em, you know, in *that* way. And when she didn't want to give him what he wanted, he tried to take it."

"Tried to...rape her?" Shady said, stunned.

"That's what she said."

"You took that to the sheriff, surely?"

"I did."

"And?"

"It was her word against Johnny's, and he denied it, of course. We could have gone to court, but Becca refused, didn't want to have to relive such a dreadful experience, and who could blame her? Although traumatized, she'd managed to stop him, and so with no—" she had to swallow before continuing "—*physical* evidence, guess who they believed?"

"Him?"

"In good old Wyatt town, the authorities believed Johnny every step of the way. And I saw how they looked at her too, the sheriff included. Becca and Tess are modern girls. I've brought them up to express themselves, dress how they want, *own* their femininity, and, granted, Becca liked tight clothing and short skirts, which she was wearing that night, the night of the visit to the sheriff's office, and, like I said, I saw the way they looked at her, like she…*asked* for it, that kind of attention. This town," she spat. "This damned town."

It was infected. That's what it sounded like to Shady. Too many bad seeds thriving.

"You'll get nowhere," Helen insisted. "You may even be in danger if you continue with what you're doing. Two of you isn't enough. You need an army to take on an army. You have a lot of life ahead of you, so my advice? Don't probe anymore, just turn around and go, you and the red-haired boy. Some things run too deep."

"But—"

"That's it, I've said my piece. I won't say any more.

Respect that, please. And if you repeat any of this, I'll deny it."

"Sure, I—"

"I'm sorry for Beth. I was sorry about Ethan too, and Kim. I *feel* for the Wick family. They've suffered, but don't get involved. Escape while you can."

CHAPTER TWENTY-ONE

The picture building in Shady's head had so many gaps in it still. There was no use trying to tune further into Johnny Latham's psyche via his photograph or to extract Kim's necklace from her pocket and try again with that—it just made everything more muddled. Now was a time for hard facts, for fleshing out Johnny's character more in his absence, a two-bit character, a bully, a man who'd attempted rape, but who'd then turned into the town's darling, a golden boy. *Untouchable.*

No longer in the turnout, she was continuing onward to Wyatt, where the heart of the matter lay—a rotten heart, it seemed—grateful for Ray's oversized hoody, which she'd found on the rear seat, so big on her she could disappear inside it.

She knew exactly where she was going: not to the library to thumb through dusty archives, but to the coffee shop where she and Ray had taken Mrs. Latham. Mrs. Latham, who perhaps wanted to forget that her golden boy didn't always shine bright, who refused to acknowledge rumors about him, both past and present, at least publicly.

Leonora was the girl who'd worked the counter in the coffee shop that day, Shady praying she was there today as well. She knew Johnny, apparently, had gone to school with him, knew too about the rumors that surrounded him and had neither denied Mrs. Latham's insistence her son was an innocent nor confirmed it.

If she'd been at school with Johnny, it meant she knew Ethan Wick too. He could also be fleshed out, meat added to his bones.

Something was very wrong in Wyatt, and the nurse had warned Shady to steer clear of it. She was just a girl, and Ray was just a boy. Neither of them were official investigators equipped to deal with situations that could take a turn for the worse. But leaving South Dakota now, it'd be too much like fleeing, giving in to the powers that be, *invisible* powers, those behind the scenes that always tugged the strings. Perhaps she couldn't topple such a sinister network, but she could find out more about Ethan, connect with him, Beth, and Kim, follow a dead girl's instructions instead of anyone else's.

One thing she couldn't do, though, was stay here for very long. She had a job to return to, a family and a life. She'd have to leave, but not today, not tonight; she'd promised herself that. And in that time, she'd pull out all the stops, do what she could.

And if she failed?

If she failed, they'd return to the museum, and the necklace would be blessed by Annie's friends, the exorcists, although Shady and Ray had never met them, didn't know if they were even local or not. They would then place it in a lead-lined box, not using silk or a scrap of leather but something more hardcore, until its energy was completely depleted.

As for Kim's face, blood-streaked and eyes bulging, she'd have to try to forget it. Forget the threat that Shady would hang if she failed, like Kanti had hanged. By her own hand too? Is that where her gift would ultimately lead her? To ruin?

Quickly, she admonished herself. She was *not* ruined now. She was determined.

The coffee shop came into sight, opposite the grocery store, the street quiet. It was early afternoon on a Thursday, in a town of just under seven thousand people, amidst the South Dakota wilderness, most people at work, she assumed, or maybe on vacation during their kids' school break. The few people who were out and about on yet another grey day looked grey themselves, lackluster.

There were also very few cars driving by but several parked, and Shady pulled in beside one of them, retreated into her hoodie, and headed outside.

Please be there, Leonora. Please. That prayer was on her lips as she reached the coffee shop, peering in through glass windows that had become slightly misted.

She sighed with relief.

She *was* in there, and better still, there was no one else. *The gods are with you*, Shady told herself as she pulled at the door. *Or rather, Kanti is. A goddess.*

Perhaps unsurprisingly, Leonora was on her cell and didn't immediately look up as Shady entered, but when she did, the tired smile she'd forced faded.

"Oh," she said. "It's you."

Shady hoped her own smile looked more genuine. "Hi. It's Leonora, isn't it?"

"Uh-huh," the girl answered warily.

"I'm Shady Groves."

"Okay. What can I get you…Shady."

"Um…coffee, please, black." *And a side of information.*

How on earth could she approach the subject, get her to talk rather than clam up?

While contemplating, she took a seat at the table closest to the counter in case Leonora didn't linger when delivering the coffee—so she could continue to chat even if the girl backed up.

Strange thing was, she didn't. She served the coffee and then, Angie-like, hung around, was the one who kicked off asking questions.

"Do you know how Mrs. Latham is?"

"Yeah, yeah," Shady replied, somewhat taken aback. "She's still in the ICU."

"Heart attack?"

"It was."

"You're not from around here?"

"No. I'm visiting."

"Visiting who?"

Shady took a breath. Should she say it? What the hell. It was all or nothing out here, she was learning. "I'm visiting Beth. Or I was supposed to be."

"Beth Wick? Who's gone missing?"

"Yeah."

"Like her brother, Ethan, a couple of years back."

"Like her brother," Shady confirmed. "You knew Ethan?"

She nodded, bit at her lip, but only briefly. "We had a thing. Kinda."

Shady's heart quickened as she gestured to the seat opposite her. This was better than she had hoped. "Want to sit down, join me? Doesn't look like you're busy right now."

From being forthright, the girl now hesitated.

"Leonora?" Shady prompted. "Please?"

Eventually, she complied, then asked the same question the nurse had. "Are you an investigator or something?"

"No," Shady said, wondering if she had that air about her, of somebody seasoned, quite liking it if she did. "Not really. But you know what?"

"What?"

"Seems to me like there's something worth investigating around here."

Leonora looked down at her hands, Shady noticing her nails were bitten, some of them down to the quick. "You wanted to know about Ethan?"

Again, she was taken aback. "Yeah. Yes, I do."

"I liked him. He was…shy. Kept himself to himself. I was, like…his girlfriend, I suppose, but…I never really got to know him, although I tried. He just seemed so…insular. A hard nut to crack, you know?" From sounding so forlorn, she suddenly smiled. "He had such beautiful eyes. You could lose yourself in them."

Like Johnny's eyes, thought Shady, immediately disappointed with herself for thinking that, for once again succumbing.

"He was misunderstood," Leonora continued.

"Ethan?"

A frown marred her otherwise pretty enough features as Leonora pushed fair hair away from her eyes. "Yeah, Ethan. Who we're talking about, right?"

Shady nodded avidly. "Sorry, yeah."

"He didn't do well at school. I mean, I didn't either—look where I ended up working—but Ethan found it hard, you know, felt like an outsider."

"He told you this?"

"No, I kind of guessed. Not sure he got along with his

parents either, think he thought of himself as a disappointment. And Ethan, he *hated* that."

For someone who didn't really know Ethan, the girl seemed very insightful, Shady continuing to listen with interest.

"Not sure how he got along with Beth, but him and his younger sister were close."

"Kim?"

"Uh-huh. She was a cute kid. Tragic what happened to her."

To them all, thought Shady.

"Ethan was misunderstood, okay?" Leonora's voice now had a note of insistence. "He wasn't a bad guy."

Now it was Shady who frowned. She hadn't said he was.

"It's just…"

When Leonora faltered, Shady dared to interject. "He ran with Johnny Latham?"

"Johnny Latham's *gang*."

"And they were…bullies?"

"Not Ethan. But they were, the others. Yes."

"What others? What do they do now? Are they all still in town?"

"You know what?" Leonora said. "No one ever seems to leave here, not in the way of, like, catching a bus and waving goodbye, off to greener pastures. They only leave if…"

Again, Shady finished her sentence for her. "If they go missing?"

"Uh-huh," she said softly. "Ethan…"

"Ethan, what?" Shady pushed her cup aside. "Tell me, Leonora. I won't say anything, not to anyone. What we're talking about, it's confidential."

"That's the trouble," she said.

"What is?"

"No one *ever* says anything. Everyone turns a blind eye."

"Maybe not everyone," Shady replied. "Doesn't seem like you want to."

"It's just…" She took a deep breath, had lowered her head but now raised it. "Look, I don't know what's happened to Beth, okay? She was Ethan's sister, but I never really knew her. She was, like, a couple of grades below me. We never mixed. And when I saw Ethan, it was always out somewhere, never at his house, or mine either. We'd go for rides in his car. Such…*quiet* rides sometimes. Ethan was like that, really quiet." There were tears in her eyes as she recalled this, Shady wishing she could reach out and take her hand, find out more that way, that Ethan was her first love, this quiet, misunderstood boy whom she'd barely known, but what had that mattered? He'd found his way into her heart regardless.

"Leonora, I'm sorry," Shady murmured.

"It's fine, it's okay," she insisted. "Ethan could have just quit town, you know? And Beth too. The pair of them were brave enough to do something like that, get out of here."

"But their parents?"

"Ethan was a disappointment to them, like I said. As for Beth, after Kim, her parents were just too consumed with grief to notice her. I've heard her dad spends most of his time locked away in his office at home, and her mom spends most of the time in her bedroom, sleeping."

"Where'd you hear that?"

"Some things people *do* talk about in a town like this."

"Rumors."

"Yeah," Leonora said, sighing. "Rumors. But…what I'm about to say is fact, I swear it."

"Okay."

"Last time anyone saw Ethan was August twenty-fifth, his folks, when he left home around noon. It was a hot day, really hot. Most people stayed inside with the drapes closed and the AC on max. A quiet day, with nothing but the buzz of damsel and dragonflies in the air, as quiet as it is today, like it is every day in Wyatt, at least on first inspection."

Shady leaned closer. "That's the date Beth told me and what I've read too." There was such scant news on him, but there was that, at least, those timings.

"That wasn't the last time *I* saw him, though."

"What?" Shady's voice reduced to a whisper.

Leonora shook her head. "Don't worry. It's not a secret. I told the sheriff's office."

"Told them what?"

"I saw him, later that night. I'm sure I did."

"What do you mean, you're sure?"

"I have an aunt who lives in Murdoc. D'you know Murdoc?"

Shady nodded. She certainly did. Murdoc was home for now.

"I was visiting her that night. I'd taken over some of Mom's chicken soup because she was ill. I'd taken the main highway there, never the backroads. You're told from the get-go around here *don't* take the backroads at night, all sorts of stories made up about 'em. Stick to the main routes, and so I did. Why run into trouble if you don't have to? Ethan tended to stick to that rule too. Or so I thought. But...I saw him, not on the way to my aunt's but the way back. It was late, after eleven, and I was going home. He wasn't in his car. Lord knows what happened to it; that was never found either. He was in a Ranger, a *black* Ranger, the truck Johnny

Latham used to have. He was in the passenger seat, and Johnny was at the wheel. Ethan, though, was kinda slumped and just...staring. Blindly."

"And you told the cops this?"

"Yes!" the girl insisted. "I told them all that. They hauled Johnny in for questioning, but he said it wasn't Ethan, that I must have been mistaken. He said it was another of his...his...*sidekicks*." Leonora spat that word out. "And that sidekick, Caleb, who I also went to school with, confirmed it. But Ethan, I'd know him anywhere, the shape of him. I..."

It was she who grabbed Shady's hand, and held on to it tight, images flashing through Shady's head while she did so—of Ethan, the man who dominated Leonora's mind still. Another beautiful boy, such a...troubled boy. Going in the wrong direction. Lost. Scared.

Leonora spoke again. "Why was he staring so blindly? Why?"

"I don't know," she said as kindly as she could. This girl...she hurt. But then so many in Wyatt did, those she'd met, at least.

"They believed Caleb and Johnny, not me. Case dismissed. Everyone dismissed it, even my parents. It wasn't only dark, you see, that night, it was lashing down with rain, and therefore so easy to make a mistake. It was Caleb, not Ethan. And yet Caleb, he's got blond hair, a shock of it that stands out against the darkness. And it didn't."

Leonora let go of Shady's hand and wiped at her eyes and nose.

"And that's really all I've got to tell you. I don't know if it helps, and I'm used to being disbelieved, *ignored*, but I know what I saw. And I'll stand by it until the day I die.

That was Ethan in Johnny's car. And—" another hard swallow "—he wasn't in good shape."

Shady leaned back in her seat, trying to digest all she'd learned, wishing she could make sense of it, what Johnny had been up to that night, and Ethan, and what had become of Beth.

The girl had returned to her position behind the counter and was checking her cell, so Shady stood, supposing she'd better take what she'd learned back to the motel in Murdoc, get Annie on FaceTime, and discuss it with her and Ray.

Murdoc...

She was on her way to the door but swung back around and approached the counter. Leonora looked up, clear surprise on her face. Weren't they done?

"Where in Murdoc did you see Johnny and Ethan that night?" Shady asked. If her spine had tingled earlier, it was doing so again, a thousandfold.

"Where?"

"Uh-huh. Tell me where exactly."

"It was... Do you know the gas station in Murdoc?"

Shady nodded as the girl continued.

"On the way back to it from town, there's a crossroads, which I'd stopped at. Johnny's car was at the intersection too, coming from the direction of the gas station. Here's another thing," she said, putting her phone back down on the counter and once again warming to her subject. "Like I told you, no one takes the backroads around here, especially at night. There's no real need. The highway takes most people to where they want to go. If anyone's ever on them, they're just passing through, maybe got themselves a little lost. But Johnny and *Ethan*," she said, her jaw firming a little, "turned left at the crossroads instead of right. So not into Murdoc, but away from it. I don't even know what they were doing in Murdoc. My aunt lives there, but it's a one-horse town. Nothing open at night except one restaurant, Buffalo's, and that's just full of locals."

"So they turned left," Shady reiterated. "Towards the Badlands. Down the Spook Road?"

"The Spook Road?" For a moment, Leonora looked confused. "Oh yeah, the one with the bridges. Yeah, that's what Johnny drove onto."

"And you told the cops that too?"

"Of course!"

"Did they even investigate, do you know? Go down there and search for him?"

"Are you not listening either? They *dismissed* what I had to say because of Johnny, because of Caleb." She shook her head. "Because of lies."

"Because of lies *and* secrets," Shady said, almost to herself.

Leonora agreed, avidly. "A whole ton of 'em. This town is built on lies. One day…one day, I'm gonna leave too, I swear. There's got to be somewhere better."

"You can always come to Idaho Falls."

That drew a smile from Leonora. "Is that where you live?"

"Uh-huh. We've got a good crowd there. You could join us."

"Maybe I will," she said, something else on her face: hope.

"If you do, look me up."

"Okay."

"Bye," Shady said.

"Bye."

Shady was almost at the door again when Leonora spoke.

"You wanted to know the exact spot where I saw Ethan last?"

Shady frowned as she turned back. "Yeah. At the crossroads in Murdoc."

"Yeah." Leonora was also frowning. "The site of the crash too."

"What crash?" Shady asked, for a moment completely confused.

"*The* crash, you know? When Ethan's little sister lost her life. Fucking cursed, the crossroads *and* the Spook Road."

CHAPTER TWENTY-TWO

"You were going alone, weren't you?"

"No."

Ray was having none of it. "Shady, it's me, Ray. I know you. You came back to the hotel room, saw I was sleeping, fussed around a little, and then went to sneak out again, *without* waking me, to go to the Spook Road, which we've been told to keep away from at night. A road with a weird legend *meant* to keep us away. You were going to go alone despite knowing the danger involved, which you've been in before, back in Oregon when you headed out without telling anyone there. Jesus, Shady, *why*?"

"Ray, I'm not stupid, okay? I know there's danger here, and I don't ever want to get myself in the same situation as I did in Oregon. All I was going to do was go to the crossroads and maybe a little way up the Spook Road, to the first bridge or something, then turn around. I just wanted to see how I felt, knowing what I know now, whether——"

"You could connect," he finished.

"Yeah. That. Hey, you still look really pale."

"I *always* look pale."

"Not always," she said, smiling. "But you've been so sick."

"I had a hangover."

"Or food poisoning, like you said."

He shook his head. "*Just* a hangover. Think I may have been exaggerating before."

Shady raised an eyebrow. "You were looking for a little sympathy?"

"Did you feel any?"

She thought for a minute. "Nah."

Ray grinned. "Anyway, upshot is, I'm fine now. You're going nowhere without me."

"Bet you say that to all the girls, Ray."

"Actually, no. It's only ever you."

Joking, they both were. And yet, no matter how briefly, there was an awkwardness, a *frisson*. Shady felt it, but not only that, was surprised by it. *What the hell...?*

Ray asked for his hoodie back, breaking any tension that might have occurred, the redness that had temporarily enlivened his pale complexion fading. "It's the only one I brought with me, so come on, hand it over. No way the hoodie you brought will fit me."

"A fair argument," she said, complying.

He then checked his watch. "So...it's getting dark outside. When do we go?"

"Now?" Shady suggested. "And since you're with me, we can be braver."

"Braver how?"

"We can drive all the way down the Spook Road and back again. Put out *all* the feelers."

"All the feelers," Ray repeated, his voice a murmur. "Okay, it's not too late, I guess. It's not the witching hour. I'd feel differently if it was."

She shrugged. "Darkness is darkness, Ray."

"Thanks for the reminder, Shady. I needed it.

Considering."

He was being sarcastic, as was she, but it was good-natured enough as they left the motel room, stepping over yet another cockroach that had crawled out from somewhere and gone belly-up, Shady trying not to grimace. Funny how they always showed up dead. Just what were they spraying the rooms with around here?

Regarding the matter of the missing brother and sister, she'd thought she'd find out more about it in their hometown of Wyatt, and she'd been right, she had. But the epicenter was not there; it was in Murdoc. This place was guilty of *everything*, a badland indeed but with no picturesque jagged mountain range to redeem it. That was miles away, down a lonely road that, around here, you grew up being warned to stay away from or else.

That stuff about the bridges, time to see if it was true, if the night really did make a difference. And if one should disappear, why? Where'd you end up instead?

Where had Ethan ended up? He'd allegedly been driven along there at night by Johnny Latham, slumped in the passenger seat beside him, staring blindly. A boy who was misunderstood, according to Leonora, to Beth and also Kim. But was he? An innocent caught in a web? That same predator having now devoured the eldest of his sisters too?

Not Kim, though. When Shady had come back and told Ray what had transpired, after he'd finally woken, they'd googled Kim's accident some more. A mother with her own child in the car had crashed into them; like the woman who'd driven the car with Kim in it, she could have become distracted. No one was to blame, it had been decided. It was an accident, pure and simple. In the few articles that existed, all referred to the accident having happened *outside* of

Wyatt. None, however, named Murdoc, a town so small, so insignificant, it didn't *warrant* a mention. Yet something big was going down here, Shady thought as Ray drove them out of the parking lot. Something…monumental. And the reason Kim and her friend had been driven to Murdoc in the first place? Because there was a sports field, sometimes used by the school in Wyatt, that time being one of them. Leonora had told her that, when Shady had asked. A floodlit game of field hockey—so it'd been dark. And yet still Kim had seen something…Ethan? A child who was unknowingly close to death, and therefore the veil had been thin and she'd spied her brother there, disoriented, bewildered, *dead*. Had he been calling out to her, aware that she could see him? *I'm so lonely here. Find me. Please.*

And she had, only not in the form they might've expected. As something dead too.

They reached the crossroads, Ray slowing the car to a halt.

"You know about crossroads folklore, right?" he said.

"Tell me."

"All righty, the Spook Road isn't the only thing with a reputation around here, but it's kinda fitting it should lead off from a crossroads. You see, what a crossroads is supposed to represent is a location 'between worlds,' a place where spirits can make contact."

If that was so, it fit with the theory she'd devised only moments earlier.

"Seems to be a lot of places in between worlds around here," Shady said somewhat wryly. "The place in between the bridges, for one."

"I wonder which bridge allegedly disappears," Ray mused. "And if it's by night only."

"Ray, it's bullshit. All we're doing here is trying to tune in."

"All *you're* doing."

She laughed. "Yeah. Sure."

"And if we make it back?"

"Of course we're gonna make it back!"

"Okay, but if we do, then what? We can't stay in Murdoc forever."

"I know that. After this, we'll go, but we'll keep tabs on it and Beth, of course, hope to God she's found safe and well. Shit, Ray, I really hope she just took off, that those texts I got really were from her. If so, that suggests she's keeping an eye on us."

"Directing us?"

"Yeah. Maybe." She sighed heavily. "Somehow. Ah, who the hell knows? It hurts my brain trying to make sense of it. It's all just so…weird."

"And about to get weirder still," Ray said, nodding toward the Spook Road.

"Look, if you don't want to go—"

"Don't even!"

"Don't even what?" Shady replied as innocently as she could, then relented. "I would not go alone, Ray, okay? Promise. I wouldn't wait till you fell asleep again, then take off."

"Don't trust you, Shady."

"Ray!"

He was only half joking this time. "So we go now while I'm wide awake, while it's still relatively early evening. And then tomorrow we get out of here and go home, continue to work on the case, but from afar." His eyes back on the Spook Road, he added, "*Very* afar."

"Okay. You're on. You ready?"

"As ready as I'll ever be. Let's do it, let's see what happens this time."

* * *

It could be beautiful by day in the summer, this road, leafy trees creating tunnels for part of it, temperatures way cooler beneath them. Despite legend, a road you might *want* to take.

But only by day. At night, even on a warm, starlit evening, it'd be different. *Not* as inviting. Certainly, in the grip of October, it held no charm whatsoever, Shady noticing a shiver down her spine as they headed over the crossroads to begin their journey down it.

Ray'd said the veil between the dead and the living was considered thin at the crossroads, that boundary between the past and the present. It was an ancient belief, with its roots in Greek mythology, but universally upheld. Could it be that because so many believed in it down the ages, a truth had been manifested? Or was it just a simple fact, the world more mysterious than anyone could ever imagine, even someone like her with a psychic ability, who *knew* certain things to be true? If it was the former, then it would follow that the myth of the Spook Road had some truth to it too. Five bridges one way, but sometimes, just sometimes, four bridges in the other direction. The in-between existing not only at a crossroads but in many places, and not only in America but all over the world. Paranormal hot spots. Paranormal...*bad* spots.

They were on it, twin headlights already struggling to deal with the dark.

"You think it's okay to keep the high beam on?" Ray asked.

"Why wouldn't it be?"

"Just in case someone's coming the other way? It'd blind them."

"*If* someone comes, you'll spot them on high beam too, so can switch it off in good time."

"Okay, all right," he replied, somewhat relieved, Shady could tell, and she didn't blame him. The darkness out here was suffocating.

"Feel anything yet?" he inquired, shifting in his seat.

"Give me a chance. Just…give me a chance."

They reached the first bridge, the car bumping over a ridge at each end, and then, when negotiating the next twist in the road, Ray dimmed the lights for good measure, turning them up bright again as soon as he was able.

It was this route Ethan had been driven along, she and Ray following if not in his footsteps, then certainly Johnny's tire treads. She tried to imagine him, this man she'd never met, put herself in his place, found she was staring blindly too out the windshield, into a darkness with no end. *What were you feeling, Ethan? What were you thinking? Can you hear me? You connected with Kim, your sister, now connect with me. I've been sent by her to find you. Are you here on the Spook Road still? Where?*

Nothing came back at her, just more darkness, more twisting roads, an emptiness that reminded her of Johnny and the mystery of what lay beneath his charming exterior. Despite her failings, she persevered with Ethan. *You left home late morning. Where'd you go? Why'd you come here at night? For what purpose? Did you believe in the myth about the bridges?* Could it be they were simply goofing around, Ethan and Johnny, wanting to put the myth to the test, something they'd done before, perhaps, and they were stoned, hence his blind staring? When Brett was stoned back in Idaho Falls, that's how he looked sometimes, vacant, staring into space at only he knew what. Sometimes, there'd be a trace of awe on his face, sometimes a hint of horror, his brow furrowing. Brett smoked far too much weed. Maybe Ethan did too, and Johnny and their friends, practically the entire youth of America. Drugs were a huge problem. Big business…

"That's the fourth bridge," Ray said.

"The what? The fourth?"

"Yeah, what did you think it was?"

"The second."

He shook his head. "No, the fourth. I thought you'd be counting."

"I was. I am."

And yet she'd missed not just one but two bridges? She sat up straighter. This myth, perhaps there was something to it after all, but not what people thought. When you followed so many twists and turns, it made you…dizzy, unfocused.

Still trying to imagine being Ethan, she counted down the miles to the fifth bridge. When they'd first made this trip, Ray had said it was around eight miles between the fourth and fifth, and so Shady tried to gauge it roughly. *One mile, two—Ethan, I presume you came this far that night, then what? You turned around and went back? Did you lose count of the bridges too? Or were you not counting them at all? Could you not? Three miles. Four. It has to be four miles down now, right? Five—*

"And that's the fifth bridge," Ray said, interrupting her

musings. "Hallelujah."

Five miles? When it should have been eight?

"How many miles was it between them, Ray?"

"Same as before. Just over eight."

"Seemed shorter."

He disagreed. "Seemed the same to me. You got anything?"

She shook her head. "Nope."

Pulling over onto the side of the road, he stopped the car. "So, we turn back, right? Do the same thing but in reverse?"

"S'pose."

In the confines of the car, he frowned. "Shady, we *need* to turn back."

"Yeah. Of course. We do. I agree. This is no place to be after sundown. That much is true, at least." Even so, she strained to see what she knew was ahead, but there was no mountain ridge visible, the darkness concealing everything. All beauty erased. And no feelings either, no insight. Perhaps there would be on the way back. Another shot at it.

"You ready?" Ray asked this time.

She smiled. "As ready as I'll ever be," she said, echoing him in that respect too, thinking only belatedly, *after* he'd turned the car around and driven over the fifth bridge that had now become their first, that perhaps she *wasn't* ready for this, wasn't…equipped for what was to come. And not just her but Ray and anyone who'd ever ended up, by design or accident, on a road such as this, in the backcountry, at night.

CHAPTER TWENTY-THREE

First bridge down. Eight miles to the second. Then the third, fourth, and last bridge, and then Murdoc, a one-horse town, maybe, but right now it felt like a sanctuary.

She found she longed to reach it, longed for the Holiday Inn too, and being safely cocooned in what were by now familiar walls. She'd even say hi to the cockroach, perhaps step reverently over it rather than dispose of it. It all seemed so far away, though, civilization, life itself. Besides her and Ray, this place was devoid of anything that had a pulse, including the land. There were no creatures of the night prowling, no birds nestled in the trees. It was a place that those with any breath left in them avoided, as should anyone with any sense.

For this was *not* a place to be, unease once again building. How she'd lost count of bridges and miles on the way to the Badlands, she didn't know. She could only suppose it was because she'd been trying to connect with Ethan Wick, another who'd traveled this glorified dirt track at night, and although she thought she'd remained fully conscious, she obviously hadn't. She'd slipped into a kind of trance again. Now, she made a concerted effort to remain aware of not only the shades of travelers past, but what the present comprised too—a long and winding road with more bridges to come, and dense clumps of trees, what leaves remained on the branches rustling against each other.

"Shouldn't be long now," Ray's voice rang out in the hollow of the car, "to the second bridge, or fourth or whatever, depending on which way you're heading. About three miles."

She wanted to reply, say something jovial like "Hey, Ray, we'll get 'er done, then what say you to a final trip to Buffalo's for burgers with the buxom Angie and, of course, a bottle of Jim Beam?" but the words wouldn't come. Her voice had shriveled in her throat. If she opened her mouth, all she'd emit was a croak.

She stayed quiet. Ray stayed quiet. Both of them peering out the windshield and most likely thinking the same thing: *Where's the next bridge? Where the hell is it?*

Nothing but darkness met her dazed gaze, trees on either side on this stretch, but nothing defined about them. They were more like shadows and therefore a *sensation* of trees, along with a sensation of darkness and silence. On the outward journey, Shady could detect nothing of Ethan. On the way back, though, it was different. Her nerve endings were on fire, tingling madly, the world reduced to nothing but feelings, having to rely not just on her eyes but on every instinct she possessed. If she wanted to survive, that was. A dramatic thought, but it wouldn't subside.

Ray took the next bend in the road carefully but maintained speed.

He'd tried to reassure her earlier, but she guessed he was also trying to reassure himself. He was as nervous as she was, and she wondered, as they approached yet another bend in this infinite journey of bends, if she should tell him to slow down, take it easier, that they had to be *careful*. But again, the words would not come. She wanted to reach Murdoc as quickly as he did. And there was no one on the road. They hadn't seen a single soul on the way out, like the first time they'd been here.

So many shadows. And not just the shadowy trees, some tall and willowy, some shorter and more robust, but there were shadows in between. Were her eyes deceiving her? Her imagination turning mischievous again, playing tricks? When she'd first held Kim's necklace, her hand enclosing one half of a heart, she'd been plunged into a hinterland, and there'd been shadows there; she'd seen bodies hanging from trees. *She'd* been hanging. Those images plagued her now, her mind insisting on recalling them.

Here was a hinterland. Here was a wasteland. Nothing living, so she'd conjured the dead, and she shouldn't. She had to stop, calm down, her breathing slightly ragged.

"Shady?" Ray had noticed too. "It's okay, another mile or so to the second bridge."

Another mile? But it was like they'd gone a dozen already! Didn't Ray think so as well?

Everything was wrong out here. It was all distorted. The night itself was; it was just so empty. As different rules applied to Murdoc, the citizens of which lived life their way, they applied to roads like this too. It was an area of land outside of time, outside of reality too.

She remembered the construction workers—Oscar, Juan, and Luis—recalled again what they'd said about the ghost roads of the USA, that stuff about finding yourself on one, something creeping up on you and not getting caught by it, not letting it know you'd noticed it. Again, she wondered what would happen if you *did* turn around? If you stared right at it boldly? What possible harm could a shadow do?

She returned her gaze frontward. When they reached the next bridge, they'd know because the tires would bump as they passed over it; the car would shudder slightly. *She'd* shudder. Maybe Ray as well.

Nothing was wholly black, not even the night. Ray had said that in the cemetery—Heavenly Haven—when they'd been searching for Kim's grave. Everything was shades of grey. But that shadow she'd seen there, that she'd run from, was different. Ray couldn't deny it, because he hadn't seen it, only her. What if it had followed? Was it out here with them? And not just one but several, an army? Helen had said when taking on an army of the living, two of them weren't enough. What about an army of the dead?

In the silence of the car, she was falling apart. Torturing herself. Ordinarily, she'd retrieve Kanti's scrap of leather, find comfort in it, a rationale. But the chamois was doing a job of its own right now, protecting Kim's necklace and maybe—her nerves quickened further at this thought—preventing further malevolence from being unleashed.

She shook her head. Too many horror movies! That's what was happening here, her mind insisting on dredging up from the deepest depths the worst scenes from those she'd watched with her parents or on movie nights with friends, squealing when the jump scares came, blood dripping from ridiculous figures who staggered about, hands reaching out from behind to grab at them again, to snap their necks, and oh, she, Brett, Teddy, Sam, Josie, and Ray had laughed. They'd *howled*.

Nothing funny about it now, though.

"What the fuck?"

Ray was murmuring something that Shady didn't quite catch. She'd been too immersed in a horror of her own making, had even shut her eyes, which now snapped open.

"Ray?"

"What's that ahead?" he continued, his voice low, though, as if talking to himself rather than her, maybe thinking because she'd closed her eyes that she was asleep again.

She looked too, *strained* to see. "What have you caught sight of?"

Again, he didn't answer, and she frowned. There was nothing ahead, so what had spooked him? She almost giggled at that. They were spooked on the Spook Road. Aptly.

"Ray!" she said louder this time, more firmly. "What can you see?"

Not once did his eyes waver or did he turn his head toward her, not even a fraction. What was wrong with him? Why was he acting so strangely?

She'd reach out and shake his arm. Maybe he was trying to prank her. He was guilty of sometimes choosing inopportune moments to do so. But *this* moment…it was the worst.

Before doing so, she followed his gaze again, leaning so far forward now that her forehead practically touched the windshield. There was nothing but darkness; she was certain of it. Shadows in the trees, but benign shadows, surely? Natural. Just empty road, miles and miles of it, too many miles, miles she was growing sick of. *Country* miles.

Nothing at all, except…a flash of white?

Her heart lurched.

Could it be white as in a dress of some sort? A *blood-soaked* dress? Was Kim up ahead? The faintest outline of her, small, frail, *angry*.

A flash of white and no bend—so a bridge? They'd finally reached it? Ray continued to ignore her when she reached for his arm, when she shook it hard, when she as good as rattled the teeth in his head. He stared straight ahead, then gasped.

Not a figure.

Not Kim.

If it ever had been.

It was a car, she realized, that suddenly flashed its lights from low, *very* low—if they'd been on at all—to full beam, blinding them, driving straight at them. Time slowing again, or had it speeded up, become preternaturally fast?

She didn't know. Couldn't tell. Couldn't scream either. She could only feel the impact as the car collided with theirs, a huge cloud of dust and gravel rising to engulf them.

* * *

Blinded, not by darkness but a swirling mist that wrapped itself tightly around her. At first, she could only sit where she was—in the passenger seat of her Dodge. She tried to move, but it was as though her limbs were paralyzed, a cold shot of fear shooting through her in case she actually was. Slowly, slowly, though, she was able to flex her fingers, then the toes in her boots, then finally tense the muscles in her leg. She was fine.

But Ray…what about him? Was he okay?

It was so *silent* in the car!

What if…? What if…?

"RAY!"

His name burst from her, and quickly she turned, *too* quickly, a bolt of pain in her neck causing her to cry out this time.

She and Ray had been on the Spook Road, had traveled up it uneventfully, then turned the car around to drive the other way, back to Murdoc. They'd passed the first bridge and were looking out for the next when Ray had thought he'd seen something up ahead.

The road was full of twists and turns, but they'd been on a straight stretch, therefore it was easier to see what was coming. And yet they hadn't, because…because… *Think, Shady!* Because Ray had been focusing on something else, had ignored her like she wasn't there, calling his name and tugging at him. Like she'd disappeared.

Had he seen a figure too? And was it Kim? Or had it just been the lights of an oncoming car suddenly upon them? A car that had been traveling with its lights dimmed low—secretive, incognito, doing its utmost to avoid detection.

And then it had driven at them.

Why?

Was it indeed a game people around here played to liven things up a little? Because the same thing had happened before on another road when first traveling toward Murdoc and Wyatt; the driver of that car had wanted to play then too. Ole Devil Eyes.

Was this the same car?

Oh, this mist! The way it was swirling made her feel so sick.

Tentatively, she straightened her neck. Whiplash. It had to be. Reaching up a hand, she rubbed at it, another flash of pain making her remove her fingers. She could move, but she'd have to do so carefully. If there was damage, she didn't want to make it worse.

Instead of turning toward Ray in the driver's seat, she reached out a hand sideways. "I'm okay, Ray. Are you? Are you all right?"

No reply.

"Don't ignore me, okay? Not this time. Come on, speak! Are you okay?"

Silence.

Her hand having also connected with nothing, she had to turn again, keeping her neck as rigid as possible. If only she could see! She patted at the air, expecting to touch something solid. What if he was hurt worse than her? No way he'd be goofing around now. Even Ray had his limits regarding that.

"Ray, come on, don't do this, please. Answer me."

There was nothing but the mist, her hands making it swirl and eddy faster.

She wasn't the one who'd disappeared.

He had.

CHAPTER TWENTY-FOUR

It was as though she were paralyzed again, shocked at Ray's absence. And then a sob burst from her, low, guttural, and a curse too.

"Fuck! Fuck! Fuck! What's happening?"

If Ray wasn't in the car, then where was he? And why all this mist?

Her mind tried to reason, find logic in an illogical situation. If he wasn't in the car, he must be outside of it, thrown clear. But that didn't figure; he'd been wearing his seat belt. He *always* did. Leaning forward, the pain in her neck so sharp it brought tears to her eyes, she reached for the windshield. As far as she could tell, it was intact. Had she perhaps been unconscious after impact without realizing it, just like she'd been unaware of falling asleep out here? If so, he must've gotten out of the car to check on those they'd crashed into.

She had to get out too, see who was okay and who wasn't.

The car door was stiff. She had to really push at it, fearing it wouldn't yield, that she'd be entombed in the Dodge, and who knew for how long. Fact was, people didn't just happen by out here, not ordinarily. You'd take the main highway, one lined with gas stations, diners like the one she used to work in, truck stops, and cafés. This, though, was an inhospitable road, leading to an inhospitable place. She could be trapped forever!

Panic was like a rollercoaster, rising and subsiding, rising and subsiding. The door *did* open eventually, and she climbed out. Because the mist was so thick, for a second she thought there might not be any ground, and so she feared she'd fall and continue falling, into the abyss. When her feet hit the gravel, she sighed with relief.

They'd been heading toward a bridge. Had they reached it?

She couldn't remember. There was something about a myth with the Spook Road, five bridges one way and four bridges the other, but what they'd never found out was *which* bridge disappeared. Or did it change according to whim, to circumstance?

Dragging one foot in front of the other, she initially clung to the open car door for support, but then had to rely solely on her own ability to balance the farther she went.

As she'd done in the car, she started calling out. "Ray? Where are you?" When met with more silence, she shouted louder. "Is anyone there?"

Where had the mist come from? A dust cloud kicked up by the crash should have settled by now, and yet, if anything, it was growing thicker, threatening to choke her.

She came to a standstill and looked around, able to draw only shallow breaths.

They had been in a car wreck, which meant there *were* other people here. And yet no one was responding? What if…? Her mind was the thing to freeze now, the prospect too terrible to contemplate. What if they were *all* dead? She the only one still living? Wandering around on her own in this sudden mist, a mist she should perhaps be grateful for because if it parted, what would it reveal? Utter carnage?

She couldn't just stand there not knowing. People might be hurt but not dead, and so they'd need her help, Ray too. She walked again, more determined. The other car was here somewhere, a great big hulk of metal that had hit them and then maybe come to rest in the trees. Ray hadn't gone through the windshield, so he was out here too in the mist, had gone to check on the other car, and maybe…just maybe…they hadn't been grateful for his concern. They'd been alive and not so hurt that they couldn't pull a gun…

At another standstill, she whirled around and around, then wished she hadn't. No way to know which direction she now faced, north, west, east, or south. Was it wise to continue calling out when you had no idea who you were dealing with?

Panic rose, and it rose high, a tsunami that then crashed down around her.

As if trying to make herself smaller, she hunkered down, her arms hugging herself, every worst-case scenario continuing to play out in her head: Ray lying dead, drenched in his own blood, his eyes no longer able to see yet staring.

Blindly staring. Like Ethan had, beside Johnny Latham in the car.

Those boys…misunderstood. One of them, at least. The other—Johnny—someone you might not *want* to understand. Untouchable. Protected. Merciless.

Ethan had been blindly staring because… *Because he was dead, Shady. That's why. And Johnny was driving him out here for a purpose.* Burial? Somewhere along this barren stretch, there'd been a grave dug for him?

"Oh, Johnny," she murmured, tears gathering in her eyes. What she'd felt in his presence…she'd been mesmerized. It was so hard to accept evil when it came in such perfect packaging. For that's what he was, for her and for all those women who'd fawned over him when he'd swaggered into Wyatt's hospital: perfection. A pinup, a dream.

And arrogant.

And empty.

Or misunderstood? She couldn't help but seize on that notion again. Between Ethan and Johnny, who was the true bad seed?

Standing tall, she had no choice but to continue searching. She was on a narrow stretch of road with trees on either side of it. It shouldn't be *that* hard to find something here.

"Ray, Ray, Ray." She only murmured his name this time. "What's happened?"

Sweet Ray, Ray who wasn't textbook handsome, who had the craziest red hair, pale skin, and freckles, a slight paunch, even, due to his love of donuts and cinnamon buns as big as your head, but he was awesome, someone who could hug you hard, make you feel warm and contented in the circle of his arms, *safe*, who wouldn't ignore her, not unless he was in trouble. Who'd be there, by her side, had promised to be, every step of the way.

If only he could reach out and draw her to him, hug her now. She'd give anything.

Even though she was loath to admit it, she was alone out here in the mist, caught in it. Following the wreck, she'd been spat out, not out of the car, and neither had Ray, but into somewhere else entirely, somewhere between bridges, a true hinterland.

That was why you shouldn't put the theory of the bridges to the test, because that's what could happen. You'd enter another realm, and there you'd walk alone, always.

Walking Sam. She remembered telling Ray about that myth too, in connection with South Dakota's Pine Ridge Reservation. An impossibly tall and gangly figure who stalked lonely, isolated victims because he wanted their souls. He collected them because he was lonely too, hanging them from his outstretched arms, company at last.

If there was any truth to that legend—and right now, Shady thought it entirely possible, that anything could be— then she sympathized. *Nothing* was worse than being alone, so perhaps she'd resort to such means herself too, become just as desperate.

Tears fell from her eyes as she continued onward. She let them, didn't lift a hand to wipe them away. Despair was hers this night. Utter despair. What was beyond the Spook Road was sacred: the Badlands. What was on it, however, something entirely different.

It was hell.

Like Ethan, she stared ahead but saw nothing.

She'd wanted to help, but look where her good intentions had gotten her.

All she longed for now was what lay beyond the Spook Road, open plains and the mountain ridge. So near and yet so far. She could keep on walking, but she knew she'd never find it. The darkness had erased it before, and now the mist would do the same.

This place she was now, was it similar to where Hurit was? Inside of Mandy? At the point of death, her soul had rushed in there and hidden, afraid, the darkness on her tail.

If so, Shady's heart bled for Hurit too, another she'd tried to help but failed.

She'd found Annie, followed her ideals, she and Ray, because they believed. But perhaps belief was like this: a highway to nowhere.

The mist…such familiar mist. A mist she'd experienced before, albeit briefly.

The mist she'd been plunged into when handling Kim's necklace.

There, she hadn't been alone, far from it. She'd been hanging, and there'd been other bodies hanging; the mist was crammed with them. *Alive* with them.

And then Kim had come striding forward out of nowhere. Had looked straight up at Shady, whose feet had been dangling in midair, her hands at her neck, trying to ease the pressure of the rope there, trying to breathe, and oh, she'd been so vengeful, that little girl, so full of wrath. A demon. Such was the power of injustice; it could change you irrevocably. Kim had wanted help, had demanded it. Was failure even an option?

Shady wasn't alone in *this* mist either. And suddenly she regretted it. Despite what she'd thought earlier, there *were* worse things than being alone.

Ahead, to both sides, and behind her wasn't what she wanted to see—Ray, the two of them reunited at last, Shady crying and grinning, him too, falling into each other's arms to find solace there. Instead, it was those others. The ground beneath her feet wasn't solid either, so perhaps it never had been. She was suspended, *hanging*, her feet beginning to kick involuntarily, that pressure at her neck. Hanging forever, that's what Kim had said would happen if she failed. And this was her territory, so her rules. Shady was doomed, like those others around her, their limbs flailing for eternity. *Because you're useless. Because you couldn't follow the clues. Couldn't work it out.*

If only she could reach the necklace in her pocket; she could unwrap it, throw it into the mist, and that too would be lost forever.

It might even break the spell…

She kicked and kicked, trying to tip her shoulders so her hand could go lower and delve into the pocket with the necklace, but quickly she had to right herself again, the pressure on her windpipe too much. Next, she tried to haul her legs up. Impossible, the pain around her neck sharp, not just due to whiplash but ropes coiled like a snake.

Something bumped into her right side, another body. Something…whispered. Words she couldn't identify, words they were choking on.

Not dead. None of them. *Half* dead. Again, a far worse fate.

If only she could reach the necklace! A vain hope, perhaps, of release, but the only one she had. She could not, *would not*, stay like this forever. Unable to rest.

As the nurse Helen had said, she was so young, had so much life ahead of her. If she was granted reprieve, she'd never take it for granted again and let the darkness overwhelm her like it had with Kanti—Kanti, who was with her still. Even now.

She twisted her body to the side, to the someone who'd whispered.

Who would she find there?

"Kanti?"

The mist obscured them, like it obscured everything.

Shady twisted again more violently, and to hell with any physical pain she felt; it was nothing compared to her mental anguish. Doing so over and over, she gathered momentum, swinging back and forth, closer and closer.

Who are you? What are you saying?

She kept reaching for her pocket, for the necklace it contained, and Kanti's leather scrap too. To hurl both from her if necessary.

"Kanti, is it you? Is it? Your fate cannot be mine! It can't!"

Was she speaking out loud? Or simply screaming the words in her mind?

A mind so confused, a body that screamed in protest, a determination that only grew.

"I do not accept this fate!"

Her hand connected with something at last, her jeans pocket, and dug deep, making yet another connection with the chamois leather, inside which was the heart necklace—the broken heart, which, right now in Shady's mind, was a heart as rotten as this unreality was.

The tips of her fingers enclosing it, she yanked it out, and as she did, the mist cleared somewhat. She was no longer as blind.

She could see the bodies in front of her, dozens, too many to count, blackened eyes ready to pop from their sockets.

The worst of sights. Beyond imagination. And sad. So terribly sad.

And there was Kanti directly in front, her hair, once black and sleek, now grey and matted, skin no longer smooth but bulging with blue veins, around her eyes especially, eyes darker than Shady's, *pure* black. A face to horrify but also to draw tears. *All* their faces deserved tears, an ocean of them. They were the faces of the damned.

Her mouth was moving, Kanti's, whispering again:

You know what to do. Throw it. Throw it.

Break the spell.

With her free hand, Shady reached out. This was her *grandmother*. How could she leave her?

A lip curled as Kanti snarled. How darkly fire could burn in eyes. A night fire.

Throw it!

Shady obeyed. *Your fate cannot be mine.*

Immediately, the rope slackened.

CHAPTER TWENTY-FIVE

"Shady! Shady, over here, Quickly!"

She was on the ground in the dark, *just* the dark. The mist had disappeared entirely. And it was so cold, Shady's teeth chattering not just from the icy air, but the trauma too.

Everything was clearer, from the trees silhouetted against the darkness to the long track of road that twisted and turned before night swallowed it.

The cars, though, where were they? And Ray, where was he?

"Shady!"

Was it Ray calling her?

She shook her head, then wished she hadn't, the pain in her neck almost causing full darkness to return. The pain from…whiplash, wasn't it? Not rope. Lifting a hand to her neck, she felt tentatively around. There was nothing there. She'd been released.

"Shady, please. You have to get off the road. Come here!"

A voice, not whispering as Kanti had whispered, Kanti, who'd been one of many hanging beside her, who'd tried to help her—how? Shady was struggling to remember, to piece it all together. Again, she questioned if it was Ray calling. It didn't sound like him, though. After a few seconds, she realized it was a female voice.

"Who are you?" she eventually replied, her throat so sore she struggled to speak.

Out of nowhere, it seemed, the girl was by her side.

Whatever she'd just experienced, real or a dream, Shady didn't know, but this…this was just as strange. "Beth!" she said, she exclaimed. "What the hell—"

"There's no time to explain. Come back into the trees. We have to hide."

Hide? Shady allowed Beth to help her to her feet, wincing again because her legs felt bruised. Her whole body did, and little wonder; it would after being in a car wreck. *Or being hanged. Suspended from a tree by a rope around your neck and left kicking in the air.* No. That hadn't happened. If not a dream, it had been a hallucination, likely lasting seconds only, although it had felt like an age. But the mind could do that, play tricks, especially when in shock. Beth was no hallucination, though. She was solid, flesh and blood. And she was as good as dragging Shady into the trees because they had to hide. From who?

Having reached the tree line, she was pulled deeper into them and down an embankment that was steeper than she'd expected, Shady slipping a little and Beth helping her to remain upright. Then, Beth urged her to crouch down, keep low. Shady obeyed, not knowing what else to do, hardly daring to look up, either, at the boughs of the trees in case she'd see shadows dangling, in case she'd see *herself*, freedom from the noose an illusion.

"Where are the cars?" she managed.

"A little way back," Beth told her. "After the accident, I must have lost consciousness for a short while. When I came around, I went to your car and saw it was empty. You'd gotten out, had wandered pretty far. I ran into the tree line and searched for you from there."

"Ray…what about him?"

"I…" Beth shook her head. "He must have climbed out of the car too. I don't know, Shady, I couldn't find him. I could only find you. There was so much confusion, so much dust, so much…noise. And now there's this…silence. I don't know where anyone is."

Anyone?

Shady blinked rapidly, trying to clear her mind further. "You were missing!" she said. "And…now you're not. You're here." The wonder of it, the relief, hit her. "Shit, Beth," she said, reaching out to grab her by the shoulders. "You're okay! Your mother—"

"I know. Mom's in the hospital. But she'll be okay, Shady, honestly she will."

"A heart attack," Shady began, but again Beth interrupted.

"A *suspected* heart attack. She'll be fine. Don't worry about her, don't worry about me. Oh, Shady, I'm sorry to have dragged you into all this, but Kim won't rest. Not all the while Ethan can't."

Still holding on to her, Shady swallowed. "Are you psychic, Beth?"

For a moment, Beth simply stared at her, and then she shrugged. "Don't know. Never used to be before Ethan and Kim. I was…normal." Wincing slightly, she said. "Sorry."

Shady managed a smile. "Don't worry. No offense taken."

"But experiencing death, *their* deaths, it changes you, I guess. In more ways than one."

With Kanti on her mind, Shady nodded. "I guess it does."

230

"She knew you could help. So I had to trust her. Be guided by her. *We* did."

"We who?"

A beat of silence before Beth spoke again. "We, the good guys. Honestly, Shady, believe me, we *are* the good guys, but I'm sorry for putting you at risk."

If she'd been confused before, she was now even more so, was about to press for more information, demand it as willfully as Kim if she had to, when they both heard it, a shuffling, someone out there on the road, walking, both their heads turning toward it.

About to spring up, Shady was stopped by Beth.

"It could be Ray," Shady whispered.

"And it might not be," Beth whispered back. "Stay down."

It was hard to see in the darkness who it was, not until they came closer. A man, from the shape of him, a hood over his head, though, pulled low, covering his hair—a dark hood and dark clothing, ensuring he blended with the night. Was Ray wearing dark clothing? His hoodie was black, but his cargos were beige. This wasn't him.

"Who is it, Beth?"

Beth brought her hand up to her mouth and shook her head, beckoned for her to follow even deeper into the trees.

She did so, despite being desperate for more information and to find out where Ray was. Her cell…it was in her bag in the car. They had to get back there, retrieve it, call someone, the cops, they had to, unless Beth had her cell with her.

Eventually Beth stopped, so Shady asked her.

"I dropped it. When I was running. I…I think he's hurt. I hope he is. He was limping slightly. Did you see?"

"Who?"

"Him! Out there!"

"But who is he?" Shady asked, feeling as though she might wake from this scenario too, it was so insane.

"One of them. The bad guys."

"Jesus," Shady cursed. This really was the Wild West, cowboys and Indians, cops and robbers. Who the heck was she referring to? "Beth, listen to me. You have to explain things a little clearer or I'm going out there despite what you say, back onto the road. I'm finding Ray, I'm getting my phone, and I'm calling the cops."

"Don't."

That word again, *don't*, just like she'd texted.

There was a harder edge to her voice when Shady spoke next. "What's wrong with the cops around here?"

"A *lot* is wrong," Beth said. "Not all of them, but with a certain contingent. And the thing is, it's getting harder to tell who's who."

"What about the sheriff?"

Beth shook her head.

"He's a bad guy?"

"For sure. The mayor of Wyatt too. Plenty of so-called officials, actually—although, again, we don't know exactly who, but we're working on it, insiders are. Infiltrating, just as they have. There's a big old company out here—"

"Gilcrest," Shady said.

"You know it?"

"It's in Murdoc, where we're staying. I've been there."

"You've been there?" Beth was incredulous.

"Because of Johnny Latham, who works there. Your supposed boyfriend."

"My boyfriend?" Beth shook her head again,

232

emphatically. "He is *not* my boyfriend. Why'd you think that?"

"Some ladies in a grocery store said so when we were doing a little digging."

"No fucking way! It's not him. But…it is someone he knows, who he used to run with. They got the wrong gang member. It's Caleb."

"Caleb?" Where had she heard that name before? *Caleb…Caleb…* "Shit, he was the one who gave Johnny an alibi! When Johnny was seen the night of your brother's disappearance, driving Ethan along this road, this *very* road. His girlfriend, Leonora, reported it to the sheriff's office, but Caleb stepped forward, said it was him. And the cops—"

"Believed him, yes."

Shady was dumbfounded. "And you're *seeing* him?"

"He's a good guy," Beth insisted, grabbing her as Shady had grabbed her earlier. "True, he was a friend of Johnny's when they were younger, and also true, he did some dumb things alongside him, but he's changed. He saw what Johnny was getting into, the people he was getting in with, and decided he wanted nothing to do with it. He was scared how deep it could go. But he's valuable too. Johnny trusts him, especially after he gave him an alibi. And so he tells him things, runs his mouth off, tells him how *rich* they could get doing stuff, and Caleb's running out of excuses not to comply. We have to act now, rise up against them, find evidence of what they've done, *real* evidence, and expose them. And that evidence—" briefly she hesitated "—it's along here, the Spook Road. *Ethan* is. Johnny drove him out here to bury him. Leonora was *not* mistaken. It was Ethan in his car, already dead. We…" A slight crack in her voice, but she quickly masked it. "We don't know how

Ethan died, what happened after he left home. We don't even know if Johnny was responsible. I think he is, my gut tells me he is, but whoever did what to Ethan, it was Johnny who drove him along the Spook Road. Leonora saw."

"And Kim," Shady breathed, the magnitude of it all hitting her, frightening her too. "Kim saw Ethan on the Spook Road as well, I think. She was…close to death herself, although no one knew that at the time, not even Kim, and…and there's a theory: if you're close to death, the veil becomes thinner. You start to see through it. That's what happened. She saw him, and he saw her. He connected, found a way, just like the desperate do. He'd died, but she knew he wasn't at peace, and as you've said, she can't rest if he can't. She couldn't in life, and it's the same in death. Kim's along the Spook Road too. Somewhere."

There were tears in Beth's eyes. "I know," she said. "I can feel she's close by. Oh, Shady, I miss her. I miss them both. Every minute of every day."

Shady's eyes misted too. "I'm sorry."

"No, like I said, I'm the one who should be sorry. I brought you here, put you in danger."

Shady denied it, even though it was the truth. "You never went missing, did you?"

"It was all in the plan that me and Caleb hatched," she admitted. "I went into hiding."

"But your mom?"

"I told you, she'll be okay."

It dawned. "She knew about the plan? And your dad?"

"Once I got them to believe it was what Kim wanted, they went along with it. But, I don't know, seeing my bed empty again that morning, like it had been all weekend, it triggered a panic attack in Mom, a severe one, probably the stress of the ruse as well. It backfired. Kinda. Although…I knew then that I wasn't invisible. That she cared about me, loved me."

"She believed in *you*, Beth, not just Kim."

"Yeah, yeah, she did. It had come to crunch time. We had to get closure on this, whatever way we could, start to heal, or we might as well be dead too. You remember how I told you I found you?" she continued, and Shady nodded— the article Ray had written about Mandy that had gone viral and still got so many hits today. "So yeah, I read all about it, how you traced her origins and now keep her at your museum. You protect not just the public but her, try and *understand* her. When I checked your website too and saw that photograph of you with Mandy, Ray, and Annie, know what I did? I traced your face with my finger. You looked so…kind. And when I did that, you know what happened?"

"You mentioned my face kept reappearing in your mind afterward."

Beth smiled. "But what also happened was so did Kim's, right alongside yours, and her eyes, they *begged* me. We both knew you could help."

"Because I looked kind?" Shady replied gently.

"Yes. And because sometimes you have to trust someone. We knew you'd do your best. That you have tenacity. If Ethan is buried out here, then Kim, via you, would lead us to him. You had the necklace, you'd made the connection, I had to let you both get on with it, let it unfold the way it should, not be a distraction. Sorry I kept going on about him being missing rather than dead, though. I just thought it was safer to run with that angle, especially if this truly is a murder case, otherwise you might have been put off, kept well away. I've tried looking for him on my own, but I can't connect that deep. If we find him, if we can do that, then we stand a chance of ending the corruption. Caleb will admit he lied about his alibi, no matter the consequences. That's how good he is, but only if we have some proof." Another crack in her voice as she added, "That proof being my brother."

Shady was curious. "What is the corruption?" she asked and then just as promptly answered her own question. Gilcrest was a pharmaceutical company. "It's drugs."

Beth nodded. "Uh-huh. Isn't it always nowadays?"

"Ain't that the truth." She looked back toward the road, unseen through the trees. "Who is that man we saw? Johnny?"

"It could be."

"It could be?"

"He's the tip of the iceberg."

"What's he doing out here?"

"I don't know. Maybe he saw us turning down here; maybe it's just coincidence."

"The crash—"

"It was a *three*-car crash. The reason we piled into you was because of him coming up behind us, shunting us."

"Shunting who? You and Caleb?"

"Yes."

"Into me and Ray?"

A tone of exasperation in Beth's voice. "Yes!"

"So where's Caleb? Where's Ray?"

"I don't know!"

Again, Shady's voice hardened. "What I'm trying to figure out is this: You seem to trust me, but can I trust you?"

Beth's eyes widened, and she swallowed hard. "I don't know where Caleb is, okay? I hope to God he's okay, because…because…he will be. He's capable. He can look after himself. And I sure hope Ray can. A strange thing happened after the accident. There was this…mist." As she said it, Shady's skin tingled. "And I lost Caleb. Got myself lost in it too.

"*Where* was the crash, do you know?"

Beth now looked at Shady as if she'd lost her mind. "On the Spook Road!"

"But where? Had you reached the fourth bridge?"

"The fourth bridge?" Such confusion on her face. "I don't know. I lost count." She gulped as she looked around her. "I don't actually know how far along it we are."

That tingle? It refused to abate. They were in the wrong place, but maybe…just maybe, the wrong place was also the right place.

A crack of twigs caught both their attention.

"We have to go," Beth breathed.

"It could be Ray or Caleb," Shady said.

"We have to lie low, that's what Caleb said."

"But if it's Ray—"

"Shady, please. We're in danger here. We're dealing with *murderers*."

She'd wanted cold hard facts, and now she'd gotten them.

"Come on," Beth said, pulling her again in the opposite direction from the man clad head to toe in black. "This way, back to the cars."

The cars, that was where they definitely needed to go so Shady could get her cell.

She willingly followed, but she needed to know one more thing.

"Beth," she said as they continued forward, having to

alternately crouch and straighten because of the boughs, some touching Shady now and then, and again she shivered because of it, imagining they were the hands and feet of those mysterious others who were hanging. "Beth," she repeated, trying to get her attention.

"What?"

"Those texts you sent, telling me to find you just after you supposedly went missing, and then *not* to confide in the deputies just before we were taken to the sheriff's—you were in hiding, but were you also spying on us?"

To Shady's surprise, Beth whipped around, superfast. "What texts?"

Quickly, Shady explained the exact wording.

"We were keeping an eye on you, sure, as much as we could. But I never sent any texts. You sent me plenty, begging me to get in touch, but I couldn't."

"Because that wasn't part of the plan," Shady said wryly. "Because you had to trust in Kim. And me."

"Yes," Beth returned, as emphatic as ever. "But that text you sent about coming out here tonight, we had to follow you then, to…to…"

"The heart of the matter," Shady said when Beth struggled for words.

"Yes."

Shady frowned. "The thing is, I *didn't* send you a text about tonight. No one knew we were coming here."

"You did! We both saw it. Caleb and me."

"Beth, I'm telling you the truth, okay? I didn't send a text."

"Then who did?" A beat of silence before she spoke again. "Kim. It was Kim! *She* sent the texts." When Shady continued to stare at her, trying to work it out herself, Beth grabbed her arms. "You believe me, don't you? That she's helping us? Guiding us. She'll take care—"

Whatever Beth was about to say, Shady would never know, because now she heard another snap of twigs, this time from right behind her.

Swinging around, she saw a smile, a *dazzling* smile.

"Found ya!" a voice said, soft as butter. "Just like I said I would."

Then the world went black.

CHAPTER TWENTY-SIX

She was wandering along a road, and it was dark. Not even the moon was shining above, nor the stars. *Doesn't mean they're not there.* Yes! That was right. Just because she couldn't see them, it didn't mean they no longer existed. She'd heard that before, been told it. The stars were *always* there. She should have faith in that. Not keep doubting it. Who'd told her? She was struggling to recall, a hand going almost of its own volition to her jeans pocket and patting at it. Why? What did she hope to find there? The pocket was empty.

Oh, she was weary. Instead of walking, she wanted to lie down, curl into a ball, and sleep, no matter how hard the ground was beneath her. Her eyes would close, and she could lose herself, or rather lose herself *further*, because right now, she had no idea where she was. All she knew was that the road stretched on for an interminable distance, but she clung to hope; there might be something at the end of it, something…*magical.*

Right now, though, there was nothing on either side of her, just darkness. No trees, hedges, or scrub, no land at all. She was curious: What would happen if she headed toward that darkness? Would she disappear into it? Into a void. And once there, be forgotten? It *looked* like a place you'd be forgotten, by the side of the road, if you couldn't make it to the end, if you were just too weak, if you lay down and slept.

Was she weak? Physically, she felt it, down to her bones, and strangely, the back of her head hurt too, prompting her to lift a hand and touch the scalp there. Her fingers came away slick with blood. She frowned. How'd that happen? How did *any* of this happen? There was so much in her mind, nagging at the edges, but none of it—no information—came forward. Nothing except…a smile. Someone had smiled at her just before she'd found herself on this road. A dazzling smile, which had made her heart skip a beat, *enraptured* her. She almost laughed. She liked boys, had relationships, but no boy's smile had made her heart flip like that, to where it almost stopped beating. Which was okay, she was fine with that. Her mom had told her, "Don't hurry when it comes to boys, Shady. Take your time, be choosy. Don't let them hurt you. You deserve the world, so pick a good guy like I did."

Memories were returning at last through the haze, and she welcomed them. They were the only thing to keep her company out here. Her mom was wonderful, the very best. She loved Shady, fiercely, would guard her with her life. Ellen—that was her name—was a woman she hoped one day to emulate, and so she took her advice, wouldn't let herself be fooled, tried to see what lay beneath people's exterior. But with him—the one with the dazzling smile— she could see nothing. Why? There had to be *something* of substance.

A sound reached her ears. Someone humming a tune. She looked around her, tried to locate the source, but there was nothing and no one. She was alone, entirely. And yet the song continued, low and as sweet as syrup, Shady joining in, singing the words, just…plucking them out of nowhere from the depths of her mind.

Well, the boys all call me "Pretty Little Miss."
It don't ever phase me,
But every time he calls my name,
It nearly drives me crazy.

Again, she almost laughed. Apt words, considering her train of thought. She opened her mouth and sang some more.

Mama says he's not my type,
He really loves another.
But he's gonna marry me
When I turn twelve this summer.

A folk song, it had to be. As old as the hills. Like, who the heck got married at twelve nowadays? Wrong, so wrong. She'd sing just a few more lines from the song…the chorus, perhaps. How'd it go? *Come on, Shady, think.* Her mind had gone blank. A fog in it, when there'd been some clarity at last. She was so disappointed! *Come on, think…*

Another voice, the one that was humming, a voice that echoed, that belonged to no one, it seemed, took mercy on her, helped her out.

Shady Grove, pretty little miss
Shady Grove, my darlin'
Shady Grove, pretty little miss
Goin' back to Harlan
Goin' back to Harlan
Goin' back
Goin' back
Come back, Shady Grove
Come back
Back…

242

"Shady Grove"! That was the name of the song. How could she forget? *Her* name. Practically. A song she'd heard many times before and which had many variations. A song she'd been named for. Someone insisting on it. *Pretty little Shady Grove*, who was born just as the sun was setting in the sky. But who'd decided on it?

Her hand went to her pocket again, didn't just pat it, *tore* at it. As well as missing memories, she was missing something else, something…important that would keep her safe. Not one thing, actually, but two. What had she done with them? Where were they?

She swung around on her heel. Had they fallen from her pocket somehow and were now lying on the road behind her? She should check. She didn't want to, though, wanted to carry on in the direction she was going, because she knew now what lay in front of her, had caught a glimpse before— home. A spiritual home, the home of people like her, her ancestors. A type of heaven. But she couldn't leave behind what she'd lost.

With her heart like a ship in rough seas, slowly sinking, she forced herself in the opposite direction, covering footsteps already taken. Her eyes remained on the ground, searching all the while. The road was more like a track, full of dust and dirt and gravel, which she kicked at with her feet, sullenly. Would she recognize what she was searching for if she saw it? If only this mist in her mind would clear! If she could push it back.

The mist…

Rather than scanning the ground, she lifted her head. What she saw stole her breath. A mist like that in her mind but on the road too, rolling toward her.

Such a thick mist, viscous.

If they met somewhere in the middle, if she became engulfed in it, she'd never be able to find what she sought. She must drown her terror and bewilderment, search harder.

She fell to her knees and started scrabbling around, some stones sharp-edged against her hands. Unforgiving. All of it was. This land, this situation, and those in the mist too.

For it wouldn't be empty, merely a weather phenomenon. There'd be thousands in the mist, *thousands upon thousands*, and all thirsty for vengeance. Able to scream, even though they were dead things, suicides, victims, the *murdered*.

If she could just find what was missing, then she could turn, run toward a place of peace, find comfort there, not suffering, a haven.

"Ouch!"

One of the stones had cut her. If she carried on like this, her hands would soon be covered in blood. Just like…just like… Who else had she seen covered in blood?

Think, Shady! Pretty little Shady. Think!

A humming again, that song a part of folklore, and part of her childhood too. An…insistent hum, growing deeper in tone. Something else about it she recognized.

She placed her hands back on the ground, carefully this time, avoiding sharp stones intent on mauling her, that wanted to drive the poison of the road deeper into her veins, adding to its victims, those in the mist who writhed and squirmed in agony and torment.

The rhythm of the ground was what she recognized, the heartbeat of the earth in perfect harmony with the tune, keeping pace.

A sweet lullaby that woke her, not put her to sleep. Bringing her back to life.

A necklace. She was looking for a necklace. Wrapped in a piece of leather, *star-etched*, carved by a hand long ago, the hands of many others guiding the one who'd made it, invisible but towering high, all the way to another kind of heaven. The stars were there, even when you couldn't see them, when they were obscured. They were there and always would be, *beyond* the night. Finding a way to shine their light.

There was no necklace, no scrap of leather in front of her—Kanti's leather. Hers was the hand that had etched the stars, and hers was the voice that sang the tune. She was a woman of the earth but of so much more besides, who, in death, had found herself and found Shady again too—not as a baby, which was the last time she'd held her, but Shady as a grown woman—who saw something of herself in her, something unique and beautiful…and savage.

Kanti was the savage daughter of another. That's how she and her kind had been described, ever since others had come to take their land from them. Ellen, Kanti's daughter, half Native, had buried that side of her, although there were times, Shady thought, a slow smile curving her lips, that she could be formidable too, stand as tall as anyone. And then there was Shady, the daughter of Ellen, granddaughter of Kanti, who must deal with those who were *truly* savage, meet like with like.

There was also Kim, she who was blood-soaked. Who'd orchestrated all this, who'd reached out, connected, found a way, and was savage with rightful anger.

Savage daughters with one purpose: to find justice for the daughters of others, and the sons.

The necklace and leather weren't there. They were farther up ahead in the mist.

The mist that was still edging closer. That would blind her but also help her to see more clearly. She must not be afraid but head toward it, boldly stride. Right now, the only sanctuary on offer was within its folds. She must *lure* him toward it. Johnny.

But first, she must face him again.

CHAPTER TWENTY-SEVEN

She'd fought. She must have. Although Johnny had delivered a heavy blow to her head, Shady had fought before she'd fallen. Maybe just for a few seconds, but it had been time enough for whoever was with her to turn and run, to escape, once again going deeper into the trees that lined the Spook Road, huddled together conspiratorially, knowing so much about what happened out there.

He was calling after Beth, the man in front, the hood of his sweatshirt fully back now, revealing that dark hair and those handsome features that were now distorted, as everything was out here, screwed up in outrage. "Beth! I know what you've been doing. You and Caleb. How...*false* he is. I've been trying to find you. Where've you been? Hiding?" He was spitting out words, anger and injustice in him too. "You think I'm stupid, do you? That's a grave mistake you've made." A bellow of laughter now, as if he'd made some kind of joke. "You'll go the way of your brother, of the entire Wick family. You'll be wiped out."

He was shouting uselessly. She'd gone. A girl who knew perhaps every twist and turn in this road, every clump of trees and every open space, because she'd been out here many times, she *and* Caleb, two other souls that haunted it, traveling the road secretly, furtively, the lights of their car kept low if there at night, searching for a body, her brother's. She might not have found him, but those trips weren't in vain; she knew where to hide, Shady praying Ray and Caleb had found somewhere safe too, that they could call for help—the good guys, the ones who *would* help, coming out here and saving them.

Shady, though, could go nowhere. She lay on the ground, beneath his feet, at his mercy. Or so he thought. Confident. So confident. Someone who thought he was a star too. Ascending to where? What rotten heap was he so desperate to be at the top of?

Not confident, arrogant. And arrogance was like the mist sometimes; it could blind you.

He was incredulous that Beth had escaped, that she wasn't before him, cowering, or rushing to help Shady. He was unable to fathom Beth was doing exactly that, helping, for she was of no use to anyone dead. *Ah, Johnny, Johnny*, Shady thought, recognizing a pang of disappointment, *you really are stupid. Just a pawn. Just a minion.*

She was laying there, bleeding, hurting, but she was also elated. Her hand had closed over something, a rock of some sort—large and sharp-edged, a weapon as good as any, earth-given—and, pouring all her might into it, she brought the rock upward, the sharpest edge exposed, and smashed it into his groin, his *tender* place.

He screamed, a cry of anguish now rather than anger, his hands cupping that place as he fell to the ground beside her, lying there, his face as close as a lover's.

In it, though, only hatred.

"Bitch!" He forced the word through clenched teeth,

snarling at her, something feral. "You fucking bitch!"

Shady snarled right back. "You fucking bastard!" she countered before pushing herself away from him, through leaves and rubble, then climbing to her feet, no matter how unsteadily, suppressing another wave of nausea, refusing to let it weaken her.

She had to turn, not to run through the trees but to get back to the road. And he'd follow, once the pain in his groin subsided. Like her, he was determined, wanted to prove himself, but to who? *The very worst, Shady, that's who. Run!*

She obeyed her own instruction, him yelling after her now as he'd yelled at Beth. "You can't get away," or words to that effect, which she refused to listen to. *Just follow me, Johnny, okay?* she thought instead. *Get the fuck up and follow me!*

Did he have a gun? If so, then the road could be the very worst place to be, as she'd be out in the open, exposed. In here, in the trees, she could at least hide, become a shadow too, like the ones she'd seen. But something drew her on, dispelled that fear. The road was where she had to be. And Johnny too. A ghost road, like the one she'd seen just minutes ago when she'd been unconscious, that had grown thick with mist again, that would welcome her and welcome him.

So much pain in her neck and now at the back of her head, but adrenaline was master, diluting both for now. The road was ahead, straight ahead. Wasn't it? She mustn't get this wrong, take a wrong direction, pitch farther into the wilderness. She had to keep calm, think clearly, and keep moving. *Trust* in what was happening. Realize something too—that she was only a cog in a wheel. There were much bigger forces at work here, bigger than Beth, Caleb, Ray, and *all* the good guys. Evil kicked back against good all the time, never let up, not for a minute, but neither did good. It *never* cowered.

The trees were so thick and the branches low, providing coverage, especially against gunshot, but also hindering progress, trying to ensnare her. They scraped at the skin on her face, tore at it. Soon, she'd be as terrible a sight as Kim was, as wild. On the dark road she'd been on previously, she'd wanted for a minute to lie down and sleep, just sleep, she was so exhausted. And now there came that urge again, her limbs like lead, resistant to movement. If she could stop for a second, catch her breath, maybe that would help. She could summon some energy from somewhere, some final reserves.

A crack of twigs behind her. A *roar*.

He was up, Johnny, back on his feet and following her.

No time to stop, because if he reached her *before* she got to the road, evil would score a triumph.

Something touched her as she pushed her body onward, something…cold.

It was as though a hand had slipped into hers and was tugging at her. She looked to see who it was. No one visible, not yet. But they soon would be.

Gathering energy, gathering speed, Johnny was shouting again behind her, so close.

"Shady? I'm coming for ya, I've almost got ya. Pretty little Shady, but soon you won't be. And it's a shame, such a shame, because…because I *liked* you, you know. There's just something about you, something so…different to others around here. I liked you a lot."

A sob from Shady now. Because she'd liked him too. At least what was on the outside, and yet…something inside him had resonated with something inside her too, which confused her, left her colder than the touch of the hand in hers. Why did evil have such a hold on him? From what age? When had he decided he liked it, that he could use it, bend it to his will? So many made that mistake, thinking they could do that. Once again, similar to what was good, the finest of lines between them, evil bent its knee to no one.

"Shady!"

A hair's breadth away. That's all he was.

"Shady!" he screamed, and her legs almost gave way with fright. If they did, she'd fall, take a tumble, be beneath him again. Lunging at her, he'd be on top, and they would gaze into each other's eyes like the lovers they would never be. Because lovers wouldn't do what he'd do, take what he wanted without consent. His hands pawing at her, *clawing*, closing tight around her neck and squeezing.

That hand in hers, icy cold and small, like that of a child, tugged hard, *yanked* her forward, and there she was at the edge of the trees, back on the road, in the mist.

* * *

"Shady."

He was still behind her and had done as she'd intended, followed her out of the trees and into the mist, his voice not as strident as before, though, something else in it that she welcomed—a fear that was *delicious* to her ears, which she could feed on, and others too. What others, though? Who was in here besides them? Kim? Ethan? Kanti, even?

She continued forward, the pain in her neck and head now reduced to a dull throb, barely detectable, feeling stronger as she'd wished, more life in her limbs, penetrating

251

skin and bone. *Follow me, follow, Johnny, down to the hollow...to the very epicenter.*

"Shady, where are you? Answer me, damn it! Answer me!"

He didn't know the mist, not like she knew it. Hadn't perhaps experienced it before, not out here on this road. He'd driven up and down it many times, counted five bridges on the way out and five bridges on the way back, done his dirty work along it, but still all five bridges remained, that part of the legend nonsense, or so he thought, quashing disappointment about it. A bitterness. He *wanted* it to be true. A myth he'd grown up knowing. There had to be something behind it. This road was so lonely, perfect for a burial, a *secret* burial. Perhaps even he didn't know where Ethan lay anymore, for the ground had consumed him, and that lifted some of his disappointment, for what the ground had done, *eaten* Ethan, there was magic in that, at least. It had collaborated with Johnny, and he wondered how he could harness that further. Ideas brewing...

But he didn't know about the mist. Until now.

She had the advantage because she *had* experienced it before, to various degrees, and so she kept moving, was *striding* though it, confident but not arrogant, never that, no icy hand in hers now, whoever that was having confidence in her too. The mist was empty for now. But as past experience had dictated, they'd soon find others.

"Shady." Again, he shouted her name, more fear in his voice, almost weaselly. And then more words, dredged up from the depths, Johnny able to harness anger and hatred perfectly well. "Fuck you! Fuck you to hell and back. I'm turning around, getting out of here."

She stopped in her tracks. No! He mustn't do that. He had to keep following, the mist swirling about her as it always did, becoming agitated.

"Johnny," she shouted. "Johnny, where are you? Don't go. Okay? I'm here. Come and find me. You did once before. You promised. Now do it again. See if you can."

She'd thrown down a challenge. One he'd accept?

"Let's see if you're not chickenshit at heart, okay?" she continued. "Afraid of the mist. Afraid of a girl. What harm can we do to you? If you're truly what you think you are, a rising star, not someone's puppet, a nobody, always trying to get attention the only way you know how, a *bully*. If you're not that, not a coward, prove it. Come on, Johnny-boy, the apple of your momma's eye, a momma who wants to be so proud of you, but the truth is, deep down, she despises you. Show me what you're made of. *Show me what you can do.*"

Silence. So profound, so complete. Shady caught up in it every bit as much as he was, staring into the mist, praying for him to appear, willing him. Wondering if he'd take the bait. Being called a puppet, a nobody, would that cut him to the quick? Anger him some more?

"Johnny?" she called. "Two-bit Johnny, don't be a sore loser. Come and play."

Of course it would work. That kind of taunting always did with the vain.

He was striding straight toward her, his arms outstretched as if he indeed wanted to strangle her, all trace of fear gone, emboldened by what she'd said.

All Shady could do was stand and stare. He *was* beautiful, and in that moment, powerful. Like a God. "Oh, Johnny," she murmured. "What a waste. What a fucking waste."

No gap between them at all now, and his hands closed around her throat, forcing her down all the way to the ground. Snarling again.

"I'll show you what I'm fucking capable of," he spat.

It was hard to speak, but she had to, had to force a smile too. A knowing smile.

"It's nothing, Johnny. Not anymore. You're capable of *nothing*."

CHAPTER TWENTY-EIGHT

Not true, what she'd said. It was horrifyingly *untrue*.

What this man was capable of was shocking.

They'd made contact, were staring into each other's eyes, connecting, and Shady saw it, everything he'd done. The bullying and the taunting when younger, the feeling of supremacy he'd gained because of it, the lack of empathy or mercy, the emptiness of his soul. But she also saw something else, someone watching him, taking note, monitoring his actions from afar, at first. A shadow figure, *many* shadow figures, encouraging his ruthlessness. Oh, they could use a boy like Johnny.

She saw the death of Ethan too—his murder. He'd had every intention to cut loose that day two years ago, and he *should* have gotten out of Wyatt, gone far, far away. He'd taken this road, the backroad, knowing that if he didn't leave, he'd be pulled further into Johnny's grip, just as Shady was now. Because Johnny was right—once you'd done stuff, you belonged to him.

Ethan *had* done things he'd regretted, and remorse had overwhelmed him that day, the day Johnny had found him. Before Johnny had, though, Ethan had reached the Badlands, had stared at the majesty of them, feeling nothing but despair, wondering how his life had turned out the way it had, what a disappointment he was to his parents, to himself, to everyone. He'd disappear. It was for the best. He was an in-betweener. Not bad enough to be part of a bad gang, not decent enough to be part of something good. He had a girlfriend, Leonora, and she seemed to think he was good, but she was wrong. And his little sister Kim was wrong too. Kim, who adored him. That necklace she'd given him…

He'd leave them both and get out of there. Run. Go somewhere other than South Dakota, the West Coast, maybe, California, where he'd stand a chance at a better life, where people didn't know him and the mistakes he'd made, the running he'd done for Johnny because he was too scared not to. *Everyone* did the running for Johnny, it seemed, he who was in the pocket of so many, of people in authority, he'd told him, the "big guns." There was money in what he did, and with money came respect.

"And you can have it too," Johnny had said. "Just do as I do. Do what I say. Exactly."

Drugs. Ethan had taken enough of them recreationally. Enjoyed them. But to supply them, and in the increasing quantities they were doing, crossing state lines into North Dakota, Montana, Wyoming, and Nebraska, *flooding* those places with them… Where did Johnny get it all? Who was supplying him?

When he'd asked, Johnny had smirked. "Told you, the big guns."

He'd rebelled once, told Johnny to fuck off. That's when Johnny had pinned him up against the wall, just like he used to when they were younger, and he'd stared into his eyes. He had such dark eyes, was so fucking handsome, the devil in disguise, and something had stirred in Ethan, something that *shouldn't* have, and Johnny saw.

"If you leave, little guy, I won't come for you." He'd almost purred, knowing damn well the effect he was having. "I won't give you that satisfaction. I'll come for your family instead, those pretty little sisters of yours, your momma and papa. I'll bury them alive. So stick around, okay? Stick with me. I told you, I'll make you rich. You can have everything you want," and then with a wink, he'd added, "*maybe* everything."

It had sickened Ethan, that exchange, and what he'd felt for him, for Johnny, not Leonora. He wasn't like that! Yet Johnny…he just had that way about him, always had.

And so he was going to run, get out of there, and that day sat staring at the Badlands, the jagged ridge, trying to persuade himself to continue onward. No way Johnny would make good those threats and hurt his family. Would he? That stuff about burying them alive…

It was so vast, this land, so many secret places. If one disappeared, and then another, would anyone go looking for them? Or would those in power seek to bury them deeper?

Johnny was just bluffing, playing the big guy. And Ethan had to go back, try to find another way out of his clutches. Persuade the entire family to leave Wyatt if he had to, but first, get them to trust him again. Kim, beautiful Kim. How could he break her heart so badly that it resembled the heart halves on the chains she'd bought for them?

There was a way out of everything.

And so, he turned the car around—and ran into Johnny. Johnny, who was simply taking a little trip up the Spook Road, like he had so many times before, like he had this night. He had some free time so thought he'd test the myth again, five bridges out and five bridges back. Or were there? He ran *straight* into him, Johnny recognizing Ethan's car and swerving into its path. Both of them got out, Johnny asking Ethan what he was doing. He knew what he was *supposed* to be doing—running a package with Caleb down to Nebraska, so why wasn't he? How leisurely he walked toward Ethan, Ethan trying hard not to tremble.

"Get in the car," Johnny said. "Leave yours and get in mine." When Ethan stood his ground, Johnny laughed out loud. "You've disobeyed me, brother," he said. "And maybe…just maybe, so has Caleb, because he never let me know you weren't with him today. Which suggests that maybe he's not where he ought to be either."

"I called Caleb," Ethan spluttered. "Told him I was sick. He's gone alone."

Whether Johnny had bought that or not, Shady couldn't tell, not from the images still rolling in her head, coming fast, knowledge downloading like a song from the internet, moments passing, seconds, minutes, and yet she was living it alongside Ethan, his fear reeking, though he'd tried so hard to hold it all together to protect Caleb. Caleb, who *had* known what Ethan had planned on doing and who'd encouraged him. "Get out of here, and don't come back. I'll look after your family, okay? I won't let him get to them."

Would he make good on his promise? It was so difficult to know who to trust!

"Get in the car, Ethan," Johnny growled.

"But my car—"

"Don't worry about your car," he replied. And then more softly, using that charm he had, "Let's go for a little ride, just you and me, okay, *brother*? Let's…talk. I know you're scared. I know you're worried about what we do. But it's *okay*. Really. It's all worked out in minute detail. Hey, did I tell you? I've been offered a job, at Gilcrest in Murdoc! That pharmaceutical company that's just opened. We've been doing some stuff that might be a little frowned upon by some around here, and I get it, I do. You don't want to do that so much now. But guess what? There's still stuff to deliver, still money to be made, and it's legal, sort of, kosher, and that's what counts. Like I keep saying, Ethan, you'll make a ton of cash. Make your parents proud of you at last. Make 'em see running with me was *always* one of your better choices. We're going places. Straight to the top. Come on, Ethan." He was so, so beguiling. "*Be* with me. You're my friend. I like you. You know I do."

And damn it, Ethan had gotten in the car. But again, whether or not he'd believed Johnny, Shady couldn't tell. What had happened to Ethan, what came next, she wished she *didn't* know. The taunting, the bullying, the torture, the words that left Johnny's mouth as he'd played out Ethan's death, making it as slow and painful as possible, his *first* kill. She'd spend a lifetime trying to erase those images from her mind, only to fail. They would return to taunt and torture her also in the darkest hours of the night. She'd have to be strong and call on the strong to help her, Kanti, who was mightier in death than life, who'd hanged herself perhaps because she understood that this world, and those in it like Johnny, so beautifully corrupt, could be dealt with better from the other side.

There were those who'd watched Johnny from when he was a little boy, groomed him, encouraged the arrogance he clearly possessed. A lackey, the tip of the iceberg. They too were arrogant in nature, so, so confident. But what they couldn't see and what Shady could, besides what had happened, was what was *going* to happen.

Johnny was a sight to behold with his dark hair and dark eyes, his broad shoulders and dazzling smile, but beneath it—and she'd detected this before—there was nothing. An emptiness. There was no real intelligence, no kindness, no empathy, no love. And sure, that might have had something to do with his upbringing, but an excuse like that only got you so far. There was no...*emotional* intelligence. He was merely an empty but functioning vessel, the very thing evil adored, because then it could fill you with whatever it wanted.

He'd been given opportunities, and he'd wrangle more. Readily, they'd be given to him because, as well as evil, people liked beauty, were drawn to it, fooled by it, and so he'd climb as he wanted to, using any method available, trampling on others along the way, the mighty having to take a tumble at some point. He'd jump into their shoes. Be *worse* than those who currently did the devil's work, that taste for death Ethan had given him now on the rise.

When he was done torturing Ethan, he'd driven him back along the Spook Road, not a dead Ethan but alive, albeit barely, his eyes open but staring blindly. That was good, that's what Johnny wanted, for him to *see*.

Ethan's car was there still, but Johnny took no notice of it. He'd dispose of it, but not until later, after Leonora had gone to the sheriff's office...and it was when she had that Caleb proved himself. Caleb, who'd delivered the package the day he'd been told to, gone alone and been right on time. He'd said he preferred not to have company anyway, which was fair enough, Johnny thought, especially if that company was a traitor like Ethan.

On the Spook Road, Johnny counted five bridges one

way, *always* five fucking bridges, and then, reaching the end, he doubled back. That night, with what he intended to do, would there still be five bridges on the return?

At the second bridge he stopped counting, tired suddenly of the game. Of *course* there'd be five bridges both ways! It was all just bullshit, a tall tale. More fool him, more fool anyone for believing in it. He also stopped the car at the second bridge, before it was too late—before the breath left Ethan's body entirely—and dragged him out, down the embankment, into a creek that had long since run dry, and buried him. Alive.

Ethan's eyes remained open as dirt showered down on his face, such terror in them, the last sound he heard being Johnny laughing and cursing him. "Fucking faggot."

Johnny, who'd kissed him before the torture had begun, touched him in another way.

Worse than all the others combined. A lord of his empire. The bodies she'd seen hanging beside her along the Spook Road didn't line this road yet, and maybe they never would, but they'd hang from somewhere. Future deaths. People killed by the drugs Johnny and his kind peddled, *legal* drugs promising relief from pain but only ever causing more, over and over. There would be hundreds dead by Johnny's hand, thousands, but distant deaths, deaths that gave him less and less satisfaction. There was nothing like the personal touch. And so there'd be more hands-on deaths like Ethan's too. The *fun* kind. After all, all work and no play made Johnny a dull boy.

Shady was losing consciousness, so Johnny eased the pressure. Oh no, no, no. He couldn't have that. Too easy. Just as he'd dragged Ethan, he now dragged her. Where to, she didn't know. Out of the mist if he could find a way?

Would it let him? And yet…it *was* parting slightly, becoming less thick in places, transparent. If he got her out of there, back into the night and to his car, that'd be it. Game over. She'd be his next plaything.

Although she was struggling still, kicking, lashing out, he was so strong, his arms wrapped right around her, holding her tight. *Like lovers. Like fucking lovers.*

He'd noticed the mists were thinning too, had lost any trace of fear, was winning.

"It's okay," he crooned. "You'll enjoy what we do at first, I promise. *Really* enjoy it, because you know what? You want it. Come on, stop crying. I told you, it's not all bad."

She was struggling, and she was crying, tears for Ethan, for all those who would die because of Johnny, her own death now imminent too. There were those who were good in Wyatt and Murdoc; Beth had told her that and so had Helen. Those who waged their own war against the evil there, tried to bring it down, destroy it, and there were those out here, on the Spook Road, trying to do the same. But the outcome was never assured, the battle constant, weighing in the favor of one sometimes and then the other. Which way would the scales tip tonight? The mist…why was it thinning? If they reached his car…

Figures in the mist. She could see them. Ray? Caleb and Beth? They'd found a way out of their own fog at last? Found her?

How come Johnny couldn't see them? He was dragging her straight toward them.

You never knew what to trust in these parts. Not even your own eyes.

It could be a hallucination in front of her. Mere wishful thinking.

262

A child was at the forefront and, behind her, a woman with flowing black hair. Kanti. There was a man too with dark hair, his eyes wide open and staring, something glinting at his neck, and countless others, those who'd hanged beside her, now cut loose.

Almost upon them, and still only she could see them. Not Johnny.

Not until he finally looked up.

And when he did, he dropped her.

Such vengeful faces, blood-soaked, eyes and veins bulging, full of wrath, staring back at him, although on some faces snarls were disappearing, turning into smiles.

Slow, *leisurely* smiles.

Johnny brought his hands up to rub at his eyes. "What...what are they?" he asked. "Shady? What the fuck are they? Ethan? Is that you? How?"

"Because of this place," Shady said, the crowd now within arm's reach and all of them so...savage. "Because, Johnny, there *is* an in-between. It isn't a myth. You found it before, only you didn't have the brains to realize. It's where you buried Ethan. Buried him...*alive*."

Obsessed with the myth, always putting it to the test, but now he denied it, shaking his head violently. "No. No. No. It's bullshit."

Shady pushed herself upward, forced herself to her knees, grimacing. "I'm afraid not. We're here in the thick of it, the in-between. It's as magnetic in its own way as you are."

"They're dead," he whispered, beginning to trust his eyes now. "All of them."

Even Kim...Kim, who'd died in a crash at the start of the Spook Road, the crossroads, on her way to a sports field. An accident, just an accident, but the driver of the other car—

Shady understood this now, crystal clear—was a woman with children of her own, who'd taken a few more painkillers than she should have that day, *prescription* painkillers. She'd been taking so many recently for pain in her lower back. It was excruciating sometimes, and when you had kids to run after, you needed all the help you could get. Thank God for the painkillers! For a doctor who willingly signed them over to her while she waited to see someone about the prospect of surgery. When it was done, she wouldn't need so many; she would wean herself off. But for now, they dulled the pain, yet they also made her feel lightheaded, a bit…out of it. She'd *definitely* dispense with them post-surgery. It really wasn't a problem, though. If they were dangerous, if they were addictive, the doctor would have said something, warned her. The pills were manufactured by Gilcrest, delivered anywhere they needed to go. High. She'd felt high. At the moment of impact. But a *legal* high. So no prosecution. No need. She wasn't to blame, not really.

"You murdered them all," she said. "You *will* murder them all."

How Johnny frowned. "What? Them? These…these…I didn't!" He took a step back and then another, tried to retreat. "Help me. Please. Stop them."

He was terrified. And rightly so.

But then, he would terrify many.

He'd destroy them.

She shook her head. "I won't help you," she said. "I'd rather help them."

They were upon him now, driving him farther and farther back into the mist, which had congealed again, only remaining thin where she was. A veil of kinds, and in it was

Kim. Sweet, innocent Kim. Once. But, like Kanti, able to be something entirely different when she had to, when it was for a cause bigger than all of them, bigger than Shady could ever have guessed—when it was for the sake of good. The deaths she'd seen, of those who'd fallen into the pits of despair and shame, they might occur anyway, some or even most of them, unless other forces elsewhere could do as had been done here tonight: pick off acolytes like Johnny, one by one. Battles were fought all the time all over the world, in the open and in the shadows, *by* shadows, the scales forever tipping.

Oh, Johnny…he was persistent. She'd give him that. "Shady! Shady, where are you? Help. You have to! Fucking help me, will you? You can't…you can't leave me with…*them*."

But she had no choice. The mist was almost completely closed, effectively shutting her out as it shut him in. Her work, for Kim, was done.

As she stood on the Spook Road, on a clear, dark night, alone, quite alone, she found what she was looking for on the ground in front of her. The other half of the necklace that belonged to Kim. And beside it a scrap of leather, star-etched. As she bent down to grab them, to hold them in her hands, tight, so tight, she found she was no longer alone. People were rushing toward her—Beth, a man who had to be Caleb, and Ray. They'd found her.

But everything was not quite done yet. Not when there was evidence to find.

CHAPTER TWENTY-NINE

Kim's necklace led them to Ethan. Once Ray and the others had reached her, once they'd hugged it out, everyone so relieved to have found each other safe, Shady did something she'd never done before with it: she put it on, secured it around her neck. With the scrap of leather also safely stowed in her jeans pocket, she beckoned for the others to follow her. What they didn't know, not in that moment, but what she'd tell them soon, when the time was right, was that she was being pulled along, yet again, although there was no icy cold hand in hers. It was as though gravity itself moved her, all the forces in the universe combined, and she was really just a pawn, a channel, an instrument. But glad to be so. *Proud.*

They ventured back into the trees, down an embankment, and out into more open land, turning right toward a bridge.

"The fourth bridge on the way to the Badlands?" she asked Beth.

"Yeah," she said, but she sounded uncertain, had to check with Caleb. "Is it?"

"I think so," was his reply.

Caleb, who'd also put himself at the epicenter in his own way. A wayward boy who'd turned into a good man, a fitting partner for Beth, as brave. They'd be happy together down the years; Shady was certain of it. They might even stay in Wyatt after tonight, with their families. It'd be a fine place to live. Maybe even magical.

Of course they all asked where Johnny was, if he was still out there and they were still in danger, and she told them he wasn't, that his body would be found in due course.

"*You* killed him?" Ray said, incredulous.

She shook her head. "No. He attacked me. I managed to get away like Beth, but he followed me, further up the embankment, the steep part. I think he slipped. It was as simple as that. Must have hit his head or something, because he never got up again. Wasn't breathing. He's back in the trees. *Somewhere* in there."

A lie, a white lie, but it'd do. They were going to find Ethan's body, but Johnny's body *wouldn't* be found right away. And when it was, it'd be unrecognizable. Pulp. Only identifiable by his teeth. If Beth or Caleb ever asked her about it, she'd simply say she must have been mistaken; he hadn't been as dead as she'd thought. He must have regained consciousness and crawled away, an injured, pitiful thing, and then…well, then the night creatures had gotten him, coyotes that roamed this land, though you never saw them, or a mountain lion passing through. She'd tell Ray the truth, though. And Annie. In due course.

Beneath the bridge—the fourth on the way out of Murdoc, the second on the way back—it was as though the earth had been torn apart, a fissure running straight through it, deep and wide, continuing on toward the horizon and the mountains, where mist *always* lingered. Such a daunting land. A land where no one had any business being, certainly no man. Except Johnny. Except Ethan. *This* was where

Ethan was buried. They wouldn't be able to raise his body tonight, they'd need professional help, but she could find the spot and mark it, asking the others to help her place stones there, heap them up in a small mound, his body identifiable by his teeth and the necklace he wore. Johnny could have torn it off when torturing him, but he'd been so confident Ethan would never be found, so stupid and arrogant, that he hadn't bothered.

With the grave marked out, finally, Beth remained on her knees, her head in her hands and her shoulders gently heaving. "To think he's there," she said, "cold in that grave for so, so long, so alone. What did Johnny do to him, Shady? How did he kill him?"

That was information with power to destroy further.

"His spirit's not there," Shady said instead, trying to console her. "He's with Kim now."

Busy.

Eventually Beth climbed to her feet and turned to her. "Go."

"What?"

"I said go. You and Ray. Get out of here, go back to where you came from. Do it now, right now. I mean it. We're going to put in a phone call to people we know we can trust."

Shady was suddenly worried. "But what if you can't? What if you're wrong?"

The steeliness in such a young girl's eyes stunned her. "This is our business now. But…thank you. Thank you so much for doing what you have. I was right about you, Kim was." She turned then, looked up at Ray. "Thank you too. For your kindness."

Caleb stepped forward, a guy not as dazzling as Johnny

had been, or even Ethan. He had a shock of blond hair, as Leonora had described, and should be wearing glasses, Shady thought, as he was squinting slightly. "She's right. Don't get involved. You've been noticed once already; it can't happen again. That running you out of town, banning you from Wyatt?"

Shady and Ray looked at each other before Shady answered. "Uh-huh?"

"I saw you'd gone to the Wick house…"

Shady remembered the rustling she'd heard in the trees that lined the yard. Also, the sounds at the cemetery, maybe not all courtesy of apples falling from the trees to the ground, or jackrabbits. "You were keeping tabs."

He nodded. "Yeah. From a distance, though, just…wanting to make sure you were safe. When you were arrested, a contact in the sheriff's office told us you'd been banished from Wyatt, so we thought about coming clean then. That if we didn't, you'd give up, and go home. But Beth kept holding out, even when I insisted, kept saying, 'Don't.'"

"Don't?" Shady frowned. There it was, that ever-repeating word.

"Uh-huh. Anyways, she was right. You stuck around, in Murdoc, carried on with the investigation. Beth did say you were stubborn."

Shady couldn't help but smile. "She called it 'tenacity' with me."

Caleb shrugged, somewhat apologetically. "Same thing, huh? We're just glad it's true. Thing is, you've been noticed, but you'll also be forgotten if you do as we say and go now. This really is town business. We've got what we needed, evidence that we can twist and turn, just like they twist and turn everything. We've got a murder. The tide will change."

"Where are the illegal drugs kept?" Shady wanted to know. "At Gilcrest too?" There were warehouses there, so it made sense, but Caleb shook his head.

"These people are careful. They cover their tracks, or think they do. Gilcrest is a pill mill for sure, but it's just about the right side of legal. The other stuff, cocaine and ice, passes through various trailer-home sites in the backcountry, in areas as secluded as you can get."

Shady sighed as she turned to Ray beside her. "We have to go," she said, echoing Beth and Caleb, who, like the mist, were shutting them out. "Is the car okay to drive?"

"We can try it, but what about our stuff back at the motel? Our clothes?"

"I'll grab them," Beth said. "Mail them to you later. Is that okay?"

Ray nodded. "Sure. I guess."

The four returned to the road, the cars up ahead entirely visible. The Dodge was wounded with a heavily twisted scar from the front fender all the way to the rear, cosmetic damage only, though; it was functional enough to live on, to fight another day.

"What happened to you, Ray?" Shady asked. "After the impact?"

"I don't really remember," he said. "Think I hit my head on the steering wheel and blacked out. When I woke, you were gone. I tried to find you, but…yeah, my head."

"It's hurting still?"

"It's a bit fuzzy. Shit, Shady, I know you're also hurt, but…are you okay to drive?"

"Yeah," she decided. "I am. I'm just glad you're okay, Ray, that we all made it."

"Yeah," he said, looking pretty happy about it too, but tired. She wouldn't be surprised if he slept on the way, just…passed out. And when he woke, she wouldn't be surprised either if all that had happened this night would seem like a dream to him, and to her as well. Already, it was taking on dreamlike proportions. This entire episode was. Surreal.

Beth hugged Shady again. A fierce hug. "Now go. Please."

Shady made to turn, then stopped. "The necklace," she said. It was still around her neck. "Here. You——"

Quickly, Beth shook her head. "No, you have it. It's not Kim's, actually, that one. It's Ethan's. They were always swapping them around. It was like a game they'd play." She smiled sadly. "Silly, really. 'You own my heart,' she'd say, and he'd reply, 'No, you own mine,' and they'd swap necklaces. I used to watch them doing it, used to roll my eyes and wish a heart could split three ways so I could be a part of it, but anyways… It was a cute game, and I don't begrudge them. May have once, but…not anymore. I know that one is Ethan's because his had a little dent in it. Not sure how it happened, maybe a factory defect. That's another reason Kim liked to swap, so he'd have the *perfect* heart, not just her." Her voice caught a little as she added, "She was so friggin' sweet!"

"Yeah," Shady replied. "She was."

They parted, Beth promising to keep Shady up-to-date with developments, and Shady letting her know that if they ever needed them again, they knew where to find them. And *only* Beth and Caleb would know, their contact details down at the sheriff's office having already been removed and soon any evidence of their stay at the Holiday Inn too, Marsha not blinking an eyelid at such requests, happy to carry them out for a modestly greased palm.

They drove, she and Ray, not back toward Murdoc and therefore toward oncoming cops. They'd take the backroads, for miles and miles, until they reached a main highway that'd take them home. True to what she'd thought, Ray fell asleep practically the minute she started driving. He'd have to get his head seen to, and so would she. There'd be plenty of places they could stop a safe distance away, get some Tylenol to see them through. And when they finally reached home, she'd wear a baseball hat for a few days to disguise any bruises. As for the dent in the car, she'd find an explanation for that too.

It was dark on the Spook Road, the two of them passing over the last bridge and into the wilderness proper. Once there, it was different. There was moonlight, and there were stars, so bright after the darkness that Shady wished she could stop and set up camp for the night, smiling to herself about that.

It was about ten miles from the Spook Road to the jagged mountain ridges. After that, there was a turn in the road to skirt the base of the rock formations, then picking up other roads, no matter how minor, all the way out of the Badlands to places more familiar and ordinary. Right now, it was just a straight track ahead, stretching out, and with no sign of anyone else. If Johnny was Ole Devil Eyes, then no need to worry about him either; he couldn't terrorize them now. They were alone, she and Ray…

Alone, except for…shadows, up ahead.

Noticing them, her heart almost leapt from her mouth.

"Ray?" she said, but he was ignoring her again, too deep in sleep. "What the hell?"

They were the *strangest* of shadows. A bunch of them. Squat in shape. "What are you?"

She hit the brakes, skidded to a halt, and *still* Ray slept on.

She could see now what they were.

"Jesus," she breathed. "Oh my God."

Buffalo. A herd of them. Her first-ever sighting. Some moving across the plain, others standing grazing or sitting. So much life, all around her. *Sacred* life.

She switched off the motor, content to sit there while Ray slept, any aches and pains she might have had of her own forgotten. All she wanted was to watch them. *Needing* this moment, just her, the buffalo, and the land. If she could, she'd get out and head closer. But these were wild animals, which wouldn't appreciate a human approaching them, and who could blame them? It was difficult to know who to trust and who to run from. Some, though, lifted their heads to gaze languidly back at her, as curious as she was, before deciding she was of no consequence, no threat, and lowering their heads again, at peace, perfect peace. As was she. A legal high, if ever there was one. No synthetics needed.

Not alone. *Never* alone. Shady lightly rested back against the headrest, forgetting the bad, immersed only in the good, of which there was an abundance. That's when she saw them, more shadows, caught sight of them in the rearview mirror. Shapes that were more recognizable. Not static but moving toward her, coming closer.

Kim. Ethan. All those who might yet still die, although they were so much fainter than the first two. And Kanti. She was at the helm this time, her hand held high and something in it that glinted, not silver like the stars but gold, a beacon.

Oh, how regal she looked with her flowing black hair and the pale shift she wore. A true badass banshee.

As Shady turned to stare, they glided past her—and past a sleeping Ray—through the field of buffalo, toward a final resting place, a special heaven, the Badlands.

Not once did Kanti turn in her direction, or any of them; they kept their focus on the goal, some of the buffalo once more raising their heads in idle curiosity.

Shady's hand had traveled to her neck, held on to the necklace there, Ethan's, which was also Kim's, now the property of the Mason Town Museum, and she wondered something—how did *she* feel, Shady herself? Brokenhearted by all that had happened, such tragedy? Or was her heart filled to the brim with awe and love?

It was too hard to call it. She mourned the loss of those she'd seen, the *future* losses, but she was envious of where they would go, for it was a better place than this.

She was tired, overwhelmed. The aches and pains came back.

If she closed her eyes too, would it be okay?

She couldn't resist.

It *would* be okay. No one would come after them. Ole Devil Eyes was gone, maybe even Mrs. Latham too, Johnny's mother. If she lived or died, Shady hoped she'd find her own particular peace, for she was another he'd been cruel to, yet how she'd tried to love him.

This was a safe place. She could sleep till morning if she wanted, until the break of a new day. Just recline the car seat all the way back and drift away.

Ray would wake then too, and they could behold the spectacle before them, the jagged rise and fall of the mountainous range, bathed in the rays of the dawn, all the reds and yellows, blues and purples, the colors of a sunrise reflected against the colors of the rock, an artist's palette. A hostile land yet so beautiful, and so enduring. They could witness it all, side by side, together—Ray the only companion she would ever want in that moment—breathless with wonder, before finally heading home.

The buffalo having long moved on. All gone. Every one of them.

As if they had never been.

A NOTE FROM THE AUTHOR

As much as I love writing, building a relationship with readers is even more exciting! I occasionally send newsletters with details on new releases, special offers and other bits of news relating to the Psychic Surveys series as well as all my other books. If you'd like to subscribe, sign up here!

www.shanistruthers.com

Printed in Great Britain
by Amazon

39314274R00159